THE HEARTBEATS OF WING JONES

THE HEARTBEATS OF WING JONES

KATHERINE WEBBER

DELACORTE PRESS

Text copyright © 2017 by Katherine Webber
Jacket art copyright © 2017: background by Demurez Cover Arts/Maja Tupcagic/
plainpicture; shoes by Kristen Curette/Stocksy; hair by Shutterstock

All rights reserved. Published in the United States by Delacorte Press,
an imprint of Random House Children's Books, a division
of Penguin Random House LLC, New York.

Delacorte Press is a registered trademark and the colophon is a trademark
of Penguin Random House LLC.

Visit us on the Web! randomhouseteens.com

Educators and librarians, for a variety of teaching tools,
visit us at RHTeachersLibrarians.com

Library of Congress Cataloging-in-Publication Data
Names: Webber, Katherine, author.
Title: The heartbeats of Wing Jones / Katherine Webber.
Description: First edition. | New York : Delacorte Press, [2017] |
Summary: Half-Chinese, half-black Wing Jones has always worshiped her
older brother, but when he kills two people in a car accident and barely
survives himself, Wing's only solace is running.
Identifiers: LCCN 2016005580 (print) | LCCN 2016031826 (ebook) |
ISBN 978-0-399-55502-2 (hc) | ISBN 978-0-399-55504-6 (glb) |
ISBN 978-0-399-55503-9 (ebk)
Subjects: | CYAC: Brothers and sisters—Fiction. | Emotional problems—Fiction. |
Running—Fiction. | Traffic accidents—Fiction. | Racially mixed people—Fiction.
Classification: LCC PZ7.1.W418 He 2017 (print) | LCC PZ7.1.W418 (ebook) |
DDC [Fic]—dc23

The text of this book is set in 12-point Adobe Jenson.
Interior design by Ken Crossland

Printed in the United States of America
10 9 8 7 6 5 4 3 2 1
First Edition

FOR MY PARENTS

CHAPTER 1

MY FIRST MEMORY IS OF MY BROTHER. SEEING HIS HEAD BOB-
bing along in front of me as I chased him down our street, calling
after him to wait for me. And he'd turn around and grin, his baby
teeth smooth as pearls. "Come on, Wing!" he'd say to me, his little
sister.

I would have followed him anywhere.

This one time, the first time I can remember, we were at the
swings, they were bright red swings, I can still picture them. Marcus held his hand out to me. "I'll help you up," he said, using all
his six-year-old strength to hoist my tubby four-year-old body up
on the swing.

"Ready?" he said, and before I said yes he gave me a big push
and I was flying. Marcus made me fly.

"Like this, Wing! Kick your feet like this." He had climbed
on the swing next to me and was pumping his legs as hard as he
could. "We can go higher!"

And I felt like we were blasting off into the blue, blue sky.

"Higher!" he called out, and I kicked my legs as much as I could, but my calves weren't as strong as his and I couldn't get as high, no matter how hard I tried.

We couldn't have been swinging on our own for very long, but at the time, it felt like forever that it was just us, on a rocket ship, climbing higher and higher. I didn't think we'd ever come back down.

"Wing! Let's jump!"

I remember looking over at Marcus, seeing his face set in determination, his lips puckered, brow furrowed, same face he still makes right before he throws a football, clutching the metal links of the chain, and then throwing himself off the swing into the air, shouting like a warrior. He landed in a crouch and stood, brushing sand off his hands.

"Your turn!"

I should have been scared. But I wasn't. I was with Marcus. I kept my eyes on my brother, who was beaming at me, clapping, hopping up and down. He couldn't wait for me to join him back on earth.

"You can do it! Let go!"

And I did. I let go of the swing and tried to catapult myself into the air like my brother had. And for just a second, I was airborne, just like he had been.

But then I landed. And I didn't land in a crouch. I landed in a heap, my ankle under me, twisting in a way it shouldn't have.

I remember trying not to cry as Marcus kissed the top of my head and then my ankle. He said a kiss would make it better. Then he ran to get our grandmother LaoLao.

"Stay here, Wing!" he commanded. As if I could get up and walk with a broken ankle. "I'll be right back!"

He took off running, sand scattering around his feet as he left me curled up, trying not to cry, staring at the clouds.

When my dragon flew down from the sky that first time and lay down next to me, I wasn't scared or surprised. It felt like she'd always been there, invisible until now. She was so beautiful, so majestic, that she made me forget all about the pain. Green and gold and shiny all over, with steamy breath that smelled like the Chinese tea my LaoLao loved. The lioness appeared on my other side, tawny and soft, smelling like vanilla and cinnamon, like my Granny Dee, and I wasn't surprised to see her either. She curled up close, her warm head nuzzling my broken ankle.

Time is funny when you're little. I couldn't tell you how long I lay in the sand, buffered by my dragon and my lioness, but they were gone by the time Marcus came back, dragging our huffing and puffing LaoLao, our Granny Dee a few paces behind them.

"I'm sorry I left you!" Marcus was crying now, he always cried when I got hurt, he couldn't stand it when I stubbed my toe or got a paper cut.

"I had a dragon," I told him proudly, my pain momentarily forgotten. "And a lion!"

"Where are they?" Marcus sniffed and looked around. I shrugged. I didn't know. But I knew they would be back. Someday.

"I'll show you," I said, and was rewarded with a wobbly smile.

My dragon and my lioness never did show themselves to Marcus. Just to me. And it was a long time before I saw them again.

CHAPTER 2

Fall 1995
Atlanta

THE CHEERS ARE DEAFENING.

Even though I've been watching my brother do this his whole life, watching him get knocked down and knocked out, I tense and hold my breath, waiting for the four guys chasing him to tackle him.

They don't. Marcus slips through their outstretched arms like a stick of butter, and he's glossy and shiny too, I can see that from here, and he pulls back his arm like a sling and the ball goes flying and the crowd stands as one, everyone except my mother, who's sitting with her hands over her eyes because she can't stand to watch him play. My brother's best friend, Aaron, jumps into the air like a gazelle, he's all grace and power, and I get the little shiver I get watching him, a very different feeling I get from watching Marcus, and his hands grab the ball and he lands with it secure between his palms and then the crowd really loses it.

Above the roar of the people around me I hear the announcer shouting "Touchdown!" as if we haven't seen what just happened. The clock hits zero just as the scoreboard updates showing that Marcus and Aaron's touchdown has won them the game. The band starts up and the cheerleaders wave their pom-poms and all around me people are cheering, throwing their popcorn in the air, knocking over their cups of Coke, acting like they personally threw the ball or caught it or did anything at all other than stand here and watch. But Marcus says that's all they need to do and if they didn't he wouldn't have a scholarship. Wouldn't have a job playing professional football one day. So I guess the crowd is just as much a part of this moment, his moment, as anyone out there on the field.

Marcus and Aaron run at each other like long-lost lovers, their arms are tight around each other, and Aaron is ripping off Marcus's helmet and rubbing his knuckles in his hair and their smiles are so bright, I swear they light up the field more than the floodlights.

My mother finally lowers her hands from her eyes and looks up. "It's done?" she says, her Chinese accent heavier because she's scared. "He didn't get hurt?"

"He didn't get hurt," I assure her.

"And he won?" Now that she knows he's okay, she can focus on the important things. Like the final score.

"They won," I say, consciously changing the pronoun. Although Marcus once said that even though there's no I in team, there is one in win. Aaron tackled him for that, right off the front porch.

My mom stands. "I knew he would win," she says, voice confident. "Marcus always wins."

"Of course he does!" My Granny Dee, my dad's mom, sniffs. "He's my grandson, ain't he?"

LaoLao, my mom's mom, gives a sniff of her own. "He my grandson!" she proclaims, her Chinese accent even more pronounced than my mother's. Granny Dee and LaoLao have this argument at every game. As if one of them could have more claim to Marcus than the other. They look over at me at the same time, and I wonder if they notice how even when they bicker, they move like two parts of the same machine.

"Go get me a Coke," barks Granny Dee.

"For me too!" says LaoLao. "We are celebrating Marcus's win!" I sigh but don't argue. No point in arguing with Granny Dee and LaoLao.

"Mom?"

My mom gives me a tired smile and shakes her head. She digs into her purse and pulls out a wrinkled five-dollar bill. "Get something for yourself, sweetie," she says.

It might not seem like much, but that five dollars could be used for a lot of other things besides buying my grandmothers a couple of overpriced Cokes at a high school football game. I love my grandmothers, but I don't love how much they love to boss me around. I sigh again, louder this time, more of a huff, and Granny Dee's walnut face snaps up, her bright eyes narrowing.

"You got somethin' you wanna complain about? You too busy to go get your Granny Dee a Coke?"

"Me too," LaoLao adds, scooting her bulk closer to Granny Dee's thin frame. "Too busy, little Wing? Too busy doing what?"

My grandmothers put their heads together, their old laughter wheezing out of them like air out of punctured tires, a most unlikely united front. Teasing me can always bring them together. It's like when a cat and a dog forget they're enemies to come together to chase a duck. I look at them, the women—one from China, one from Ghana—who have been the stalwart forces of my life since before I even took my first breath. Granny Dee, barely five feet, gray and brown all over. So thin she looks like a gust of wind could knock her over, but my money, if I had any, would be that the wind would break before Granny Dee would. And LaoLao, as round as a dumpling full to bursting, her sleek black hair still dark as my mother's, tied in a tight bun in the back of her head. She looks like she could withstand a hurricane.

"Them Cokes ain't gonna get themselves," says Granny Dee as she fans herself with a flyer. "My Lord, it is hot tonight."

I shake my head at them and go down the stairs to get them their stupid Cokes. As soon as I turn away they start to bicker about something else. Now that I'm gone, they don't have any reason to team up. Silly old ladies, I think, affection for them blooming in my chest.

The stands have emptied out, and I'm grateful. I don't like having to make my way through crowds, pushing myself against them or asking them to move aside, feeling too big and too small at the same time. Watching their eyes go up and down me, trying to figure out what it is about me that is so *off*. What it is that works so well in Marcus but didn't quite come out right in me. Same ingredients, different result. Like a cake that came out perfectly one time and a little squashed the next. I know I don't look like anyone else at this school, or maybe even in all of Atlanta. Hell, maybe in all of Georgia. I know I don't look like my mom, with her bird bones and silky black hair. I don't look like LaoLao or Granny Dee either, as Granny Dee will tell you when she tries to do my hair. "Child," she'll say, pulling out one of my curls and watching it spring back with a bemused expression. "How can your hair be so fine but so tangly at the same time?" It never stays in braids, wisps of it coming out, but it won't straighten either. Granny Dee doesn't know what to do with it. Or with the rest of me. She'll cluck at my hips and my butt, like I asked to have a big butt, and then she'll look up at me, because I'm more than just a bit taller than her, or LaoLao or my mother for that matter, like she can't believe any granddaughter of hers takes up so much space. And even though LaoLao is one of the fattest old ladies I've ever seen, even she always has something to say about my size. "You are too big," she'll say, all three of her chins wobbling as she shakes her head. "Like a horse. And your skin is so dark!" I don't know why she sounds so surprised. It's not like she didn't know my daddy was black.

Of course, no one ever says Marcus is too big. Marcus couldn't be too anything. Marcus is perfect.

Marcus. I glance out on the field, hoping to catch a glimpse of my brother, but he's disappeared with the rest of the team. I probably won't see him till tomorrow. He'll be going out with the team to celebrate the win tonight. Out with Monica. Out with Aaron.

Thinking about Aaron makes my heart skip like a little girl with a jump rope.

CHAPTER 3

I'M AT THE FRONT OF THE SNACK BAR LINE AND AM ABOUT TO order when someone slips neatly into the narrow space between me and the counter, the way a nickel does in the slot of a gumball machine. Someone fair and small with wavy red hair, mermaid hair. Mermaid hair to match her mermaid green eyes. Someone who reeks of cheap perfume and too much hair spray.

I clear my throat; I can't help it. It isn't fair that Heather Parker thinks she can waltz right to the front without even a hint of an excuse me. Heather turns, wavy hair fluttering around her like she's got an invisible servant fanning her, and glares up at me. It is a special skill, to glare up at someone who is a whole half a foot taller, but it's something Heather Parker has perfected. She's had a lot of practice over the years.

"Ew," she says, her tiny nose wrinkling. "I didn't know they let the freaks come out tonight."

You'd think that after hearing something over and over again the blade would dull, but it goes into me every time. Every. Single. Time. *Freak.* Sinking into me, staining me, like hundreds of invisible tattoos. Freak on my forehead. Freak on my chest. Freak on my arm. Freak on my feet. *Freak, freak, freak.*

I used to stare at myself in the mirror, wondering what made me so different. I don't know what it is exactly, but I can't blend in, and I don't stand out in a good way like Marcus. I stick out. Marcus, he manages to *stand out*, to shine when he wants, but he can blend in too. Not me. I can't blend in but I don't stand out. And I guess that's enough for Heather Parker to call me a freak every chance she gets. Enough so everyone else has started to believe it too. Just like when Heather decided that butterfly clips were cool last year, and all the other girls started wearing them. Or when she shunned Lily Asquith for daring to kiss a boy Heather had laid claim to and the next day Lily's diary was passed around school and the word slut was chalked all over her driveway. It doesn't hurt that Heather's father is our local weatherman, which doesn't sound that glamorous to me, but apparently it's enough to make Heather practically famous. She says she's gonna be a news anchor on CNN because she's got "the face for it" and "all the right connections." She's also vicious, but I don't know if that's a required qualification to be a news anchor.

The student behind the concession stand is watching our interaction the way someone would watch a wildlife documentary. The kind where the hyenas take down a giraffe. His expression is a mixture of expectation and pity. He knows what's going to happen but he's powerless to stop it, and part of him is a little bit excited to see the hyena take down her prey. He isn't going to get between Heather Parker and one of her victims.

I could step on her. I could pick up one of my *freakish* legs and bring it down on her pretty little face and squash her like an insect. I imagine the scene comic-book style, playing out on my own personal projector, and it makes me smile.

Smiling is the wrong thing to do. Heather's face flames red and she leans closer to me.

"What are you laughing at?" And she calls me something else—something worse than a word. The sound of it makes the person in line behind me, someone I don't know, inhale sharply.

I flinch. I've got this word all over me too.

"Wing!" I look up and see my brother's girlfriend, Monica, jogging toward me. Her long blond hair is streaming out behind her and she's out of breath. "There you are! Your mama and grannies have gone home already and told me to tell you. They said you took too long getting the Cokes."

She stops and takes in the scene. Heather standing right under my nose, the silent boy behind the register, the group of freshmen gawking and giggling next to us. The silent echo of what Heather just called me ringing in all our ears.

"You causing trouble, Parker?" Monica says, her voice dangerous sweet, like sugar laced with poison.

"Your daddy know where you goin' tonight?" Heather shoots back. "I heard he doesn't like who you've been hanging around with."

Monica doesn't rise to the bait. Instead, she smiles, lips pressed tight together, so tight they almost disappear, and grabs my hand. "Come on," she says. "We don't need to stick around with this trash."

Heather looks like she's winding up for another insult—I can hear the gears inside her clanking—but Monica is pulling me away, so fast and so far that whatever Heather yells out after us is eaten by the wind. I wish the wind would eat all of her.

"What is her problem with you?" says Monica when we're almost out of the stadium. "You never done anything to her. You never done anything to anyone."

I shrug. It doesn't matter what I have or haven't done. Heather Parker is one of those people who feeds on other people's pain. It's what keeps her skin so clear and her hair so shiny.

"Thanks for rescuing me back there." I feel awkward saying it, but I want Monica to know that I appreciate her getting involved. She didn't have to.

"Wing, baby girl, you're family," says Monica. "If anyone messes with you, they're messing with me." Her eyes soften, melting from the laser blue she was shooting at Heather to gentle blue, like laundry detergent.

I manage a smile. "Are y'all going out to celebrate?" I ask, changing the subject.

Monica shrugs. "There's a party at Trey's place, but I'm not in the mood," she says lightly. I know there is more to it. Trey lives in a pretty dangerous part of town, even more so than where we live, and Monica doesn't want to venture there at night, even with Marcus and Aaron by her side. "But I still wanna celebrate the win."

Marcus and Aaron appear out of nowhere, emerging from the darkness and coming into sharp focus under the parking-lot lights. Marcus is shouting over his shoulder at another one of his teammates. "Nah, not tonight. I'll make up for it next weekend!" He turns toward Aaron.

"You go on, man. You don't need to miss out because I'm not going."

Aaron shakes his head. "Nah, Dionne will be there, and I'm not in the mood for her shit tonight."

Dionne is Aaron's ex-girlfriend. Even though they haven't been together for over a year, Dionne still likes to start drama with Aaron. Especially when she's been drinking. At least, that's what Marcus says. I feel a sharp spike of jealousy mixed with relief. Jealous because Aaron is still so clearly tied up with Dionne. Relief because he doesn't want to see her tonight.

Out of the corner of my eye I see someone else approaching. Someone I've seen around but don't know well. Don't want to know well. Someone who casts shadows everywhere he goes. He wears his Braves cap (with the big silver sticker circle still on it, just like all the rappers do) low, so low you can't see his eyes. Just his sharp chin and soft mouth. His mouth doesn't match the rest of him.

"What's this? Our golden boys"—he steps on the word *golden* so that it comes out dull, not gold at all—"ain't goin' to the party? Ain't gonna celebrate? But I got the goods for tonight myself. Just for my favorite cousin and his favorite little friend."

No one else would call Marcus *little*. Monica takes a step closer to Marcus and I wish I had someone to take a step closer to. Jasper makes me nervous. Not just me. I can tell by the way Marcus has sewn his lips shut that Jasper makes him nervous too.

Only Aaron is relaxed. His posture is the same, his breathing even. You might wonder how I know what his breathing is like, but if you spent as much time as I did watching him, you'd be able to tell too.

Jasper is Aaron's cousin twice removed and once hopped over, or something. Jasper has got no parents to speak of, but the ones he did have, once upon a time, if we are to believe that he was ever a child, were somehow related to Aaron's daddy. He looks older than us by years and years. I think he's only twenty-one or twenty-two, but the years are heavy on him, heavy with things that make Marcus watch him like he's a snake.

"Jasper," Aaron says, moving forward to clasp his somehow cousin in a boy hug. "Man, where you been? I didn't know you were comin' to the game tonight. It's been a while."

"You're too busy for your old buddy Jasper these days," Jasper says, spitting out the side of his mouth as he does. "One of your little teammates called me up, said they needed some stuff for a party tonight. I assumed you would be there."

"Ah, sorry, man." Aaron's voice is taut as a tightrope wire; one wiggle and the walker will come crashing down. "I'm really not up for it tonight. But hey, good to see you. Been too long."

Jasper shrugs. "Your loss, my man."

"Next time," says Aaron, grinning.

"Next time," Jasper agrees as he slips away into the dark parking lot.

I feel rather than hear Monica exhale. She opens her mouth, but Marcus shakes his head at her, once, and she presses her lips together and rolls her shoulders back as if she just took off a backpack full of rocks.

"So," says Aaron, voice bright as sunshine, "where *are* we going, then?"

"Where do you want to go?" Marcus asks. In the shadowy parking lot he looks so much like our daddy that I have to look away.

Sometimes I think about how our daddy will never get to see Marcus growing up into him. His lashes are curly like our daddy's were, and his lips are the same shape too. He's got our mom's high cheekbones, though, and if you are really looking you can see how his eyes tilt up just a little bit at the corners.

I'm the opposite. I got my daddy's dark skin and wild hair and my mom's Chinese eyes and straight lashes. I don't understand how a person can have such curly hair on their head and such straight eyelashes, but genetics are a mystery. And I definitely didn't get my daddy's or my mom's high cheekbones and sharp jaw lines. The kind models in magazines have. But almost all the models in magazines are white.

I've never, ever seen a model who looks anything like me. Not black, not Chinese, certainly not white. Marcus was approached last summer down at the mall by a modeling scout. She said he looked exotic and would photograph well. That didn't sit too well with Marcus. He doesn't like being called *exotic* or *unique* or *different*. All Marcus wants to be is the all-American golden boy.

No one has ever asked me to model. And I look even more "exotic" than Marcus.

Marcus's voice snaps me out of my tumbled thoughts. "Moni, what do you want to do?"

"I wanna go to Gladys's," says Monica, in that tone that's right between a whine and a demand. "I've never been. And everyone's always talking about it."

She means Gladys Knight's chicken and waffles restaurant, the one downtown. She pronounces it "Gladees," the way everyone around here does. Like they're all personal friends with Gladys Knight.

Marcus raises his eyebrow in a silent question to Aaron.

Aaron shrugs in response. Monica stamps her foot like a little girl and pouts, her glossy lips puckering prettily.

"Come on. It'll be fun. We can all go. Wing, you've never been, have you?"

I shake my head. "I thought y'all were going out to celebrate." They always go out after games and I always go home. With my mom, Granny Dee, and LaoLao. The only reason I'm here now is I took too long getting the Cokes, and Lord knows my Granny Dee and LaoLao have the patience of a two-year-old throwing a tantrum when they want to go home. Sometimes I wonder if they were born with so much in common or if years of living together at our house has slowly melded them into the same person. Not that I'd ever tell them that.

Monica leans toward me and grabs my arm tight. "We are! We're celebrating by going to Gladys's. No better way for Marcus to celebrate than by being with his favorite people in the whole world." What she means is, there is no way in hell that she is going to the party at Trey's with Jasper, so this is the next best thing. But still. I like that she's included me. As one of the favorite people.

"Don't let Granny Dee or LaoLao hear you say that," I say, but I'm smiling and I feel a warmth glowing inside me, like a little spark that Monica has lit with her words.

Marcus wraps his arm around Monica's shoulders and pulls her in and kisses the top of her head. They are beautiful together. I wish I had a camera so I could freeze this moment of them. Marcus in his letterman jacket, eyes bright and laughing as he looks down at Monica. Monica in her blue sweater dress, long blond hair tumbling down her back, snuggled up against his chest.

There's a light cough next to me and I glance up and across to Aaron. "I don't really care where we go as long as we go soon. I'm starving. Come on, you two," he says, rolling his eyes with a smirk. "Although I don't really think you want to go there with me and Wing. I think you want to go somewhere just the two of you. . . ." He finishes his sentence in a warbling croon and Marcus lets go of Monica and is next to Aaron in a second, wrapping his arms around him and holding him tight.

"Is this what you want, man? Don't worry. I've got plenty of love for you too."

Monica laughs, the sound tinkling out into the night like fairy bells chiming, and grabs my hand, pulling me toward her Jeep. "Come on!" she says, tossing her keys to Marcus. "Marcus, you drive." She gets in the front seat, still laughing. Aaron climbs in behind the driver's seat, muttering under his breath that she didn't call shotgun.

I get in behind Monica. I can't stop grinning. It isn't that I don't ever hang out with them; I see them all the time. Monica or Aaron or both of them are always over. But this feels different. It doesn't feel like I'm just Marcus's kid sister. It feels like I belong. The feeling is like a hard butterscotch candy in my mouth, smooth and sweet, and I want it to last forever.

CHAPTER 4

Going into Gladys's feels like going back in time. The walls are wood paneled and the lights are dim and everyone but us is in a suit or nice dress, and one woman is even wearing one of those fancy hats that people wear to the races. A low laughter floats in the air—it's unclear who's laughing or if it's multiple people or if it's the room itself—chuckling away at some inside joke long gone.

The restaurant is warm. Not hot, but warm like the inside of a freshly baked biscuit. It smells like maple syrup and hot fried chicken and my mouth starts watering. I inhale deeply, taking in the sweet and savory scent.

Monica is the only white person in here. Even without her, we'd stand out, the way Marcus and I manage to stand out everywhere we go. I feel the eyes of the nearest table taking us in.

Aaron. Tall, black, wearing a black hoodie and jeans. And gorgeous. I see a girl—no, a woman, probably in her early twenties—

eye him up and down more than necessary and I have to stop myself from stepping in front of him and blocking her view.

Marcus. Almost as tall as Aaron. Letterman jacket. Eyes wide, lashes curly, hair short, but it's still obvious that his curls are soft. When his hair is longer, they coil away from his face like on a Greek sculpture. He grins easily around the restaurant, as if he's saying hello to everyone. As if he's an old friend. His arm stays tight around Monica's waist. Less possessive and more protective.

Monica. Shorter than all of us. White. Blond. In here, her skin looks so pale she's practically translucent, the way Nicole Kidman looks on the red carpet. Her hair seems to catch the light and reflect it back, glowing a hundred different shades of gold. She's got a coy smile on, like she's been let into a secret club, and maybe she has been, maybe we all have.

And me. Taller than Monica, only a few inches shorter than Marcus and Aaron. I'm in the back of our little group, both black and Chinese like my brother, wearing faded black jeans and a long-sleeved white shirt. My dark hair is loose and bobs around like something living right above my shoulders.

The server takes us to our table and we sit down in the plush leather booth. I end up next to Aaron and across from Monica. Monica's eyes are about the same size as the steaming plates coming out of the kitchen. She leans over to me and lowers her voice. "Is this place for real? I feel like I'm on a movie set or something."

I grin at her and shake my head, but her enthusiasm is catching. I don't just feel like I'm on a movie set. I feel like I'm *in* a movie. The dim light that makes everything cloudy and soft around the edges, that laughter in the air, sitting next to Aaron, so close we're practically touching, my brother smiling with his arm around

Monica, even the jazz playing in the background . . . There *should* be a camera rolling somewhere.

I barely get a chance to look at the menu before the server is back. Marcus and Aaron already know what they want, and Monica giggles and says she'll have chicken and waffles with a side of bacon, corn bread, and mac 'n' cheese. This is one of the things I love about Monica. Girl can eat. I say I'll have the same and Aaron pats me on the back and whistles.

"Big M, I think our ladies have gone and out-ordered us."

The "our" floats out of his lips like a cloud. I can see the shape of it in the air, the softness of it, and I inhale, not wanting to let it slip away or evaporate; I want to keep it inside forever. I'm smiling so big that I feel my eyes crinkling at the corners.

"What's so funny, Wing-a-ring-ling?" Aaron punches me gently on the arm, kid-sister-like, and I wish he'd put his arm around me the way Marcus has his arm around Monica and that we were out on a proper double date. Not just the little sister tagging along with her big brother, his girlfriend, and his best friend.

I'm saved from having to answer by Marcus starting to sing the song he used to chase me round and round the house with. "*Wing, Wing can do anything! Wing, Wing, make the bell ring, ring.*"

Aaron laughs, a low sound that rumbles up from his chest. If the "our" was a cloud, his laugh is lots of bumblebees, coming up out of his mouth one after the other. "I forgot about that damn bell," he says.

I laugh too, and it sounds like feathers floating in the air. I picture one landing on Aaron's shoulders, on his chest, and wonder if he can feel my feather giggles.

"What bell?" says Monica, sweeping her hair over her shoulder.

Aaron lifts his hand to his chest and I think maybe he does

20

feel one of my feather laughs. He leans forward, the movement pushing him closer to me, and puts his elbows on the table.

"They used to have this bell, like the kind at the front desk of a hotel or something, I don't know where the hell they found it, and that bell was the end goal of everything. Instead of hide-and-seek, we'd hide the bell. Race in the yard? Have to hit the bell or else you didn't really win. Win at a board game? Not until you hit the stupid bell." He shakes his head. "Marcus was always making Wing or me compete with him at something."

"You used to always win the races," I say, remembering Aaron as a little kid galloping across our backyard, his legs too long for his body. He's grown into them now.

"Of course he did," says Marcus. "You gotta be fast to be a good wide receiver." Aaron is the guy who runs and catches the ball when the quarterback throws it. My brother is the quarterback. They've been throwing balls and racing around for as long as I can remember.

"You gotta be fast to get a track scholarship," says Aaron.

"Come on, man. You've got football scouts looking at you."

Aaron shakes his head. "Nah, Marcus. You've got football scouts looking at *you*. Sure, they see me out on the field, 'cause I'm with you. But I've got a hell of a better chance getting a track scholarship than I do as a wide receiver." It's true. Aaron's fast, real fast. Last year he broke the school record for the 100-meter and 200-meter dashes.

Marcus looks like he wants to argue the point, and I can tell that this is a conversation they've had before, but Monica grabs his hand and squeezes. "Marcus," she says, "you'll be able to throw a football even if Aaron isn't there to catch it."

"Nope," says Marcus, "it's gotta be Aaron." But he's smiling as the waitress arrives and puts down plate after plate of steaming food until I'm surprised the table doesn't buckle.

It is a feast. My first bite of waffle is perfect, buttery and warm, and I wonder if the food really tastes as good as it does, or if we're all so happy that our joy is sprinkling onto our plates like some sort of exotic spice, making everything that much tastier.

Aaron nudges me with his elbow. "Wing, can I get a bite of your mac 'n' cheese?"

I nod and push the small bowl toward him. He digs his fork in and I get a little tingle thinking about the two of us sharing the same bowl.

It's stupid. I know it's stupid. It isn't like we are sharing the same fork or anything, and it isn't even like I'm going to be taking a bite of something he's taken a bite of, like a cookie, he's just taking some macaroni and cheese out of my bowl, and it really isn't any different from when he's at my house and we're all eating family style, we always eat family style in my house, and we're getting food from the same bowl, but this feels a little different, a little more intimate. Maybe it is my imagination. My stupid, hopeful, overactive imagination. Pretending that sharing a bowl of macaroni and cheese is the same thing as sharing a milk shake with two straws.

I would love to do that. Maybe down at the Varsity. We'd get peanut-butter-banana-chocolate for sure. My favorite flavor.

While I've been daydreaming, or whatever it is you call daydreaming when you do it at night but you aren't actually sleeping, my waffles have gone soggy under the chicken and syrup. Aaron points this out.

"Your eyes bigger than your stomach, little girl?"

Marcus has called me little girl my whole life and it's never bothered me. Hell, I'm pretty sure Aaron has called me little girl occasionally. But for some reason, tonight, it irks me. It reminds me who I am. What I am, and even though I'm almost sixteen, everyone still sees me as the little sister. The tagalong. That this is in no way any kind of double date and I need to stop pretending.

I hack at my waffle with vigor. "Don't you worry," I say. "I'll finish."

"Of course you will," says Marcus, blissfully unaware of the turmoil going on inside me. "Y'all remember when Wing beat me at a dumpling-eating contest, right?"

"There you go, always making everything some kinda competition," says Aaron, shaking his head.

"I was eight," I say, stabbing my fork into my macaroni and cheese.

"And I was ten! And I got outeaten by an eight-year-old. How many dumplings did you have, Wing? Thirty-eight?"

"Forty-one." I'm unable to stop my lips from turning up into a smile.

"Damn, girl," says Aaron. "I'm not even sure I could eat forty-one dumplings now. You should definitely be able to finish those waffles."

I want to be dainty and feminine. I want to push my plate away and flutter my lashes, my stupid straight lashes, and say that I'm too full and I couldn't possibly eat another bite. And maybe pout like Monica. I wonder how she knows how. Did she study *Cosmo?* Thinking about Monica reading *Cosmo* makes me think of the *other* things she might learn, and that makes me think of her and my brother and I need to stop this train of thought real quick because I do not like where it is heading.

The waffles are cold and soggy and not nearly as good as they were when we sat down. Nothing is. The grease is congealing on top of the macaroni and cheese and the skin on the fried chicken has gone limp. Even the booth seems to have lost some of its luster.

Everyone else has finished their food, even Monica, who ordered as much as me but you don't hear the boys teasing her about her appetite, Monica wouldn't stand for it, and I feel like the little kid at the table who is taking too long. I duck my head and focus on finishing my food as fast as I can, only half listening to the conversation around me.

"Why did you say you'd see Trey next weekend?" Monica's tone is casual, but I know she doesn't like when Marcus makes plans without telling her first. Especially plans with people like Trey or Jasper.

"Ah, it's Lamar's birthday next week. His nineteenth. Party at Trey's. It'll be fun."

"Was I invited?" says Monica pointedly. I'm still staring down at the remains of the chicken carcass on my plate, but I can picture her expression perfectly.

"Of course you were! Anywhere I'm invited, you're invited."

Monica makes a sound that's a little bit like a rhino getting ready to charge. A small rhino, but still a rhino. Marcus makes a similar sound back, and it's like some sort of bizarre mating ritual I haven't learned yet.

"Anyone else invited that I should know about?" I don't know what Monica is getting at, but whatever it is, it makes Marcus frown and glare back at her.

"Wing, if you're finished, why don't we go get some fresh air and let these two chat?" says Aaron. "Not that I wouldn't love to play referee to your little tiff."

"We aren't fighting," says Monica. "We're still celebrating.

We're just taking a little break, you know, a little halftime, whatever you wanna call it, to figure out next weekend's plans. And find out why Marcus would accept an invitation on my behalf without talking to me about it. Especially without telling me who else might be there."

Now she's less like a rhino *about* to charge and more like a rhino actually charging.

"Maybe we should *all* go get some fresh air," I suggest, digging around in my pockets for that five dollars my mom gave me earlier. I hope it's enough to cover my share. It is all I have.

"No," says Monica. "You two go outside. We'll get the bill and see you in a few minutes."

Marcus hasn't said a thing. He's leaning back in the booth, a small smile on his face. He finds Monica's tantrums amusing. It must be from all the years of hearing Granny Dee, LaoLao, and my mom shouting about one thing or another that he's able to find the humor in it. Or maybe it's because he loves them all so much and he knows how much they love him, so it just doesn't get to him.

I don't find it amusing at all. It stresses me out when people shout or get upset. Which is why I slide out of the booth after Aaron and hurry out of the restaurant, keeping my head down with my hair in my face so I don't have to see the expressions of the other diners.

When I get outside, Aaron is leaning against Monica's car rubbing his fingers together, and I know he wants a cigarette.

I go as close to him as I dare, wishing it were closer.

"I think that bum back there is pissing. Don't look over your shoulder," he says, squashing any romantic notions I have. I can hear the pee hitting the ground and now I do move closer to

Aaron, less because of how I feel about him and more because I'm nervous about who else might be hiding in the dark.

"I'm guessing you don't have a cigarette," he says.

"Good guess," I say. "You know what my mom would do if she ever caught me with a cigarette? What either of my grandmothers would do? What Marcus would do?"

"Yeah, I know what Marcus would do. He's the one who made me quit."

"Then why'd you just ask me if I had any?"

"Because I knew you wouldn't."

The conversation seems like it's going round and round in a way I don't understand.

So I do what I do best. I keep quiet.

"I was just messing with you," Aaron says. "Don't worry. I don't ever smoke anymore. Just feeling tense. I don't know why Monica had to go and blow up like that."

"She didn't 'blow up' like anything," I say, feeling defensive, even though she kind of did. I hope she and Marcus have made up by now. And that the reason they haven't come outside is because they're sitting making moon eyes at each other.

"You think they're perfect, don't you? Monica and Marcus?"

Aaron and I don't ever talk like this. He teases me, he asks how my classes are going, occasionally he'll even compliment me, some throwaway comment like "nice scarf" that didn't cost him anything, and I'll reach out and grab it as fast as I can and hold it close and put it in my pocket and take it out when I'm feeling low. But for as long as I've known him, which has been as long as I can remember, we've never had any kind of deep conversation between just the two of us.

"I don't know what you're talking about," I say. I'm flustered by the question, even though it's nice to be talking to Aaron, just the two of us. Marcus is perfect. And he's found the perfect girl. And they are perfect together. Sure, Monica can flare up sometimes. And every once in a while Marcus will be kind of an ass. I can admit that. But if they aren't perfect they're as close as any humans can be. This I am more certain of than I am of anything.

"Girl, you got stars in your eyes every time you look at them."

"Marcus is my brother," I say. "He's the only one I got. The only one I'll ever have." I pause. "You wouldn't understand."

"He's my brother too . . . ," Aaron starts, but I turn and look at him with a fierceness that cuts him off midsentence.

"No, he's not," I say, surprised by the steel in my voice. "He's my real brother. He's your best friend. He's your 'brother.'" I put my fingers up in air quotes. "But he's my brother. He's all I've got."

"What about your mama and your grannies? You got them too, don'tcha?"

Aaron has his mother and that's it. No grandmas, no daddy, no aunts, no uncles. Just his hardworking, hard-drinking, depressed-as-hell mother. I've only met her a handful of times and I don't need to meet her any more than that.

And Jasper, I guess. Not that he does Aaron any good. Or is good for him.

I don't know why I'm picking a fight with Aaron over something so silly. And as much as I proclaim that Marcus is more *my* brother than *his* brother, I know they're connected by something that goes just as deep as blood. And in the same way that Aaron will never really understand the connection between me and Marcus, I'll never know what it is that makes them so close.

"Look," I say, finally turning and looking directly at him. "I know Marcus isn't perfect. And neither is Monica. But . . . they're as close as anyone I know is going to be. Why you wanna ruin that for me?"

Aaron just gazes at me awhile, his expression still. He nods toward the restaurant. Marcus and Monica are coming out, arms around each other, snuggled and smiling. He sighs and shrugs. "Just something to think about, that's all."

On the way home we blast the radio and roll down the windows and sing at the top of our lungs. The night air tastes like starlight. I haven't had a drop to drink and don't know what being drunk feels like, but right now I swear I'm tipsy. The edges of the moment are blurred like an old photograph. Just enough that I can't quite see Aaron's expression, and I force his words into the music box in my brain, slam the lid, turn the key, and forget about them.

CHAPTER 5

I should have known that Heather Parker wouldn't be satisfied with how Friday night went. I used to try to figure out why she hated me. Now I know there is no why. Hating me is like . . . sport for her, like shooting skeet out in the countryside. Just another extracurricular activity. I picture it on her college application, between all her pageant awards and hours of community service: Ten Years Tormenting Wing Jones.

There was the time when we were on a field trip in fourth grade and she dumped an entire jug of sweet tea on my head because she "wanted to see what would happen" to my hair. And the time when she asked our teacher why I had a "such a dumb name." She got in trouble for that one, but she got a big laugh from the class. I didn't know how to explain that for some reason my parents gave Marcus an American first name and a Ghanaian middle name, and I got a Chinese first name and a Ghanaian middle one. Then there was the time my mom came to pick me up from school and Heather told her that she couldn't be my mom because she didn't look like me. Or when she used to pull on the corner of her eyes and ask how I could see. And every time she said or did anything, she'd look around to see what kind of impact it was making, how many people were laughing. The more people laughed, the louder she got, and the louder she got, the smaller I tried to make myself.

As I'm passing Heather's desk on Monday morning, I hear her whisper something I can't quite make out, but the word gross jumps out at me loud and clear. I hurry past her, but she sticks one leg out and I see it but I don't stop in time and the next thing I know I'm sprawled out on the vomit-colored carpet, trying to ignore the stifled laughter around me. And it isn't just Heather's little crew, it's the whole class.

"Jesus, watch where you're going!" Heather says loudly as the door opens and our history teacher, Mr. Poller, walks in.

I can't decide if the teachers at my school are as dense as concrete or if they purposely ignore what they see. In the case of Heather Parker, I think most of them are probably just as scared as the rest of us. Last year, her mother got our English teacher fired. No one crosses Heather Parker.

Which is why I'm so surprised when Mr. Poller opens his mouth, his liver-spotted cheeks shaking slowly, spittle flying out, and says in his monotone rumble, "What is going on here, ladies?"

"Wing." Heather says my name like a swearword as I haul myself up, feeling like my limbs are everywhere. "She wasn't watching where she was going and tripped on my leg. I can feel the bruise forming already. I can't have a bruise. I've got pageant practice tomorrow."

"Please be more careful, Miss Jones," Mr. Poller says as I slide into my seat, trying to ignore Heather's victorious smile.

You know what's even worse than class with Heather Parker? Lunch. I shuffle around in the cafeteria every day, looking for an open spot next to someone with a book or some kids who won't mind if I sit next to them, and I eat my lunch, and then I find a quiet spot and get started on my homework or put on my headphones and listen to music till the bell rings. Marcus got me a Walkman last year for Christmas. Sometimes I wonder if it's because he knows I don't have any friends.

My mom asked me once why I don't sit with Marcus at lunch when I told her I didn't have anyone to sit with. "He's your brother, isn't he?"

As I line up to get my lunch, I try to imagine what would happen if I were to prance over to the table where Marcus is sitting with Monica on his lap and Aaron to his right and Dionne is throwing her weave over her shoulder trying to catch Aaron's eye, and Trey and the rest of the football team are throwing food at each other and Dionne's crew is laughing at something she's said and Monica is trying to ignore them—they've never really accepted her, even though she's been dating Marcus since the eighth grade. Dionne did try a little bit, when she was dating Aaron, I think they went on a few double dates but they were never going to be best friends, and then Dionne heard that Monica knew that Aaron was going to break up with her and didn't tell her, and that pretty much shattered any chance of them ever being any kind of friends. I'm impressed that they still manage to have lunch together every day. But if Monica is willing to defy her daddy to be with Marcus—and her daddy isn't the nicest man in the world, not by a long shot—then Dionne must be nothing more than a little gnat she has to swat at occasionally. Sometimes Tash sits with them, and when she does Monica doesn't sit on Marcus's lap, she'll sit with Tash. Because Tash is the closest thing Mon has to a best friend.

Other than me and Marcus. She told me that once. She was a little drunk, I could smell the tequila on her breath, and she leaned toward me and kissed me on the cheek and told me that I was her best friend and she was my best friend. And that one day I'd be her maid of honor at her and Marcus's wedding and that she loved me so much (right about then she belched so loudly I thought she was going to vomit all over both of us but she didn't, she just blew the air all over my face) that she wanted me to walk down the aisle right before her.

"With Aaron, because he'll be the best man, of course," she added, and I felt my heart expand inside me, expand so much I was certain it was going to burst right out of my chest and keep growing and expanding until it burst through the walls of our little house and it wouldn't stop, it would grow, grow, grow, so full, until it took over all of Atlanta and maybe Georgia and it wouldn't stop there, it would float up into the air, my big beating heart, and it would go higher and higher until it was up among the stars, creating a new constellation. That is how happy I was. Just imagining Marcus and Monica's wedding, and me being a part of it, the maid of honor, and Aaron being the best man. My mom says they can't get married till they both graduate from college because we aren't backwoods hicks, but I wish they could get married right now.

And at their wedding, unlike in the cafeteria, I would sit with them.

Because, going back to my imagining, if I were to walk up to the table now, Marcus would bolt up, eyes wide, and think that I needed him. Really needed him. And Monica would rush toward me and cry out "Wing, Wing! Baby girl, what's wrong?" and the rest of the table would go as still as statues and watch, and their judgment would be like dark smoke coming at us, enveloping us, because even if Marcus is my big brother I'm still a sophomore loser. But Monica and Marcus wouldn't notice the smoke, because they have their anti-judgment gas masks on that they always wear, that they've been wearing since they first kissed in the gym in eighth grade. I've figured that's the only way they've gotten this far, wearing their masks to keep the poisonous fumes from going into their mouths and their noses and up to their brains. So they wouldn't be able to smell it coming off their friends at their table, but I would. I don't have a handy anti-judgment gas mask.

And then when nothing was wrong, if I just smiled and said, "Oh, I just thought I'd join y'all for lunch," Marcus would frown, not in an upset way, but in a confused way, because why would I want to sit with the seniors for lunch? It isn't that he doesn't care that I don't have friends, he just doesn't really know what to do about it. Because even though he's my brother, it would be weird for me to sit at the football table with a bunch of seniors. But he'd tell Trey to scoot down and say "Of course, come sit," and then I would sit and the table would be silent except maybe for Trey snapping Dionne's bra strap or something, and I would try to smile but the smoke would be stinging my eyes and I wouldn't be able to stop them from watering, not crying, never crying, from all the poisonous fumes.

It isn't that everybody *hates* me. I just don't really fit in anywhere. It might be 1995, but at my school the white kids sit with the white kids, the black kids sit with the black kids. Only exception being Marcus and Monica, but Marcus is the exception to everything. There isn't a table for half-Chinese, half-black kids. There aren't even any other Asian kids at my school except for my brother, and the school hierarchy rules don't apply to him.

It wasn't always like this. I used to have a best friend.

April Tova Roth. Only Jewish girl I've ever met.

April and I met in the seventh grade, at the mandatory seventh-grade cotillion. We were both hiding in the bathroom from Heather Parker. Sure, I'd had some friends before that, but no one who got me. It was like all the friends I'd had before were polyester and April Roth was imported silk. Neither of us belonged with anyone else, so we belonged together. There wasn't room in my life for any other friends, not with April around. Between her, Marcus, and Aaron (always Aaron, he was always there, I can't remember him not in my heart), my heart was always full to bursting.

Other than Heather, April wasn't scared of anybody. She was born in New York but moved to Atlanta when she was ten, and said that the hobos in Atlanta have got nothing on the hobos in New York. She would talk back to teachers and tell them that they were wrong and she knew because her mother was a professor and her father was a banker and didn't those professions require more brains than it took to be a seventh-grade science teacher?

And freshman year, when Ryan Cork asked our biology teacher how someone like me could possibly have come into the world, using nasty names for both my mom and my daddy, April threw a textbook at him.

Ryan Cork was suspended for two weeks for saying what he did. And April was suspended for four and nearly expelled.

April didn't come back to our high school after that. Her mother quit her job at Georgia Tech and took her old position at NYU. They said they didn't want to live in a place like this. And it wasn't like there was a line of people jumping at the chance to become my new best friend. We write letters sometimes, and she says she wants me to visit, but we both know I don't have the money for something like that.

The week after April left, I sat down at Alicia Howard's table. Her brother sometimes hung out with Marcus and Aaron, so I thought that might be enough for us to get along.

"Girl," she said, looking me up and down, "we didn't invite you to sit with us." As I walked away, keeping my head down so they couldn't see my expression, I heard one of the other girls say "Isn't she from China?" and someone else said "Nah, I think it's Japan." "I thought Japanese girls were supposed to be all little? Wing's ass is bigger than mine." Their laughter chased me across the cafeteria.

Lunch really isn't my favorite time of day.

After lunch, I have ceramics. I'm not very good at it, but I've got to take something to get an art credit, and there was no way I was going to take drama or chorus or dance or anything where someone has to look at me. And I don't mind ceramics. There's something relaxing about molding the clay, even if everything I make comes out ugly. And it's better than gym, which was my other option for this year. I'll have to take it eventually, my school requires two years of some kind of athletic activity, but I want to postpone it for as long as possible. I don't want to have to deal with Heather Parker in the locker room.

The ceramics studio is down past the track, away from the main campus. As I walk, I hear loud laughter and instinctively freeze, sure that it's directed at me. But when I look toward the sound, I relax. It's Eliza Thompson, striding out onto the track like she's strutting on a catwalk. Three girls flank her.

Eliza Thompson is so fast and so fine that sometimes I think maybe *she* should be with Marcus instead of Monica. She's not just the fastest girl at our school but in our whole county. She's all long brown limbs and slender neck and sleek short hair, and I can hear her laugh bubbling up from the track as she stretches, leaning this way and that. All grace and power.

She bends down and touches her toes, the movement so smooth it is like watching a river bend down over a cliff and make a waterfall, then snaps back up, so quick it makes me blink. She takes off running in a burst of speed, and my own feet tingle.

I watch and I wonder what it feels like. To be so fast you can get away whenever you want and to be so sure of yourself that you don't care who is watching.

CHAPTER 6

I'm not invited to Trey's party.

Everyone has been talking about it all week. Everyone is going. Even people like Heather and Laura who normally wouldn't dream of going anywhere as sketchy as Trey's neighborhood are going. I overheard Heather today in history.

"Everyone slums occasionally. Come on, it'll be a riot. And I heard he's got two kegs."

Her minions nodded their heads like those Chihuahuas you see on truck dashboards.

But nobody thought to ask me if I wanted to go. Not even Marcus or Monica or Aaron. It isn't that I want to go. I've never been to a party like this, and I don't think I'd enjoy it. But it does hurt a little bit to know that I'll be home with my grannies while everyone else at my school is at the same party together.

Trey has the "hookup" when it comes to booze. That's what I hear, anyway. And he also has a gun that his cousin or his uncle or someone he isn't even related to got for him. Probably Jasper, now that I think about it. It makes me anxious to think about Marcus, Monica, and Aaron at a party with a gun.

They probably already have been. There's so much I don't know about their lives. And my whole life is them. It's like we're kids again in the swimming pool and they can come hang out with me in the shallow end and it's great, the best ever, and we play Marco Polo and spider and dolphins and pirates and all my favorite games, and then they swim in the deep end and I'm not a good enough swimmer to go, so I sit on the stairs, because swimming in the shallow end by yourself isn't fun, and watch their heads bob up and down as Marcus dives and Aaron cannonballs, and sure, I can tell you that it looks fun, but I can't tell you if it actually is fun.

I don't tell my Granny Dee this when she asks me why I'm pouting like a trout. I also don't tell her trouts don't pout. I don't even think they have lips. There is no point arguing about anything with my Granny Dee. I know she's trying to be nice, though, especially when she pushes a plate of cookies toward me.

"Where's Marcus tonight?" she asks, and I sigh.

"Out."

"That boy always out."

"It's Friday night, Granny. Everyone is out."

"You ain't out," she says, peering over her spectacles at me. They aren't glasses, by the way—she'll tell you that. They're her spectacles.

"Thanks for reminding me."

"You usually ain't so broke up about it either," she says, taking one of the chocolate chip cookies. "Something goin' on that you wanna tell your Granny Dee about?"

I take a cookie and bite into it. Stale. Made yesterday. Or the day before.

"These cookies are shit," I say, standing up so suddenly that my chair squeals in protest against our linoleum floor.

"You watch your language, little girl! That is no way to speak to your grandma. I'm not like your other one. I understand you. You can't get by saying bad words in front of me."

LaoLao speaks English just fine, but she still has a heavy accent and Granny Dee likes to pretend that she doesn't understand her. And LaoLao swears plenty too, but she does that in Mandarin. Practically the only Mandarin words I know are swearwords.

"If you don't apologize right this second for that filthy language, and for insulting my cookies, I will ground you."

I laugh. "Ground me? What difference will that make? It isn't like I'm going anywhere—or have anywhere to go."

"Where is all this sass coming from? I don't like it one bit." Underneath her anger is a note of hurt. Her conflicting emotions come at me like a steam train, but when I look harder I see that they're nothing but a puff of smoke, leaving a little old lady in its wake.

I go around to my Granny Dee and squeeze her shoulder. "I'm sorry," I say, not quite in a whisper but almost. I don't have much experience apologizing. I don't do things that require apologizing too often.

She reaches her veiny hand up and pats my own. "You know what you could do to make it up to me?" She looks up and her eyes are magnified beneath her spectacles. I smile at her encouragingly. "Make me a fresh batch of cookies. You were right, these are shit."

"Where are Mom and LaoLao?" I ask as I break an egg into our green mixing bowl. The kitchen is small and dark in the daytime, but at night, it's warm and feels like home. With the curtains drawn over the small boxy windows, some jazz music on for Granny Dee, the oven making everything nice and toasty, I can pretend we are anywhere. I don't need to see the bars on the windows of the house across from us or our overgrown front lawn, if you can call it a lawn, or watch people hurry by, not wanting to stick around in our neighborhood. I've lived in this house my whole life. It was my Granny Dee's house, the same one my daddy grew up in, but I won't be sad to say goodbye to it when Marcus gets drafted for the NFL, and I know he will because he isn't just good, he's magic, and when he's rich we'll all be rich and we'll move somewhere real nice, somewhere bigger and better, somewhere we all have enough space and there aren't bars on the windows and the light shines in every room.

"Your mother took a late shift tonight," says Granny from her chair as she nods back and forth to the jazz. "And your other grandmother"—I have yet to hear Granny Dee refer to LaoLao as LaoLao—"she went to bed early. Lazybones."

I nod and crack another egg. Right as the bright yellow yolk falls on top of the white flour, I hear it. A knock. And then another. Urgent. The kind of knocks that the Gestapo use in war films. The kind of knocks that make my Granny Dee's hand fly up to her heart.

The kind of knocks we've heard only once before.

I glance at the clock above the old oven. It's only 10:17. Not that late. Maybe it's my mom. Maybe we locked her out. This is what I tell myself as I walk to the front door, even though I know I haven't dead-bolted the door yet. And my mom wouldn't knock like that. And she doesn't have a shadow like that. And she wouldn't ever come home in a car with a red and blue flashing light on top of it.

When I open the door it is like I've fallen into a nightmare, one I've had over and over again.

Only it's worse than a nightmare. It's happened before.

CHAPTER 7

Officer James Northrup is standing at our door, his fist raised, ready to knock again. I feel all the air go out of me, looking at his craggy face and solemn eyes. He's got more wrinkles since the last time he came knocking on our door.

"Wing," he says, and I know what he's going to say next because he's said it before, this has all happened before, and I want to slam the door in his face to keep him from saying it because maybe if I don't hear it, maybe it won't be true.

"There's been an accident."

I remember the first time I heard those words. Seven years ago. And he didn't say them to me. He said them to my mother. "Winnie," he said. My mother's Chinese name is Fu Yin and somehow that turned into Winnie when she came to the States. "There's been an accident."

I had been sitting on the couch watching Power Rangers, a show I couldn't stand to watch after that night. I still don't think

I could stomach watching an episode. Because all I could think that night was the Power Rangers should have been there instead of my daddy.

They should have been the ones going to the drug bust; they should have been the ones who broke into the derelict house in College Park and shined their flashlight around and had their specially trained German shepherd tight on a leash and called out "This is the police!" except they would have said "This is the Power Rangers!" and the Power Rangers would have been prepared for anything. Prepared for the shouting and the shooting and the bullets.

But the Power Rangers weren't there. And those bullets went straight into my daddy's face, my daddy's handsome, perfect face, and blew it all to bits.

This was all I could think that night as I listened to Officer James talk in a low voice, glancing over at me and Marcus to make sure we weren't listening. Marcus wasn't, he was wrestling with Aaron on the floor, but I opened my ears as big as I could, turned them into sound-catching tunnels, and heard every word.

That's how I knew what happened to my daddy's face. Officer James was as delicate about it as he could be, but there are only so many ways to sugarcoat that someone was shot in the face. My mother's face was pale, pale, pale, the kind of pale on the tubes of whitening creams my LaoLao gets sent over from China.

That wasn't the first time my daddy had been shot. Or even the second time. Part of the job description, he said when he came home with his arm wrapped in layers and layers and layers of bandages. Part of the job description, he said when he came home with stitches snaking down his back.

But Officer James had never come to our house to tell us.

"Winnie," said Officer James, "I'm so sorry." He paused, let my mother take a deep breath, probably the worst breath of air she ever took in her whole life, and then went on. "I'm going to need you to come with me. To identify him."

Still, even as my eight-year-old brain was starting to process what this meant, my mother clung to a frail sliver of hope. "Where is he?" Her voice was trembling like a spiderweb in a thunderstorm.

"Winnie," said Officer James again. "I'm sorry."

This was when my mother reached out and slapped Officer James in the face, the sound so loud and unexpected that it made Marcus and Aaron look up from their wrestling match. Made LaoLao rush in from the kitchen and Granny Dee run down the hall.

"My husband is dead and all you can tell me is that you're sorry? Where the hell were you? Where were you? You're his partner, damn it!"

The word *dead* echoed in the room. It ricocheted around all the corners. It stopped and whispered in all our ears and then it screamed in our faces and then it went out the door before we could stop it. Before we could stomp on it and cut it into a million tiny pieces and make it disappear.

Officer James didn't move. He just kept staring at my mom with that same somber, solemn expression. The Power Rangers started battling one of the bad guys, and it was loud, so loud in the silence left by the word *dead*, and my mom turned toward the sound, and I'll never forget how her face looked. Her eyes were dark tunnels that led to nowhere and then she screamed "Turn that thing off!" and threw a book at the TV.

It was a heavy book, and the corner went straight into the

screen and then the TV started smoking and my Granny Dee, who had been rocking back and forth and whispering to herself, praying over and over and over again, her words spiraling and spilling until all she was saying was "Lord Lord Lord Lord Lord," started screaming like someone was dragging nails down her back, and LaoLao ran to my mother and took her in her arms and my mother started sobbing against her own mother's chest and Marcus and Aaron were cowering and sitting so close they might have been conjoined twins, and I was on the couch alone while the blue and red lights in front of our house flared and blared and made our living room look like a circus.

My mother did go with Officer James eventually. Granny Dee went with her. LaoLao stayed with us.

She took us all upstairs, Aaron too, I don't know why no one thought that he should go home but nobody was thinking any kind of sense, how could we, when nothing was making any kind of sense, and she started running a bath, a scalding hot bath, and stripped the boys down into their little-boy boxers and told them to get in, and they still hadn't said a word, they were like zombies, and they got into the tub and she poured a whole bottle of shampoo in there, so much that the water frothed and foamed over the sides of the tub, and then she sat down on the rug and pulled me into her lap and enveloped me in herself and held me and rocked me and petted my hair and every once in a while I would feel something wet drip down her face and onto my head or the back of my neck.

Eventually Aaron spoke up.

"Ma'am," he said. "Why are we in the tub?"

My LaoLao didn't hesitate. "Because I cannot hold you all at the same time."

Aaron thought about this and then said, "So the bath is holding us?"

LaoLao nodded. "It's holding you and keeping you warm. Like how I am doing to Wing."

Aaron nodded. "But, ma'am? It's getting cold in here."

LaoLao took the boys out as if they were just little things, wrapped towels around them, dried them, then got out some old bathrobes and made them put them on. They didn't protest once. They were ten-year-old boys and they let my old Chinese grandmother wrap them in threadbare terry-cloth robes. She put me in my pajamas and herded us into our parents' room.

"Get in bed." She pointed at the bed in case it wasn't obvious.

And we did. We all got in my mom and dad's bed. Aaron and Marcus clambered in first, sharing a pillow, and then I squeezed in between Marcus and LaoLao. I saw the shadow of my dragon dancing on the wall. No, not dancing. Raging. I heard my lioness growling under the bed. It was the first time I'd seen them since I'd fallen off the swings, and even though I was hurting so bad, hurting more than when I broke my ankle that time, more than when Heather Parker was mean to me, more than I'd ever hurt before, knowing that my lioness and my dragon were there with me and that they were angry and hurting too made everything just a little bit better. The way having a thin blanket with holes in it was better at keeping out the cold than having no blanket at all. I wanted to peek under the bed, to see my lioness, to pet her and ask her to get in bed with us and keep us safe, but LaoLao was holding me too tightly for me to move.

"It is okay," LaoLao said.

But nothing was.

Now it is seven years later and Officer James is at my door, telling me that there's been another accident. I realize I haven't breathed since I saw who was at the door.

"Wing?" he says, and his tone is the exact same tone as when he said "Winnie?" to my mother and then announced that my father had been shot and killed, but he can't be here to tell me that because that already happened and it isn't like it can happen again.

"It's Marcus."

CHAPTER 8

I HAVEN'T SAT IN THE BACK OF A COP CAR IN OVER SEVEN years, not since I used to ride in my daddy's car when he finished a shift. It makes me dizzy. It makes me sick.

LaoLao and Granny Dee are on either side of me, LaoLao's girth spilling over onto me while Granny Dee's bony hip digs into me with every turn.

"My mom," I say as we fly through a red light, the sirens on and the blue and red lights flashing. I raise my voice to be heard over the rise and fall of the echoing siren. "My mom!"

"I sent someone to the restaurant," says Officer James, keeping his eyes on the road as he swerves around a pickup truck. "She'll meet us at the hospital."

He hasn't given us any details except that there was a car accident. Marcus was driving. They had to use the jaws of life to cut him out and he was rushed to the hospital. There were two people in the car with him. Officer James doesn't know their names. One of them was killed instantly.

There was another car too. Just the driver was inside. Officer James doesn't know if she survived or not—just said that the car was wrecked "real bad." And then he closed his mouth and wouldn't tell us anything else.

As we swing into the hospital parking lot, our siren trying to scream louder than the ambulance sirens in a piercing discord, he looks at me with red-rimmed eyes. "I came as soon as I knew who it was," he says. "I recognized the car. I sent someone else to the restaurant and I came straight to your house. I had to."

"Thank you," I say in a wooden voice, which is the strangest thing in the world to say to someone who has shattered your family with their words not once, but twice. A weird thing to say to someone who should have saved your daddy but didn't.

"It's the least I can do," he says, and I wonder whether my daddy's death haunts him.

I nod but I don't say anything. I can't say anything.

Then I scramble out over Granny Dee and run as fast as I have ever run into the hospital, leaving Officer James to help my grandmothers.

The sliding doors open and I nearly knock over an old man wearing a blue hospital gown and someone is screaming so loudly that for a second I think it must be me and I just don't realize it because that kind of thing is always happening in books, but my mouth is shut tight so it can't be me. But there is something familiar about the scream and I turn toward it and then there are arms around me, holding me so tight I'm worried I won't be able to breathe, and there is hair in my face, hair that smells like beer and cigarette smoke and a perfume I'd recognize anywhere.

It's Monica, and she's shattered.

Another pair of arms comes up and engulfs me, arms that are familiar too but in a different way, and Monica is still screaming and a nurse is running toward us and she's saying something but it's like someone has turned off all the sound in the room except the sound of Monica's howls. Which are starting to take shape into words, the way clay slowly forms into cups and bowls. I don't want to hear Monica's words, but I can't cover my ears because my arms are pinned to my side because I've got two people pressed against me like we're trying to make a human sandwich.

The words slowly piece themselves together in my brain.

"I saw it! I saw everything! Marcus! Marcus!"

Then I see LaoLao and Granny Dee, and they look so scared and lost under the bright hospital lights and they are huddled together in a way I've never seen them. I manage to slowly push Monica off me. Her mascara is running down her face to her chin and she's panting like a wounded animal.

The other arms are Aaron's arms. He relaxes his grip on us but keeps one hand on my lower back, supporting me. It occurs to me, the thought coming from very far away, that it's shocking that I was able to support Monica when she flung herself at me, that I didn't fall straight over, but then I realize that Aaron was there supporting both of us the whole time.

"Where is he?" I say, my voice coming out strange and harsh.

"They won't let us see him!" Monica sobs. "But I saw. I saw. He's dead, Wing, he's dead and they aren't telling us!" Her voice is getting higher and louder with every word.

"Monica! Stop that! He's not dead!" Aaron is shouting, and an old white woman winces and steps away, scared of a young black man shouting. "Stop it!" he roars again.

LaoLao and Granny Dee have shuffled their way toward us, moving like one creature, their arms entwined. "Where's my daughter?" says Granny Dee, and I blink, not knowing what she means.

"My daughter," says LaoLao. "Where is she?"

"She's my daughter too now. Winnie is mine too," says Granny Dee, and now that they're closer I can see that she has tears coursing down her cheeks, turning her wrinkles into rivers.

A hospital representative in scrubs comes up to us. "Could I ask y'all to follow me?"

"What is it? Is it Marcus? Do you have news?" Monica throws her questions at the woman; her eyes are wide and desperate, like a fish's gaping mouth as it lies on a dock, drowning in the air. The woman gives her a patient smile. "I'm not sure yet. We won't know for a while. But . . . you are starting to alarm the other patients and people here. I understand this is a very hard time for your family. Why don't you come with me into a more private room?"

"Screw that," says Aaron, starting to back away. "I'm not going into a room. I know what those rooms are for. They're for telling you that someone is dead. Mon, maybe you're right."

The woman in the scrubs smiles again, this time with a little less patience. "I understand you are frightened for your friend"—I wince at hearing Marcus referred to as Monica's friend, as my friend, but don't interrupt her—"but he is fighting very hard for his life right now, and we think it would be best if you all came and sat in another room. Otherwise I need to ask you to vacate the premises."

"And if I don't?" Aaron looms over the woman. She doesn't bat an eye.

"Then we'll call the police to escort you out."

She looks at Aaron, at me, at Monica, at my clinging grandmothers. In quick succession. And back again. Trying to untangle the thread of how we relate.

I wonder how the ambulance called in Marcus. Black male, they'd have said. That's what people see first. And then maybe they'd have squinted down at him. Mixed race. Some kind of Asian.

And before I can stop myself, I wonder if he was in any kind of shape to be identified as anything at all.

I force the thought out of my head, force it out hard and fast like yanking a plug out of a socket, shutting it down, and stare back at the woman.

"The police escorted us in," I say, hoping this will keep her from calling them back in to escort us out. I don't know if we should go into this room, because maybe Aaron is right and the hospital is thinking that if we're acting like this when we don't even know what's wrong with Marcus, then they sure as hell aren't going to tell us he's dead, because who knows what we would do . . . but maybe we should go into the room because I really would like to sit down and there aren't any free seats out here.

"We'll go," I say, and the steel in my voice surprises me.

The room looks like a crappy boardroom. Pleather chairs, worn carpet. The worst part is the smell. Disinfectant crossed with illness. We don't speak; we don't even make eye contact. LaoLao and Granny Dee are holding hands. Monica has her arms wrapped around herself and is rocking back and forth in her chair and Aaron is sitting slumped forward with his head in his hands. My body is getting heavier and heavier with each breath I take.

The door creaks open and my mom steps in, her face set in

stone. She doesn't look at anyone but me, and when she gets to me, she wraps her arms around me and holds me tight, like I'm trying to get away from her even though I'm hugging her right back.

"I love you," she says, but it is more like a command than an endearment. "Do you hear me? I love you."

And then she goes to her mother and to Granny Dee and hugs them too.

"I've spoken to his doctor," she says, and Monica whips her head up.

"They talked to you! They told you how he is? They wouldn't tell us anything!"

"Monica," says Aaron. "Be quiet."

"Mom!" I say, losing my patience. "Tell us!"

My mom takes a deep breath and sits down. She looks smaller than I remember her looking this morning. She shuts her eyes briefly, presses her palms to her forehead, and then looks up at us.

"He's alive," she says, and it should be cause for celebration, but there is something in the way she's just said those amazing words that makes us all pause and wait. "But he's bleeding internally, his ribs are broken, his leg is shattered, and"—she takes a deep breath and I know she hasn't told us the worst part yet— "his brain is swelling and he's in a coma. They have to operate on his brain." Her voice wobbles, and she must hear it because she presses her lips together and shakes her head. "They say there's a very good chance he'll wake up. Hopefully with all his motor functions and memories. But they don't know for sure."

There is no jumping. There is no celebrating. My Granny Dee gets up from her seat and goes to my mother and rubs her shoulders.

"It'll be all right," she croons softly. "It'll all be all right."

My mom nods and looks at Monica and Aaron. "You two should get home," she says. "It's been a long night."

Monica is shaking. Shaking all over. "I shoulda been in that car, Mrs. Jones. I shoulda been with him. I shouldn't have let him drive. I'm so sorry."

"Sweetie, this isn't your fault," says my mom, but Monica still looks stricken. "And I am so grateful you weren't in that car." She swallows. "One of the boys who was . . . he died. The other one is in surgery right now. And the car Marcus hit . . . that woman died too."

I am filled with an overwhelming sense of relief that the boy who died wasn't Marcus. It's an awful thought. One I wish I could push away as soon as I think it, but it stays and gets cozy in my brain, making itself at home, until it is the only thing I can think about. I've already lost my daddy; it wouldn't be fair for me to lose Marcus too. A person can only lose so much.

There's a polite but sharp knock at the door. Aaron opens it.

There's a policeman standing there. Not one I recognize. He nods curtly to us all and comes in. "This Marcus Jones's family?"

"Yes, sir," I say. He glances at me and then my mother, his eyes ping-ponging back and forth a few times before flying over my head and landing on Granny Dee and LaoLao, and a slow understanding dawns on his face. Figuring out that I'm half Granny Dee and half LaoLao and that's why I don't look much like my mom.

"Did any of you see the accident?"

Monica clears her throat. "Yes, sir." Her voice is the calmest it's been since we arrived at the hospital. "I did."

"And you?" The man gestures at Aaron.

Aaron shakes his head. "No, sir. I was still at the house party when the accident happened."

"Then how did you know about it?"

Monica answers. "Our friend Roddy, who was driving the car that I was in, went back to the house to call 911. And to tell everyone else what had happened." I think about what that must have been like for Roddy, to be the messenger. Bursting back into the party, turning off the music, and announcing what happened.

"And I asked him to drive me here." Aaron's face is grave, like he's giving testimony in court.

"I stayed on the scene until the ambulance got there and then went with Marcus." Monica is twisting her ring round and round her finger.

I stayed on the scene. I wonder how long she sat there, alone in the dark, on the side of the road, with nothing but dead and broken bodies for company.

"I'm going to need to talk to you some more," the officer says to Monica. A dark, cold feeling is spreading through me like frost on a windshield on a winter morning.

"Sir," says my mother. "It's very late. We've all had a very, very hard day. Can it wait?"

"I'd like to get her statement while it's fresh," says the officer.

"Her statement?" My mom frowns, her forehead creasing.

"Yes, her statement. Marcus Jones is potentially being charged with underage drinking, possession of false identification, driving while under the influence of alcohol, and possibly vehicular manslaughter."

"Oh my sweet Jesus," whispers Granny Dee.

There is a thump behind me and my LaoLao cries out. I turn,

expecting to see my Granny Dee on the floor. Instead, I see Monica lying in a heap, her eyes rolling back in her head.

Turns out that a hospital is a good place to faint. As soon as Monica collapses, the police officer opens the door and shouts for a nurse. When the nurse comes bustling in, my mom hurries over and speaks in hushed, hurried tones, pointing at the officer. All I hear is "interrogating," "exhausted," "intimidating," "collapse," "breakdown," "witnessed."

I'm starting to feel faint myself. I don't know what time it is. I hope I remembered to turn off the oven.

I wish my daddy were here.

I wish Marcus were here.

The officer's words play over and over in my head like a song you hear on the radio that you can't stop humming. In my addled and exhausted brain the words run together, but I try to focus on the charges.

Possession of false identification: This I can believe. I'm pretty sure I've seen Marcus's fake ID. This one can't be so bad. Everyone has got a fake ID.

Underage drinking: What's the point of a fake ID if you aren't going to use it to drink? These two seem like they should be the same charge.

Driving while under the influence of alcohol: This is the one that shocks me. It sends tentacles of doubt through me, uncurling like octopus arms. I can't believe Marcus would be so stupid.

Vehicular manslaughter: Two people died. What I want to know is how come the police are blaming Marcus? What about this other driver?

It isn't like anyone can ask her, though. Since she's dead.

CHAPTER 9

THE HOUSE FEELS STRANGE WITHOUT MARCUS IN IT. NOT A home but a house. A container, holding us in it, trying and failing to protect us from the outside world.

I don't remember leaving that room, how we got home. Who drove. Who said what. If anyone said anything.

My mother goes straight upstairs and into her room and closes the door, the click of the lock ringing loud in our empty, empty house.

How can a place feel so empty with four people in it? I breathe in my grandmothers more than hear them. Tonight they have disappeared into the shadows; they will sink into their small twin beds, deeper and deeper, until all that is left is an imprint of them and the lingering scent of flour and spice. Without Marcus there is no one in the house.

As the door to their room closes behind them, they do not even turn to me. Doors are closing all around me, leaving me alone in our corridor. I look down the hall, it seems infinitely long, and the door to Marcus's room at the end looms large, and the emptiness behind it is like a black hole that will expand and eat our whole house and suck everything into its emptiness. My brother's room with his trophies lining the bookshelves, pictures of him and our daddy, cards from Monica, letters from colleges, newspaper clippings of games he won. It was sacrosanct before—Marcus needs his sleep, he needs to get his rest, he needs a place that is his alone, away from all the women in this house—and now, now I know it will be even more so, it will be a shrine. No one will sleep in there. I wonder if anyone will ever go in it. I find myself walking toward it, the emptiness calling to me, and I know I shouldn't go in but I can't stop.

I put my hand on the doorknob and suddenly it feels like opening this door will unlock all the others in the house and my mother and my grandmothers will stumble out and run at me like zombies, saying stop stop stop, don't go in there. Don't open the door to all that emptiness, don't disrupt his room, he'll come home soon, and he is the only one who can stop the emptiness. . . .

But I turn the handle and they don't come out. Their doors stay shut, the air stays heavy and still, and I push the door open. His room is exactly as he left it. I should leave now, leave it undisturbed for him so when he comes home—

When he comes home
When he comes home
When he comes home
—it will be exactly as he remembers it and we can all pick up where we left off. With Marcus being the perfect child, the

perfect brother, as perfect as the little gold man on the trophies all over his room, as unchangeable, incorruptible.

He's coming home he's going to come home and he's going to be so mad that I was in his room.

He's left his window open and the sky outside is a violent violet and the air smells like thunderstorms. I breathe deeply, smelling the storm, the boy smell of his room, the deodorant and the cologne and . . . incense?

On Marcus's nightstand there's a small incense holder. The ends are burnt; he's lit these before.

I have a sharp, unkind thought: Did he smoke and drink in here? Secretly? Light incense to hide the smell?

Marcus isn't who I thought he was, and I'm starting to wonder if I knew him at all.

Fear and anxiety and anger race through me, each one trying to make it to the finish line and dominate my feelings. It makes me spin. My breath catches and I realize I'm crying, not making a sound, but crying so hard that it's taking all my energy. My legs give way as I sit on the edge of his bed and then curl up on my side, not trying to stop the tears, because I know I can't stop them, letting them leak onto his pillow until it's as soggy and waterlogged as my insides. But my tears keep coming.

These aren't the kind of tears that give you a sense of relief or wash the pain away. These tears hurt. Each and every one has made the perilous journey from my heart to my eyes. I feel like with every tear I'm losing a little bit more of who I thought my brother was, but I can't stop them. I don't think I'll ever be able to stop.

But then I do. They slow to a trickle, each one still as painful as the last, and I am left carved out and drained. I take a deep shuddering breath, letting the air whistle around my empty insides.

I am so tired. So very, very tired. I'll close my eyes just for a second, give them a rest.

Just for a second.

CHAPTER 10

SOMETHING IS NUDGING ME. NO, NOT NUDGING ME, HEAD-butting me. I open my eyes and gasp.

My lioness is gently pressing her head against mine. Purring as she does. I can feel her hot breath on my cheek.

And I can sense something else behind me. Slowly, so slowly, I turn my head until I'm looking at my dragon. Her eyes are glowing amber almonds, slit pupils, green lightning snaking through the fire. My lioness's eyes are round and yellow as the sun, with warm brown pupils. She blinks at me and I swear her mouth turns up in a smile.

I sit up and the lioness repositions herself so she's lying under my arm, supporting me, keeping me up. Her purr rumbles through her, warming me. I tentatively rest my palm on her back, feeling her fur, simultaneously coarse and soft, under my fingers.

The dragon is staring at me, and I stare back. She isn't smiling.

"I haven't seen you in a long time," I say. Because I haven't, not even a shadow or a glimpse, since my daddy died. They were there that first night, and again at his funeral, but they didn't come this close. They didn't wake me up in the middle of the night.

My dragon tilts her head and bends her long neck so her face is close to mine. She doesn't answer, but raises a dragon eyebrow.

I don't know if it's the weight of my lioness or the hot breath of my dragon, but I'm suddenly overwhelmed with heat. So hot. The air in the room is so thick and heavy I can taste it.

"Why are you here?" My voice comes out in a ragged whisper, like old cloth being ripped down the middle.

The lioness growls, low in her throat, for just a second, and then pulls away from me, padding over to the closed door of Marcus's room.

I shouldn't be in here, that's what they're telling me. I stand up and follow the lioness, feeling the dragon right behind me, hearing her claws crunching into the carpet. I pull open the door as quietly as I can, but still it creaks, the sound screaming in the empty hall. I wait a second, and another, before exhaling.

It's just as hot out in the hall as it was in my brother's room. I need air. Fresh air. I can't breathe. I need to get outside.

It seems my dragon and my lioness have the same idea. The lioness is pacing back and forth next to the front door, and the dragon—she's too big for our little kitchen—is trying to fold in on herself to make herself smaller, but she can't, and that makes me smile because I'm always trying and failing to make myself smaller too.

"Move," I whisper to the lioness, adding a belated "please" as I tug open the front door. The lioness squeezes past me and dashes down the porch into the street, then rolls around on the asphalt like a kitten.

I look back into the kitchen for the dragon but she isn't there. She's already outside.

"If you didn't need me to open the door in the first place . . . ," I mutter, but it makes me glad to see her outside, stretching her wings, waggling her tail, lengthening her neck. I go to them, wanting to be close to these old friends I haven't seen in so long.

The night air embraces me, pulling me into itself, and I find myself stretching out my own arms, lengthening my own neck, moving just like my dragon. The sky is endless above me and looks low enough to touch. It looks like it would feel like velvet.

"Why are you here?" I ask again, and in reply the lioness comes over and nudges the back of my knees. My legs are taut and tense and weary, like the rest of me.

I wonder if anyone will wake up and look out their window and see a girl, not just any girl, the sister of the fallen Marcus Jones, out in the middle of the street with only her dragon and her lioness for company.

My dragon starts to flap her wings, the air rushing against me, and rises above me into the low, low sky. I want to join her; I want to fly. To get away. To go somewhere this hasn't happened. Somewhere safe. Somewhere new.

My lioness nudges me again, her sandpaper tongue brushing against my hand. "You can't fly," I murmur, bending down to feel her warm breath against my face. I wrap my arms around her, feeling her strength. Needing her strength.

She responds with a low growl before pulling away from me and crouching low to the ground. She glances at me once, and then she is running, running, running, running, down the street after my dragon. She is beautiful to watch, her body is music in motion, and I feel my own limbs responding, my muscles tensing, wanting to join her. I watch my lioness and my dragon until I can't see them anymore. Until I'm not sure I ever did see them.

When I slip back inside, the heat in our house is still stifling; I feel like I'm in a coffin. I go back into my brother's room because there is nowhere else for me to go.

CHAPTER 11

"Wing? Wing!"

I start. I'm lying on Marcus's bed, over the covers, and sunlight is streaming in through the open window, making the dust in the air shimmer like gold. The pillow is damp beneath my cheek.

"Wing?" My LaoLao is getting louder, which for her means more anxious. She must have gone to my room and seen that I wasn't there.

I clamber out of my brother's bed and pull open the door.

"Wing?" LaoLao's tone is incredulous. She stares at me, her eyes wide and round, her mouth open, the rolls under her chin tucking into her neck. For a moment I think I see a dragon's tail behind her, but then I blink and it's gone, and there is only my LaoLao staring at me.

I close the door behind me firmly.

"What you doing in your brother's room?" She frowns and

then shakes her head. "It is okay. I understand. But you know his room is for him. And now we keep it waiting for him. Go into the kitchen. Make tea. Today . . ." She sighs deeply. It's so similar to the sound the dragon made last night that I take a step back, half expecting fire to come out of her nose, but instead she puts her small, callused hands on my back and pushes me out the doorway. "Today will be a hard day."

It is the first of many hard days.

I try to be there for my mother, but there isn't much I can do. Officer James comes. Other police come. Ones we don't know. A lawyer comes. We can't afford him. A reporter comes. Granny Dee chases him off the porch with a broom.

Only my mom is allowed to see Marcus. He's still in critical condition and needs to be in a private room. Our insurance doesn't cover it. My mom says we'll make it work. LaoLao asks Mom if she can come help at the restaurant. "I too old to work, but for Marcus . . ." LaoLao shrugs and I know what she means. It's been three days and the hospital bills are already mounting, and apparently even though Marcus can't go to court—he can't go anywhere, might not ever go anywhere—he needs a lawyer. Someone to defend him for this indefensible thing he did. I don't see how a lawyer can be of any kind of help to anybody. But Officer James says we'll need one, and when my mom asks, in a strained, dead voice that doesn't sound like her own, how much we're looking at in terms of legal fees, he names a number so high I think he must be kidding, but all my mom does is nod and write it down on the yellow legal pad she's started carrying around with her everywhere.

I know that when my daddy died, we got some kind of life insurance. But that was seven years ago, and my mom doesn't make that much at the restaurant. I know that these numbers they're whispering that they don't think I can hear don't add up. I see them dancing above our heads, laughing at us, gloating at our misfortune. I want to get a broom and chase them out like Granny Dee chased that reporter, but I know they aren't going anywhere.

Two years ago, one of the other guys on the football team got some kind of rare blood disease. The kind insurance didn't cover. The team did car washes and the cheerleaders had a bake sale and people in the neighborhood donated.

When I suggest to my mom that we hold a bake sale for Marcus, she puts down the yellow legal pad and asks me to come sit next to her on the couch.

"Wing," she says, her voice soft and slow, watching me carefully. "Sweetie, you know . . . you know that people blame Marcus for this, right?"

"Well, it was his fault," I admit, because he was driving, after all. "But that doesn't mean they won't want to help him."

"Honey, it's such a nice idea. But I don't think it would be very well received. This is different from when that boy got sick."

I must still look confused, because she sighs, not like she's frustrated with me, but like she's sad that she has to have this conversation.

"I didn't want to show you this, but I think you need to know how people are feeling."

She goes to the bookshelf and pulls out a manila folder that's sitting on top of some books. Inside are newspaper clippings. Newspaper clippings about Marcus.

LOCAL FOOTBALL STAR KILLS YOUNG MOTHER

SCHOOL SHATTERED BY DRUNKEN QUARTERBACK'S
DECISION TO DRIVE

COP'S SON HEADED FOR PRISON

OP-ED: STAR ATHLETE THOUGHT RULES DIDN'T APPLY

DRUNK DRIVER SHAMES HERO FATHER'S MEMORY

Dotted throughout the article are quotes from kids at our school. Kids in Marcus's class, other guys on the team, all eager to give the "inside story" on Marcus.

"Don't you see, sweetie?"

And now I do: no one will want to help him after what he did.

I remember how different it was when my daddy died, how the very day after we got the news, and for days and days after that, we were inundated with casseroles and fresh-baked bread and cookies and whole weeks' worth of meals we could put in the freezer and reheat. Like we could eat our way out of grief. I didn't understand how a casserole was going to help us feel any better, but I realize now that it's what we lived on. We survived on food made with love, made to comfort by other people who cared about us and weren't so racked with grief that they couldn't find their way around a kitchen. And my mom got time off from the restaurant. Paid time. Bereavement.

She hasn't gotten any time off work now. Even though she's grieving. And no one has come by with anything. Nothing at all. It hurts just the same. Maybe worse. Because when my daddy died, that was it, he was dead. And it was the worst thing that had ever happened, ever. It was like our house was swallowed up by a sinkhole of pain and we were never going to get out of it. But we did, somehow. I don't even remember doing it, but we did. And now the not knowing if Marcus will wake up is a different kind of hurt. Everyone said my daddy was a hero who died honorably. There is nothing honorable about what Marcus did. If he does die, it won't be honorable. It'll be shameful. And if he lives, that'll be shameful too.

But I'd rather he live a shameful life than die a shameful death.

I don't go to school on Monday. I wonder if Monica and Aaron are there.

I don't go to school the next day either. My mom says I can stay home this whole week. Tuesday night we're sitting at the table when there's the horrible sound of something hitting our windows. I think we must be getting robbed, not that we have anything worth stealing, and we cower in our chairs, not one of us moving, sitting silent, fear loud on our faces, and the sound goes on and on, and then I hear something else. Shouting. Jeers. Laughter.

By Wednesday morning the egg yolk has run and dried down the windows and the door and all over my mom's car. Across our porch someone has sprayed

M IS FOR MURDER

On Thursday my mom meets with the doctors. We have to make a decision. The only thing keeping Marcus alive right now is the machines. The doctors can further induce his coma, keep the machines going, but our insurance doesn't cover it. They don't know how much it'll cost.

My mom doesn't pause, doesn't flinch.

"Do whatever you need to do. He'll wake up."

My brother, once the hero, the Prince Charming, has somehow turned into Sleeping Beauty. If only a kiss could wake him.

Some people think he's worse than that. Some people think he's the villain in the story.

M is for Murder.

M is for Michael. The boy who was in the car with Marcus who wasn't wearing his seat belt and went straight through the windshield and was killed instantly.

M is for mother, which is what the woman in the other car was. To a two-year-old boy. I've seen his photo in the papers. I want to reach into the photo and pull him out and hold him on my lap and brush his hair out of his eyes and tell him he'll be okay, that I lost my daddy and I'm okay. I want to tell him I'm sorry that he won't know his mama. But I don't think his family wants anything to do with our family.

M is for Marcus. My brother, who changed his whole story.

On Friday we go see him.

The ride to the hospital is somber. Granny Dee and LaoLao don't say a word, not even when I get in the front seat. Usually they squabble like little kids over who gets to sit in the front.

"We're here to see Marcus Jones." I wonder if anyone else can hear the heartbreak in my mother's voice. Hear the hope.

The woman behind the registration desk glances up at my mother, down at paperwork, back up at my mother.

"I'm sorry, ma'am, family only."

My mother's face crumples. "Excuse me?"

Granny Dee puts her bony hand under my mother's elbow, because it looks like my mother's body might follow her face and crumple too. LaoLao moves closer, frowning like thunder.

"We are family," says Granny Dee, and LaoLao nods, her frown deepening so it almost gets lost in her face.

The woman behind the desk purses her lips, stares at Granny Dee, stares at my mother. I step forward, the missing link. The thing that connects them.

"He's my brother," I say softly, even though inside I'm screaming. "We need to see him."

The bright pink color that creeps up the woman's neck almost perfectly matches her shirt, but it does nothing to appease Granny Dee. Neither do her mumbled apologies.

"You heard my granddaughter." I watch the word *granddaughter* tumble out of Granny Dee's mouth and slap the woman in the face. "We need to see him."

Once we're inside his room, the first thing I notice is that the body in the bed looks both small and gargantuan at the same time, like some kind of fun-house mirror trick. The next thing I notice is that it isn't my brother.

"Talk to him," says the nurse as she bustles around the prone and plastered body. She is cool and competent. I'm envious of her busyness. Envious that she can help him. That she has a job. We stand in a line by his bed. Staring down at the person who was once Marcus. This *thing* we're looking at, this bloated and broken

71

thing, isn't my brother. His eyes are still swollen shut and his head is wrapped in miles of gauze and he's in plaster from the waist down. He has so many wires attached to him, going through him, he looks more robot than boy.

My mother crouches down next to him, takes his hand, the one that isn't in a cast, and holds it.

"Hi, Marcus," she says. "I'm sorry I've been your only visitor this week. We're all here now."

"And we'll be here as much as we can." Granny Dee's voice rings out loud and true in the small room. If anyone is going to be able to wake Marcus, it'll be her. I look at his face expectantly, waiting to see his eyes open, the way they do in the movies.

Nothing happens. His face has the same dead expression that looks nothing like the brother I remember. The Marcus I remember.

"Wing? Do you want to say anything to Marcus?"

Marcus. Marcus. This is Marcus. This is my brother.

I want to say so much. I want to shake him and scream at him and hit him for doing this to himself. To us. To Michael and his family. To the mother who was killed, to her family. Because as much as him being in here is hurting me, at least he *is* here. I can't imagine, won't let myself imagine, how much more it would hurt if he weren't here. Even thinking about what could have been makes me scared and angry, but more than that it makes me grateful, guilt-ridden grateful, painful grateful, that he is here right now. It's like walking barefoot across broken glass to get to him, it hurts so bad, each step piercing me with tiny slivers that I don't know if I'll ever be able to get out. He shattered other people's lives and all I've got to do is wade through the mess he made, and as painful as each step is, I know it could be so much worse. All this just proves how much I love him, because I know this was his fault. He's ruined more than I can even get my head around, but I love him even fiercer than I did before. I want to cuss him out for being so selfish. For being so stupid. But I also want to see him on the field again. I want to cheer for him. I want to hold on to him and never let him go.

"Wing?"

I feel like I'm onstage and my mom and Granny Dee and LaoLao are all watching me, waiting to hear what I have to say.

"I'm sure he wants to hear your voice," my mom prompts.

"Hi," I say, not taking his hand because I'm scared that it won't feel like his hand, it will feel like a stranger's hand, because it looks like a stranger's hand.

"Hold his hand," suggests the nurse, more cheerful than she ought to be.

I slowly reach over and pick up his hand, and it is deadweight, a mannequin's hand, but at least it's warm. At least it isn't actually dead.

"I miss you," I say. "Wake up soon, okay?"

Again I stare intently at his face, wishing, hoping, praying for some response.

No response. Nothing at all.

"I think he heard you," says the nurse. I scowl at her, because it isn't nice to say things that blatantly aren't true. It isn't fair to wake up our hope like that. She smiles at me and says, "Oh, sweet pea," which I don't think anyone has ever called me in my whole life, "his heart rate just picked up. He heard you. And he's fighting to wake up."

I want to ask her if she really thinks that, and if she does, then why the hospital asked my mom if we wanted to turn him off, but instead I look at my brother's face and smile, hoping that he'll feel it even if he can't see it.

Granny Dee and LaoLao sit with him too until visiting hours are over, and then we make our way back to the car. The hope I felt looking at my brother is blooming into something bigger, yet fragile, like a bubble. When I sit in the front, Granny Dee hollers at me that I'm in her seat, so she must be feeling better too.

It's Sunday night and I'm trying to read in bed but the words aren't making sense and are jumping and blurring all over the pages. My door creaks open and my mom walks in. She comes over and perches on the edge of my bed.

"Wing," she says. "I know this is hard for you. And I'm sorry I haven't been more . . . there for you." She's pulling at an errant thread on my bedspread and won't look at me. "It's hard for me too." I want to wrap my arms around her but I'm worried if I do that one of us or both of us will start crying and won't be able to stop, so instead I stare at my hands.

"On Friday the nurse said his heart rate went up. . . . That's a good thing, right?" I ask. "Do you think he really could hear us?"

"I'm not a doctor. I wish I knew. I hope he did. But, Wing, even if he did, even if he wakes up . . ." My mom pauses.

"*When* he wakes up," I correct her.

"When he wakes up . . . things will be very different. We need to be ready for that. And it could take . . . a very long time."

"For him to wake up?"

"Yes. And for him to recover."

"He's got us," I say.

My mom smiles and leans toward me, brushing my hair off my forehead like she used to do when I was little.

"Yes," she says. "He does."

"Mom?" I finally look up from my hands. "I love you." My mom smiles, the first smile I've seen on her face since the accident, and pats my cheek.

"I love you too. Now get some sleep. You've got to go back to school tomorrow."

"I don't want to," I say quickly. "Can't I withdraw? Be home-schooled?"

"Honey, we need to maintain some kind of normalcy. You have to go back to school. Our lives can't stop because Marcus is in the hospital."

But I could barely manage school with Marcus, I want to say. How will I manage it without him?

"You have to go back, Wing," says my mom with an air of finality. "I know it's going to be hard, but you can do it. Be strong. You've always been my strong girl."

I nod because I don't know what else I can do.

She tucks me in like I'm little again and says "Sweet dreams" as she flips the light switch.

Since the night of the accident, the night my dragon and my lioness visited me, I've been having the same dream. Not about the accident. Thank goodness I can't picture that; even if I try, my brain shuts down, fades to black. I wonder if Monica sees it in her dreams, and when she wakes up, she realizes that it isn't a nightmare, that she's living it. Thinking about how awful that must be for her makes me shudder. Does she reach out for Marcus when she wakes up? (I know she used to sleep in his room with him almost every weekend. She used to creep down the hall, slip into his room after dark, and be gone by morning. Marcus said he slept better with her next to him, and when he told me that, he sounded so grown-up, and it made me feel so far away from him, this brother of mine who wanted to fall asleep next to the girl he loved, and now who knows when he'll get to fall asleep next to her, or if he ever will again).

No, I don't dream about the accident. I dream, over and over again, that I'm running. Running like I've never run before. Running like Eliza Thompson. Running like my lioness. Running as fast as my dragon flew that night, up into the sky and away from here. The setting changes—I'm on grass, on the beach, on the dirt track at school, on the road—but I'm always running. So far and so fast that my dream lungs ache and my muscles scream, but I keep going. I can't tell if I'm running away from something or if I'm running toward something.

Tonight is no different. I wake up drenched in sweat. Every beat of my pounding heart is a command.

Run. Run. Run.

CHAPTER 12

I HOPE NO ONE AT SCHOOL NOTICES I'M BACK. I HOPE NO ONE says anything to me. I hope I can fade into the walls and be invisible for today and tomorrow and all the days left.

It doesn't happen like that.

No one talks to me, but everyone notices me. They talk *around* me, they talk *about* me. I hear the whispers, the jeers, and I try to tune them out. I've had a lot of experience, so it shouldn't be so hard, but this is different. I never realized how much it could hurt to hear hateful things about someone else.

I wonder if Marcus has felt like this his whole life, hearing hisses and whispers about me. I wonder how he managed it. Because hearing people saying such horrible things about him, things I know are true, hurts me more than all the taunts and insults tossed at me ever did.

I keep my head down, don't make eye contact, and head for my locker. Someone is staring at me. People have been staring at me all morning. But this feels different. This feels like a laser going into me. I try to ignore it and focus on opening my locker.

"You aren't even going to pay your respects?" someone spits. It's Alicia Howard, the girl who wouldn't let me sit at her table. Her brother is friends with Marcus. Was friends with him. She's scowling at me. "After what your brother did?"

What your brother did. Like because he's my brother I'm somehow to blame.

I guess I never got to share in his glory, but now I can share in his shame.

"Wh-what?" I stammer. She's leaning so close to me that a few of her long dark braids brush against my arm.

"You just walked right by it. Pretended you didn't see it. Show a little respect."

"Show respect to what?"

"His memorial!" She points over my shoulder and I turn, slowly turn, and I don't know how I missed it.

There must be hundreds of carnations, white ones, in a pile on the floor. Michael's picture has been taped to his locker, and all around it are Post-it notes with messages on them. "Michael's dead," Alicia says, real slow, like I'm stupid. Like I hadn't realized it.

"I . . . I know," I say.

"Your fool brother killed him and you can't even take the time to show him some respect."

"I'm sorry," I whisper. I take a few steps toward Michael's locker, toward the mound of flowers and his smiling face. I can feel Alicia's eyes boring into me. Other people are slowing down to see what I'm going to do.

I tentatively reach out, when someone smacks my hand down. A girl I don't know.

"You can't touch that! Get out of here!"

I stare at her for a moment, her words piercing through my shocked daze. I'm not allowed to touch the picture, not allowed to show my sympathy, because my brother did this. Marcus isn't here, but I am. And all these people, they're mad at me just because Marcus is my brother. I'm filled with an unfamiliar fury, a boiling anger I've never felt before.

Not toward the people in the hall.

Toward my brother. He did this. To Michael. To everyone. To me.

"What? Are you stupid? I said get out of here!" The girl shoves me, hard, away from the locker.

I turn and I go as fast as I can down the hall, careful not to step on any of the white flowers, and I'm walking faster and faster and people are moving out of my way and shouting at me as I go and I move faster and then I'm jogging and then I'm running.

I'm running.

I'm running like I do in my dreams. My legs are pumping and I don't think my feet are even touching the floor and I see the exit and the bell is ringing for class but I can't stop and I keep going. . . . I think I see a dragon tail whipping around the corner and I go faster, trying to catch it. Wait for me! I want to cry out, but I stay silent and keep running, my books clasped to my chest.

I keep going, past the cafeteria, away from the memorial, away from Alicia, away from everything. I chase after the dragon's tail and I end up at the track. No dragon and no lioness in sight. Only thing down there is someone sprinting around the track. Whoever it is, they're fast. Like nothing can catch them. I lean against a tree and try to calm my breathing.

"Wing? Is that you?" someone shouts behind me. I tear my eyes from the runner and see Aaron jogging toward me and his face is scrunched up in confusion and concern. I haven't seen him since the night of the accident.

"Wing? Where are you going? Alicia Howard is hollering that you were disrespecting Michael's memorial . . ."

Aaron is close enough now that I can see he hasn't shaved recently and his eyes are bloodshot.

The bell rings and Aaron looks at his watch. He glances over his shoulder at the school and then back at me. He sighs. "I'm already late to chemistry, so I guess it doesn't matter if I'm a little later. Here, sit down," he says, and sits under the tree where I've dropped my books and pats the ground next to him.

I hesitate. I'm also late, for English, but I wasn't there all last week, and right now the last thing I want to do is go back into that building. I sit down next to Aaron, but not in the space he indicated because that spot is way too close to him.

When Aaron speaks, it's in a low voice. "Michael was drinking that night too. He was in no state to drive either. Him and Marcus rock-paper-scissored for it."

"That doesn't make it any better." The words are choking me. Most of the guys on the football team ignore me when they see me in the hall, but Michael would usually say hey. And now he's gone and never coming back.

"I know," says Aaron. Then he looks up at me. "How is he?" I know my mom called Aaron and Monica after we saw Marcus last Friday at the hospital and told them there was no change, he was still in a coma.

"He's . . . hooked up to all these machines. They don't know when he'll wake up. Or what . . . state he'll be in when he does."

I don't say if. I say when. Because it has to be when.

Aaron nods. "I tried to visit him a few days ago . . . but they wouldn't let me in. Said family only." He runs his hand over his short hair and sighs. "I wanted to come see you too, you and your mom, but I didn't know what to say. I should have come."

"How's Monica?" I ask.

Aaron shrugs. "A wreck. She wasn't in class most of last week, and then on Friday, when she finally showed up . . . she looked like a ghost. Wouldn't talk to no one, went straight home after school. Tash said she hasn't been eating or anything. I thought . . . I thought maybe she would have been by your place?"

"No," I say, shorter and sharper than I intended. "I thought maybe she would have been by too." I thought she'd want to see me like I want to see her.

"Well, we all know how her dad is. I doubt this has improved his opinion of Marcus."

"Did you go to Michael's funeral?" I ask, not wanting to hear any more about Monica and all her very valid reasons for not coming to the house. I definitely don't want to hear that Marcus might have proven her nasty, racist dad right.

Aaron shakes his head. "I couldn't, you know? Everyone there was thinking it was Marcus who killed him. . . ."

"Marcus *did* kill him." As I say the words, the reality of them sinks in and I feel bile rising in the back of my throat and tears crowding behind my eyes. "He killed him and that woman."

Aaron looks away. Closes his eyes. Closes himself to what I'm saying. Even though it's the truth. And we both know it. When he opens them again, he forces a smile.

"I almost forgot to tell you the good news. Oakie is out of the hospital."

Oakie. The other guy in the car with Marcus and Michael. He was sitting in the backseat.

"I'm glad." Then, before I can stop myself, I say the true thing, the horrible thing: "I wish it was Marcus, though."

"Wing!" Aaron says. "You can't say that! It's a miracle Oakie wasn't more hurt. As it is, his leg is so busted he'll probably never play football again. He's lost his shot at a scholarship."

I pull my knees to my chest and look up at the sky. It's perfect autumn blue. Crisp and clear and bright as a robin's egg. Who cares if Oakie can't play football again? I'd trade Marcus being able to do pretty much anything, I'd trade me being able to do pretty much anything, if it meant he could come home.

Still. It wasn't Oakie who crashed the car. He didn't deserve to die. But neither does my brother. I don't care what he did. He doesn't deserve to die.

"I'm sorry," I say. "All right? I'm sorry."

I'm not expecting Aaron to put his arm around me and pull me toward him.

"You got nothing to be sorry for," he says, his voice low and urgent. "You know that? You got nothing to be sorry for."

I let my head drop to his shoulder, let my weight relax against him, and try to think of nothing but how blue the sky is and how good the sun feels on my face.

I end up missing all of English. History too. I can't bring myself to go back into that building. I can't bring myself to walk past Michael's smiling face knowing he'll never smile again.

When I get home, I let myself in quietly so Granny Dee doesn't know I've cut class. The vacuum and the television are both blasting in the living room, so it's easy for me to slip up the stairs and into the cloister of my bedroom.

I crawl into bed and will myself to sleep, craving the comfort of my dreams. My mom comes in at some point, and I tell her I don't feel well, that I don't want dinner. She puts her hand on my forehead and kisses the top of my head and lets me go back to sleep.

I'm dreaming of running when something jolts me awake. My digital clock is blinking red at me. 3:18 a.m. Next to my clock, my dragon is staring at me, unblinking. She leans forward, her neck long and graceful, and presses her nose to mine. It's surprisingly cold, for a dragon. And smooth, like silk made solid.

She puts one wing around me, the heaviness of it enveloping me like a cloak, and pulls me toward the edge of the bed.

Then she flaps her wings once, making wind rush against my face. It feels the way the wind does in my dreams. I want to feel that wind.

I roll off the bed, moving like I'm still in a dream. Maybe I am. My lioness is under my bed, and she presses herself against my legs, moving me toward the door. Down the hall, through the kitchen out the front door, and then . . .

I'm suddenly, so suddenly I don't even remember getting here, back at the school track.

It's eerie at night. The only sound is the scream of the cicadas and the occasional car going by. I don't know if I'm allowed to be here. . . . It sure as hell isn't safe. This thought occurs to me with a sharp clarity, but it's overridden by what my feet and legs want to do. Then I'm on the track, and it's like I'm asleep again. I shut my brain down and let my body do what it wants, and what it wants to do is *run*.

My feet start slowly at first, one step, then another, one foot in front of the other, and it isn't like it is in my dreams, it takes effort, and this is how I know I must be awake, that I really am down on the track in the middle of the night. And with my dragon on one side and my lioness on the other, I stretch my legs out, and as my feet hit the track, heel-toe, heel-toe, the wind is in my face, just like in my dreams, and my dragon takes off, flying low above my head, just out of reach, and my lioness is going faster, daring me to go faster. I can, I know I can, and the feeling takes over, and I'm vaguely aware of the sound of my feet hitting the dirt track, of the jolt that goes up my body every time my feet connect with the ground, and then I'm going faster, faster. My legs know what to do. I'm going so fast I'm sure I'll spin out of control. My body won't be able to keep up with my feet. I'm going so fast I've got vertigo, the way I used to when I ran downhill as a kid, but no, I'm going faster than that. It's like I'm biking down a hill. Gravity is taking over, but the track is flat and it isn't gravity, it's me, *it's me*, I'm pulling and pushing myself at the same time, I'm the force. I don't think I've run like this since I was little. I don't think I've ever run like this. And all I want is to go faster.

Faster.

Round and round and round the track, my thoughts flying as fast as my feet, the night air slapping me in the face with every turn, and I've lost count of how many times I've gone round and I sense some sort of invisible barrier in front of me but I'm sick of barriers and I'm going to break through this. Drawing on something inside, I find that I can push harder and I feel myself tearing through that barrier. It shatters all around me, and I come through it and it's like I've entered some new realm of sheer bliss because if I thought I was flying before I am soaring now.

I feel like I could go forever, but at some point the stars have dimmed and the sky has gone from black to purple to pink and I don't want to get caught down here. I don't want anyone to see me. And now that I've stopped running, it all catches up to me. My limbs are trembling all over and I can barely stand and my throat is parched and I don't know why I didn't bring water. Probably because I never meant to be out here, running alone.

My dragon and my lioness are nowhere to be seen. They've disappeared somewhere I can't follow. I collapse on the grass next to the track and let my body slow down, one part at a time. My lungs expand, my heart thumps, my feet ache. I'm more aware of my body than I've ever been. I lie there, staring at the lightening sky, and all the thoughts I left behind when I was running come rushing in, now that I'm still. And one thought is the loudest.

Marcus.

I haven't thought about Marcus all night. The realization is like a punch in the stomach, but at the same time I'm grateful. I feel lighter.

I have to run again.

CHAPTER 13

THE NEXT DAY I TELL MY MOM I'M STILL NOT FEELING WELL and sleep all day. I get up to have some broth Granny Dee makes me for lunch, and then some soup LaoLao makes for dinner, each of them sure that their soup is going to be what makes me better. They don't know that the only thing that's going to make me better is to run again. I'm scared my dragon won't wake me up again, so I set an alarm for three a.m.

I shouldn't have worried. Exactly three minutes before my alarm goes off, my lioness nips at my ear. And my dragon is already waiting. I can see her shadow outside my window.

I jog down quiet tree-lined streets, avoiding the ones I know are notorious for trouble. I stay off the main roads too but hear the occasional squeal of tires in the distance. I'm glad I'm not alone, that my dragon and my lioness are with me. It makes me feel safe. I'm more awake tonight, so I'm more aware. I imagine what my mom will do if she finds my empty bed, and I shove the thought away. She's got enough to worry about. She won't think to check on me. Why would I be anywhere but in my bed? I've never snuck out before. She has no reason to think I'm sneaking out now.

There are no clouds tonight, and the moon shines bright, watching me. I don't mind. The moon can watch all it wants, but I don't want anyone else to see me.

I don't know how I was able to run like I did last night. The last time I was on a track was in eighth-grade gym class with April. April wasn't much of a runner, so I matched my pace to hers. I remember the gym teacher, Mrs. Turrick, saying she thought I'd be more of an athlete like Marcus. I shrugged and said Marcus was the athlete. Because he was. He is.

As I turn onto the track, I slow down. I should stretch. I try to touch my toes, and I can't, and even this simple failure makes me glad there's no one but the moon, my lioness, and my dragon with me. April's mom made us do a yoga video once, and I've never felt so awkward. And that's saying something. April and her mom both laughed at me, they couldn't help it, so I must have looked as awkward as I felt.

There's one stretch I remember that I wasn't too bad at. Probably because you do it sitting down. I sit on the damp grass, touch the soles of my feet together, and lean forward as far as I can for a count of ten. My lioness comes over and presses her head against my back, stretching me further.

That'll have to do. Maybe tomorrow, I'll see what kind of stretches the girls like Eliza Thompson do down at the track.

A car whizzes by, the headlights shining like searchlights and I freeze, sure that whoever it is will see me and make me stop.

But the car goes on, leaving me with my heart pounding before I've even run a step. My dragon rises into the air and circles me, and my lioness prances—that's the only word for it—out onto the track and looks back over her shoulder expectantly at me.

I ran last night. I can do it again. One foot in front of the other, one step, another, and another, and now my lioness is running ahead of me, and I want to catch her, I want to be as fast as her, so I push, and it feels . . .

It feels amazing.

I start to laugh, a little breathlessly because my lungs are working so hard to keep up with my feet, and it's hard, and it hurts a little, my lungs are burning a little, my calves are protesting a little, but it isn't a bad hurt, it isn't a hurt like the way my heart hurts when I think about Marcus.

Marcus.

Thinking about Marcus does something to me. It's like just thinking about him is enough to light a flame behind me, because I'm really running now.

Marcus.

I picture him waiting at the finish line. Cheering me on. The way I've always cheered for him. And I go faster.

I picture him running a little ahead of me, he's always been a little ahead of me, and I go faster. Damn it, Marcus, why aren't you here?

Damn it, Marcus, why did you do this?

My face is salty wet, tears or sweat, I don't know but I don't care. I wipe it away with the back of my hand without slowing down and I keep running.

Faster. And faster. And faster.

I run until I can't run anymore, until my legs are quivering like Jell-O and I'm drenched in sweat, my shirt sticking to my back and my front and even my knees are sweaty. I didn't know knees could get sweaty.

My dragon and my lioness have gone, leaving me alone with the moon. Now that I've stopped, I feel like an idiot for running around in circles, like that is gonna get me anywhere. Like that is gonna do anything.

But when I'm running, I don't feel like an idiot. I feel free, like anything is possible. Like I'm not running from something, but for something.

"I'm running for you, Marcus!" I shout into the night at the moon. Because maybe the stronger I am, the faster I go, maybe it'll be enough to wake him up.

I think I'm running for me too. Because I've never tasted anything like the night air, never felt so free, never done anything that felt so natural. But I don't need to shout that. No one needs to hear that. Not even the moon.

CHAPTER 14

Daytime doesn't feel like real time. The only thing real is running.

I can't shake the feeling that if I can run fast enough, Marcus will wake up. And since he isn't waking up, I'm not going fast enough. So I keep running. I feel like every time my feet slap against the ground, his heart beats.

Running with my dragon and my lioness by my side is my only reality. Daytime is like a blurred dream. Sometimes I hear Heather's helium-high laugh, I can tell it's directed at me, but her words are like pebbles now. They ping off me and lie in a pile at my feet and I step over them easily.

I don't speak at school unless a teacher calls on me, and even then I reply in one-word answers. Every night I go farther, longer, faster.

On Sunday we visit Marcus. His vitals are the same, which apparently is a good thing. I get antsy sitting next to him, my feet speaking their own language, a tap-tap-tap, tap-tap-tap against the floor.

When my mom isn't looking, I lean in close and whisper in his ear. "Marcus, I'm running. Wake up so you can see. I want us to race. I'm good."

Hearing that I want to compete against him, that I think have a shot at keeping up, should be enough to wake him up. The idea is laughable. And Marcus is competitive enough that he'd want to show me that he's always the best. But his vitals stay the same; there's no twitching finger or fluttering lids or anything to show he can hear me.

"Wake up," I whisper. I don't know why I whisper. Nobody ever woke up anyone with a whisper. I want to shout, but the quiet of this room, the somber seriousness, presses like a muzzle on my mouth. It isn't just me. My mom, Granny Dee, LaoLao, we all speak in hushed voices. Like we're trying not to wake him.

You'd think we'd be yelling and shouting and shaking him. Even Granny Dee keeps her voice to a low rumble. And LaoLao barely says a word, just stares at him, drinking him in with her eyes, patting his hand in an uneven beat that almost matches the tapping of my impatient feet.

And my mother. She's all smiles in the hospital room. Not real ones, though. She contorts her face into something that once upon a time resembled a smile. Imagine a carved smile on a pumpkin, like a jack-o'-lantern. Now imagine that pumpkin starts to rot, to sink in on itself, to smell. And then some punk kid comes by and kicks it in, and the jack-o'-lantern is still smiling, but it isn't a smile anymore.

My mama doesn't stink and she isn't rotting, but I think something inside her has broken and might never get fixed again.

As soon as we step outside the hospital, the pumpkin grimace falls off, leaving her face bare and raw, but that's better than the rotting smile.

I don't know if Monica has been to see him. Would they let her in? She still hasn't been by the house. I see her at school and she looks like a different person. Her hair hangs lank and greasy and her eyes are always red. She wears one of Marcus's old sweatshirts over a ratty pair of jeans every day. She doesn't sit with the football players anymore. She sits with Tash in a far corner. She hasn't said a thing to me since I came back to school. Not *hello*, now *how are you*, not a thing.

Maybe she's waiting for me. I'm thinking about this while I'm in a stall in the school bathrooms one day, grateful for the privacy and solitude the flimsy walls provide. Then the toilet flushes next to me and I recognize Dionne's voice. She's talking about Monica. My world goes from fuzzy to clear, reality rushing back in. Bright and loud and painful.

"You seen Monica? Girl looks like shit," she says. I freeze in my stall, actually stop peeing so I can hear her better.

"At least she's not sniffin' around Aaron now that Marcus is gone." I don't recognize the other girl's voice.

"Please. What are you trying to say? That the two of them are the same person? Anyway. Aaron ain't the same anymore. Haven't you seen him? Moping around and shit. Can't even catch a ball these days. Told the coach that he wanted to drop football, and this is his senior year! He's got colleges looking at him. Fool boy."

"Aw, come on, Dionne. He's got colleges looking at him for track. Not for football. He probably just played football because Marcus did. Always did follow him around."

"Yeah, well, he can't follow him where he is now. He's wandering around like a lost puppy."

"Maybe he needs some lovin' . . . some comforting. . . ."

The girls giggle in a way that makes me uncomfortable; then Dionne says, "Nah. I'm over that. For real this time."

Her voice fades away as they walk out. I'd forgotten that Aaron runs.

I wait another minute just to be sure the bathroom is empty before going to wash my hands.

My timing isn't great, because just as I'm drying them, the door flings open and almost into me.

It's Eliza Thompson. She gives me a quick nod of acknowledgment. I nod back, unsure what else to do. She passes me and is about to go into a stall, when she stops.

"Hey . . . ," she says, and her voice is softer than I expected. I realize for all the times I've seen her run, we've never spoken. "I'm real sorry about what happened with Marcus."

No one has said they're sorry. Not one of my teachers, not a single person on the football team. I feel my eyes prickling and I blink rapidly so Eliza can't tell how much it means to me.

"How are you?" she says, tilting her head to the side like some sort of exotic bird.

I shrug. "I've been better," I say.

She presses her lips together and shrugs. "Yeah, I bet. Sucks."

I nod. I want to ask her if when she runs she feels like she's flying and like it's the only thing that matters and if it makes all her problems float away like wispy clouds, but now she's looking at me with a slightly different expression, less pity and sympathy and more an "I've got to pee . . . are you just going to stand here staring at me?" look. It's a subtle difference, but I get it.

"Thanks," I mumble, and go out the door. I can run! I want to yell. You wouldn't believe it but you should see me!

As I'm walking down the hall, I wonder if anyone has asked Monica how she's doing. Is she waiting for me to reach out to her, the way I've been waiting for her? She did say I was her best friend. I wonder if that still stands. And how do her and Marcus stand? It isn't like she can break up with him . . . but it isn't like he's . . . around either. Maybe it's kind of like being in a long-distance relationship, one where you can't call or even write letters. And you don't know how long the other person will be gone. So pretty much like being in a long-distance relationship with an astronaut. Except that you didn't know they were an astronaut.

But if Eliza Thompson, someone who barely knows me, can ask how I'm doing . . . I can ask how Monica is doing.

It's the end of the day, so she should be in the back parking lot. I know where she parks. Or I could wait until tomorrow. But the thought of going up to Monica in the cafeteria is even more daunting than going into the back parking lot.

Where all the seniors park.

Where Heather Parker parks, even though she is only a sophomore and shouldn't even have a school parking permit but somehow wangled one from someone.

It isn't like I'm not familiar with the parking lot. After all, until last month, this is where Marcus parked and I got out of his car every morning.

I pull up my hood, as if that can protect me from anything, but it makes me feel better.

Monica's car is in the same spot. Next to Marcus's spot. His empty parking spot.

I never saw the damage to his car. It was totaled and hauled straight to the junkyard.

Marcus saved for that car himself, by working two summers in a pizzeria downtown. He didn't want to work in the Chinese restaurant my mom works at, because he didn't want my mom to be his boss, and he didn't want my mom to see him flirting with the customers to get a bigger tip. I wonder what Monica thought of all that flirting over orders of pepperoni pizza and pitchers of Coke.

His car was ugly, ten years old already and a rusty orange. He loved it, though. Even started teaching me to drive in it. I got my permit a couple weeks after I turned fifteen.

I'll never drive that car again.

I always thought my brother was such a good driver. He got a perfect score on his driving test, and never got pulled over. Not even once.

I see Monica hurrying across the parking lot, head down, hair hiding her face, so she doesn't see me standing next to her car.

"Hi," I say when she reaches me, and I swear she jumps a foot in the air.

"Shit! Wing! You gave me a heart attack," she says, her hand on her chest, and her face is so pale it's easy to believe that I have. She stares at me, eyes harder than I've ever seen them. I force myself to remember that this is the same Monica who threw herself against me in the hospital waiting room, who has brushed my hair, baked cookies with me, taken me shopping.

"Um," I say. "I was wondering . . . um . . ."

"What?" she says, and then panic flits across her face, distorting her features. "Oh my god. Is it Marcus? Has something happened?"

"No, no, no," I say quickly. "That isn't it."

She exhales loudly. "Oh, thank God." Then she squints at me. "So what is it?"

I stare at the asphalt. "I, um . . . just wanted to . . . you know . . . see if you were okay."

She makes an ugly rasping sound, and I look up quickly, worried that she might be choking, and then I realize she is doing some sort of twisted pantomime of a laugh, and it is nothing like the laugh I know.

"Okay? If I'm okay? What do you think? Are you okay? Seriously. Am I okay?" She makes that sound again, the one that isn't a laugh, the one that sounds like she's spitting out the broken parts of herself on the ground.

"I'm not okay," I say, so quietly I think that maybe she didn't hear me. "And I know you aren't okay. I thought . . . I thought . . ." This was so stupid. Marcus isn't the person I thought he was. Maybe Monica isn't either. The Monica I knew wouldn't stare at me with dead eyes and make me uncomfortable.

"You thought what?" Her voice is so full of venom I'm sure that when I look back up I'll see Heather Parker behind her, and Monica won't be Monica at all but a ventriloquist's dummy.

"Nothing," I say, turning so she can't see my face. "I thought nothing." I don't want to pass her, so I push myself between her pickup and the SUV next to it, but the space is too tight and I can't fit through it and now I have to turn around. I turn and nearly step on Monica. She's right next to me and she's biting her lip and her fists are balled up in her sweatshirt. Marcus's sweatshirt.

"Wanna go get some ice cream?" she says.

CHAPTER 15

I TRY NOT TO THINK ABOUT THE LAST TIME I WAS IN MONICA's car. It is too painful. When she puts the keys in the ignition, I can't help but notice her hands are shaking.

"I didn't think I'd be able to drive. After seeing the accident," she says in a conversational tone. As if she's telling me she has a hair appointment. I don't say anything. I can sense she wants to talk.

"But what else am I gonna do? Take the bus? Take MARTA? My mom let me stay home for four days, but then it was back to school. Back to life. 'Maybe it's for the best,' she said. . . ."

I inhale so sharply she glances over. "I don't think that," she says. "But you know my parents. . . ."

"No, I don't," I say, looking out the window. Maybe this wasn't a good idea. "I've only met them a few times."

"I don't think that! This is the worst thing that has ever happened to me. Do you understand that? And it isn't ever going to get better. It's a nightmare. No, it's worse than a nightmare. Because you can wake up from nightmares. It's like my whole life has been some sort of dream and now I've woken up and all I want is to go back to sleep, back to how things were, but I'm never going to. He killed two people, Wing! Two people are dead and it's Marcus's fault. And he's . . . he's whatever the hell he is right now. What am I supposed to do? All I want to do is be with him and I can't. I can't." She hits her steering wheel. "It's so unfair. Why did this happen? We had plans, you know. We had plans." She's crying now but I don't think she notices and her tears keep falling and there's snot running down her upper lip.

"Typical Marcus," she says, and the bitterness in her tone makes the air taste like burnt toast. "Royally screws up and can't handle the consequences so goes into a goddamn coma." She slams on the brakes at a red light and I wonder if maybe she shouldn't be driving. If maybe she should be on some kind of medication. Because this Monica, this is a stranger. A crazy stranger.

"Do you know how people look at me now? Like I'm somehow involved. Like I'm just as much to blame for Michael's and that woman's death. Like by being with Marcus, it's just as much my fault."

"Are you still with him?" I venture. She turns the car into the strip mall parking lot.

"Of course I'm still with him! Look, we weren't married yet, but I'm his girl, all right? Forever." She holds up her right hand, brandishing the ring he got her for her last birthday. "I didn't go through all the shit that we've been through to not be with him."

"What are you talking about? You two . . . you two have the perfect relationship." I almost slip and say that they *had* but catch myself at the last second.

She makes a sound like a horse neighing. It's a sound I've never heard her make.

"Oh yeah. Like when he hooked up with Carla Torres. Twice. And then when I found out, the bitch wanted to fight me. Me! Like I did anything to her."

"Oh," I say. I wouldn't want to fight Carla Torres. There are rumors that she brings a blade to school.

"It was awful. But I love him and so I forgave him. And then he goes and does this!"

I feel the old defensiveness waking up inside me. "He didn't do it on purpose," I say.

"Like that makes it any better. You know he said the same thing about hooking up with Carla? He was drunk then too. Being drunk isn't a get-out-of-jail-free card, you know."

"Did . . ." Before I can finish my question Monica throws her door open and gets out and slams it shut again all in the same second.

"Hurry up," she calls over her shoulder.

We walk into the ice cream parlor, the bell jingling over our heads as we go through the door.

"One chocolate chip cookie dough and one mint chip," says Monica to the girl behind the counter without hesitation. She pays, and when I try to give her a dollar she pushes my hand away.

"How did you know I like mint chip?" I say once we've got our cones and are back in the safety of her car.

"Wing, do you know how many times I've picked up a tub of ice cream at the store for Marcus? For you? Hell, how many times I've gone to Chick-fil-A for you with Marcus? You both love mint chip ice cream. Neither of you likes pickles on your sandwich. Marcus hates them so much that I stopped getting pickles on my sandwich because he wouldn't kiss me. Would call me pickle breath."

She looks at me and reaches over and squeezes my hand. "I'm sorry." She doesn't say anything else, doesn't say what she's sorry for, but she tries to smile. She doesn't quite make it because her lips go all wobbly in the corner, but I squeeze her hand back.

"It's okay," I say. It isn't, not really, but there isn't anything else to say. "I'm sorry too."

Monica turns and looks out the window, and even though I can't see her face I know she's crying again. I wonder how many hours a day she spends crying. I wonder if I should be crying more.

I wonder what else Marcus has done that isn't perfect. What else is there about him that I don't know?

That I don't want to know?

"Let's talk about something else," she says, as if I've been talking even though I've been sitting quietly, licking my mint chip. Monica's ice cream is melting already, dripping down the sides of the cone, getting her hands all sticky, but she doesn't seem to notice.

"Like what?"

"Like anything. Look, my whole life has fallen apart ... I need a reminder that there are other things out there. You know? Things other than Marcus."

"Like what?" I ask again, and she rolls her eyes. At least she isn't crying anymore.

"Wing!"

"All right. Give me a second," I think, nibbling on my ice cream until I get to the cone, which has gone soft and chewy at the top. "Where do you want to go? Like, in the world?"

"New York. London. Milan. Paris. Tokyo. Hong Kong.

Shanghai." She lists them off so quickly I know this isn't the first time she's thought about it. "I wanna go to all the big cities." She shrugs and swirls her tongue around her ice cream. "I don't even have a passport, though, so it isn't like that's going to happen anytime soon."

"Really?"

"Yes, really. It isn't that uncommon. Most Americans don't have passports. Not everyone is as cultured as you."

"If by cultured you mean different." I take a bite out of the end of my cone to get the bit of ice cream wedged down at the bottom.

Monica finishes her ice cream, cone and all, in a few quick chomps, rolls down the window, and burps. It's pretty ladylike, for a burp.

"I'm still hungry," she says.

"You could come over for dinner," I offer. "LaoLao is making dumplings." Monica loves LaoLao's dumplings.

"Is your mom mad at me? For not coming by?"

I shake my head, even though I have no idea if my mom is mad at Monica. She has so much going on in her head right now I doubt that she has enough space, or enough energy, to be angry at Monica.

"She'd like to see you," I say, and I know it's true.

"Okay," says Monica. "I'll come over."

CHAPTER 16

IF LAOLAO IS SURPRISED TO SEE ME WALK IN WITH MONICA, she doesn't say anything. She's sitting at the kitchen table filling dumplings. The table is covered with flour, delicate dumpling wrappers, and balls of the minced pork filling.

"You want to help?" she asks Monica. Monica nods and sits, helping LaoLao pinch the dumplings shut. I sit down next to her, and for the first time since I've started running, I'm content doing something else.

"No, no, no. All wrong." LaoLao reaches over and takes Monica's most recent dumpling. It looks more like a pyramid. "Fingers must be gentle and firm," says LaoLao. "Like this."

Monica nods and redoes her dumpling.

LaoLao grunts. "Yes. Better."

After a while Monica stands. "Can I use your phone?"

"You don't have to ask for something like that," I say. As she walks out of the kitchen, I see her glance down the hallway, toward Marcus's room. His door is still shut. I haven't been back in there since the night of the accident, when my dragon and lioness first returned. I don't know if anyone's been in there.

I'm not trying to eavesdrop, but Monica's voice rises so suddenly and so shrilly it's impossible not to. "Daddy, I'm having dinner at the Joneses' house. All right?"

I resist the urge to pick up the other phone to hear what her father is saying back to her, but whatever it is, it makes Monica raise her voice even more.

"I don't care," she says. And then, "Daddy, they're my family! Don't say that."

A pause.

"Well, fine! Maybe I won't come home tonight." She slams down the receiver, startling LaoLao so much that she nearly drops the dumpling she's filling.

Monica comes back in and sits down in the chair.

"Wing? Do you think I could stay here tonight?"

Monica could have slept in Marcus's room. But she didn't ask to. She didn't even ask to see it. Instead, she's sleeping in my room. On a blow-up air mattress. Like we're having a sleepover. I watch her brush out her long hair and put on moisturizer. It's like having a sister.

"Is your dad mad?" I ask.

Monica blows out of the side of her mouth, sending her bangs up into the air. She looks a little bit like a pony. "That's an understatement," she says.

"Why doesn't he like Marcus?"

"Because he's black," Monica answers immediately and without shame.

"He's also Chinese," I offer.

"I don't think that helps," says Monica. "And also, he doesn't like that I pay for stuff for us." She looks away from me, voice lowered. "I don't mind. I've got money from my grandparents and from working last summer. And I know Marcus can't get a job during the school year because he's always got practice. And I know how it is for your mom. But my daddy . . . he says it isn't right for a girl to be buying dinner." She pauses again and I close my eyes, embarrassed that Marcus couldn't afford to take Monica out the way she deserves. "Wing! I don't care. I promise. That is total bullshit. Like a woman can't buy a man dinner. I'm not some simpering Southern belle, no matter what my daddy thinks or what he wants." Her Southern accent is getting heavier with every word. "I had gotten used to it. Almost. The snide comments. The glares. The threats that there was no way in hell he would pay for my wedding, and possibly wouldn't even walk me down the aisle. Sometimes, when he'd had a beer or two, he would come around. Not about Marcus, but about me being his daughter, and tell me that he loved me no matter what. But then, after the accident . . . I thought it was bad before. But really, he was holding in all this awful vitriol."

"What does vitriol mean?" I ask. It sounds awful.

"Wing, you gotta start studying your SAT vocab," says Monica. "Vitriol is like . . . verbal poison. Literally an acid, but people can be full of it too. And my daddy is just brimming with it. Especially when it comes to Marcus. I've been telling him for so many years that Marcus is a good guy. More than a good guy, that he's a great guy. But now ... now he'll never believe me." She pulls her sleeping bag up over her head and when she finally speaks, her voice comes out muffled. "I don't even know if I believe me anymore."

CHAPTER 17

I DIDN'T THINK MY DRAGON AND MY LIONESS WOULD COME IN my room with Monica in here, but my lioness wakes me up by nuzzling my feet, and I spy my dragon's eyes glowing in the dark. She's squeezed into the small space between Monica's air mattress and the door.

"Go away," I whisper. "I can't go running tonight!"

My lioness growls softly and tugs on my pajama bottoms with her teeth, and my dragon snorts. I fling back my covers.

"Fine," I whisper, but I'm glad they woke me up. I want to run. I look over at Monica, who's sprawled out on the air mattress, hair everywhere. I think she's snoring.

I wonder if I can get up without her noticing.

Get up and get dressed and get out the door.

It isn't like I'm doing anything wrong. Still, I don't want her to know about it. Not just yet. I don't want anyone to know about it.

I sit up. "Mon?" I whisper, quietly at first. And then, "Monica!" She mutters something in her sleep, something that might be "Marcus," and rolls over, away from me. I reach under my pillow and pull out the ratty sports bra I've been wearing every night. I need to wash it, but I'm worried my mom will see it in the laundry and ask me what I'm doing that requires a sports bra. For now, it hides under my pillow, a silent, lumpy reminder of my new secret life.

I swing my legs over the side of the bed, careful not to kick Monica's mattress, and tell myself to relax. If she wakes up, I'll say I'm going to the bathroom. Nothing wrong with that.

I step over her, my foot landing with an audible thud, and I cringe, freezing with one leg on either side of the twin-size mattress. If she wakes up now it will be a little awkward. I lift my other leg over and tiptoe to the door, pulling it open as gently as I can, and step out into the hall.

I'm still in my pajamas. I can't go running in my pajamas. I mean, I guess I could. But I don't really want to. I glance down the hall, toward Marcus's room. I swallow, look over my shoulder at Monica sleeping. The air mattress is pushed against my dresser. I won't be able to open it without waking Monica, no matter how heavy a sleeper she is.

I close the door behind me and shuffle down the hall. I went to sleep in socks, so it's easy to glide along the floor without even lifting my feet.

Marcus's door opens without a sound. I grab the first things I see: his jersey on his desk and a pair of running shorts. The shirt goes past my waist, but the running shorts fit snugger than I'd like. My big brother might be taller and stronger than me, but my butt is way bigger than his. I leave my pajamas in a bundle on the couch under an old blanket Granny Dee knit when I was little.

My Converse are by the door, the laces worn and full of holes, and the soles feel as insubstantial as the thin dumpling wrappers. But they grip my feet in a way that's familiar and comforting. I need to get proper shoes sometime. If this keeps up I'll wear out these shoes by the end of the month. But for now, they're my midnight shoes. I'm like one of the Twelve Dancing Princesses from that old fairy tale, where the twelve sisters go dancing in a magical world every night and dance so long and so hard that they wear out their shoes. Except I'm not a princess and I'm all on my own.

And running is way better than dancing.

But I do feel a little bit magical.

The night air wraps its arms around me as I silently jog down the street and away from my house. With every step I feel freer. I let my breathing come naturally, my breaths kissing the night. The night kisses me back, butterfly kisses made of mist. The sky is cloudy, not a star to be seen, and feels so low that if I could run just a little bit faster I could leap up and touch the heavy night clouds. No, not just touch them. Pop right through them. Like a mermaid emerging from the sea, I'd come up headfirst, spraying clouds everywhere, and up there in cloud world they would welcome me like a queen. No, like a goddess. I'd run all day and the best part would be when I sent down a special cloud to scoop up Marcus in its fluffy embrace and bring him up to my cloud kingdom and he'd be healed instantly.

Monica and Aaron can come too. And my mom and LaoLao and Granny Dee. And they would be so impressed with the kingdom I'd created that they would hug me tight and say they should always have known I was special, and Marcus would say he couldn't have gotten better without me, and that he'll never do anything as stupid as drive drunk again, and then he and Monica would have a beautiful cloud wedding over the ocean at sunset and I'd wear a dress made out of clouds and we'd all live happily ever after forever.

That's how low the clouds are. That's how fast I am. Anything, absolutely anything, seems possible.

I get to the track and run round and round, skipping every once in a while to see if I can jump into the clouds. I don't reach the sky, and I'm not really that surprised, but it makes me giggle, so when I see the dark shape running at me, I think I'm imagining it, so I keep going straight toward it. It's slowly materializing into the shape of a man wearing a dark sweatshirt and sweats and his hood is up and it's too dark to see his face and I'm moving fast so as long as I keep going we'll pass each other and then I'll be running away from him, and even if he turns, tries to talk to me, I'll outrun him because I can run forever and—

"Wing?"

I stop so suddenly I nearly fall over.

It's Aaron. Aaron is on the track. He's staring at me like I'm crazy, and maybe I am. Why else would I be running around the football field wearing my brother's old football jersey? Chasing a dragon and a lion? In the middle of the night?

I stop, aware that I'm panting and sweat is running down my forehead in little rivers. Aaron looks at me, his eyes traveling up and back down the length of my body.

"What the hell?" he says, but not in a mean way.

"What are you doing here?" I ask.

He snorts. "What am I doing here? What are you doing here?" He pulls his hood off and I'm glad because now I can see his face.

"What does it look like I'm doing?"

He quirks an eyebrow. "I'm not really sure." And I remember

my laughing and leaping and I want to bury my head in the sand like an ostrich and not get up until he has gone away.

Except have you ever seen an ostrich do that? Or a picture of one? It is straight up ass-in-air. Which probably isn't the best move if you're trying to play it cool when you run into the boy you've loved for your whole damn life in the middle of the night.

"I was running," I say, shrugging, like it's the most natural thing in the world.

"Since when do you run?" He's all shadows and sexy mouth and quirking eyebrows and proud nose and it is *distracting*. Especially when I'm trying to answer such a simple but impossible question.

"You don't know everything about me," I say, and I'm glad that I've stopped panting and can form a sentence without sounding like I'm about to pass out.

He's thinking so loudly I can practically hear the gears in his brain whirling like the inside of a clock, trying to figure out what's going on. "He's not dead," he says, so quietly I almost don't hear him.

"I know that," I say, and my voice comes out raspy. So much for not sounding like I'm dying. My lungs feel like they're about to explode, and I'm sure Aaron can hear my heart pounding away like the hooves of a thoroughbred about to win the Kentucky Derby.

He nods and puts his hand up to his chin, pondering, and he looks so much like that sculpture *The Thinker*, and in all the years I've known him I don't know if he's ever looked more adorable.

"How long has this been happening?" he asks.

"You mean how long have I been running?"

"Yeah."

"A few weeks. After the accident."

"Why are you wearing . . . that?"

I look down at the jersey. When I was grabbing it in the bedroom, it didn't seem strange, but now, out here, with Aaron, it seems . . . weird. More than weird. Borderline deranged. Obsessed.

"I mean, you look good in it, better than Marcus does," says Aaron, and there's a hint of playfulness looped around his words, like the frosting on the edges of a gingerbread house.

"Don't tell him that," I say, and as soon as the words are out of my mouth they fall to the ground and I wish I could pick them up and swallow them because they are exactly the wrong thing to say.

"I wish I could," he says, and there's no sugar in his voice now. Just sorrow.

"Yeah. I know," I say, and it is the most inadequate response in the world, it doesn't come close to how much I wish I could tell Marcus everything, anything right now. But there isn't anything else I can say.

I don't get cold when I run so I don't have a coat, but we've been standing here for several minutes now and the night air, my earlier lover, must be jealous of Aaron because it's giving me the cold shoulder and chilling the film of sweat all over my face and neck and arms and legs. I shiver.

Aaron pulls off his sweatshirt, and as he does I see a wide expanse of dark skin above his shorts, and it looks like it was molded by a master sculptor, which makes sense because that's what his face looks like, and I'm so distracted by that hint of skin I almost don't notice him press the sweatshirt into my arms.

"Here," he says.

"I'm all right," I say, even as my nipples (my *nipples*!) poke out to declare that they are cold and would appreciate the sweatshirt. I doubt Aaron is looking at my nipples, though.

I don't know if I want him to look or not.

I'm so embarrassed by my rapid spiraling of thoughts that I pull the sweatshirt on, mostly to hide my face, because I'm scared he'll be able to read my thoughts there. And to hide my stupid nipples.

"Wing." He wraps his arms around himself and I almost regret taking his sweatshirt, except for the fact that I love how it feels against my skin and how it smells and the fact that I'm wearing his sweatshirt. "What's going on?"

I want to tell him everything: How my dragon and my lioness visited me the night of the accident and I followed them outside and ever since then I can't stand to be indoors, all I want is to be out, running, where it is just me and the sky and the feeling of my feet hitting the ground. I want to tell him that I'm doing it for Marcus, because I'm sure somehow my running is keeping Marcus alive, that my footsteps are making his heart beat, way more than the machines he's linked up to. I want to tell him that when I run I don't see the giant numbers that are bigger and bigger with every hospital bill, every legal fee. I want to tell him that when I run, I run away from all that and I'm free. Running was a secret inside myself that I didn't even know was there, and now that I've found it I don't ever want to let it go.

I don't tell him any of that. Instead, I tug off Aaron's sweatshirt, making sure to hold down the football jersey underneath so it doesn't ride up, toss it on the grass, and look him straight in the eye. "How about I show you?"

CHAPTER 18

I DON'T THINK. I DON'T EVEN BREATHE. I LET MY BODY TAKE over and I soar. I can sense Aaron behind me, and I wish I had eyes in the back of my head to see his expression, to see his face as I glide along in front of him.

"Wing!"

I slow down the tiniest fraction, and it takes almost more effort to slow than it does to speed up, and glance over my shoulder.

It is worth the effort.

Aaron's eyes are bright and he's grinning a mile wide and shaking his head and he's still running, still trying to catch me, and I don't know if I slow down or he speeds up but suddenly we're running side by side.

"Damn, girl," he says between breaths, and I roll my eyes but I'm smiling as wide as he is. The clouds have risen, out of my reach, but now I can see the stars and they wink down at me like they're saying "You go, girl" and I tilt my head back and smile up at them, and I hope that from way up there my smile looks like a bright shiny star winking back at them.

I lose track of how many times we go round, but then Aaron veers left, toward where I've tossed his sweatshirt, and collapses on his back, arms and legs spread out like he's about to make a snow angel in the damp grass. He's breathing heavily, and all I want is to go put my head on his chest, I don't even care that it's drenched in sweat, and listen to the drum of his heart.

But I don't. I sit next to him, leaning back on my hands, legs out in front of me, and revel in the ache that goes from my toes up through my shins and along my thighs. It's an ache I never knew before I started running. A bone-deep satisfaction I can't get enough of and I wake up craving.

"Who knows?" His eyes are closed and I'm glad because I can stare at his face, drink it in, without him noticing.

"It isn't a secret."

Aaron's eyes fly open and lock onto mine. I love how his lashes curl up. How dark his eyes are. I want to dive into them and swim as far as I can and then dive deeper and never come back up.

"Wing? Did you hear me?"

I blink and pull myself out of his eyes. "Sorry?"

"I said, if it isn't a secret, how come I didn't know you could run like that? How come Marcus didn't know?"

"I told you. . . . I didn't start running until after the accident."

"And you could just . . . run. Like that." His voice is flat with a hint of sharpness. Like a knife on its side, smooth and safe, until it flips.

It stings. That he didn't think I could do this. That he can't quite believe it.

He sees me like everyone else does. Like someone who can't.

Someone who is content to be on the sidelines. He sees me the way I've always seen myself, but now I know I'm different, not just different the way I've always been different but I'm a good different, I've got something special inside me, not just speed, not just strength, but something more.

I hope Aaron sees me like that now.

He stretches his arms over his head like he's making the wings of his grass angel, and then he laces his fingers through mine. It sends a jolt through my whole body and I gasp. The sound is louder than I expected and he gives a soft chuckle. I let my fingers close around his and I'm so aware of his fingers, so aware, and then he pulls them away and I wonder if I did the wrong thing, if I should have let my fingers lie like dead fish in his hand, if he was just stretching and happened to brush against my hand and his fingers wrapped around mine just out of some sort of evolutionary response, like *touch woman hand, hold on*, and then he realized what he was doing so he let go.

"Who else knows?" he says again, not mentioning the hand thing, excitement rippling in his voice. Like this is some big secret. Like he feels special that he knows.

"No one."

"Why? You can't hide this, Wing!"

But hiding is what I've always done. And why would I want to tell anyone? Or show anyone? It's just running. One foot in front of the other, again and again. I don't know why he's making such a big deal about it. Besides, even if I wanted to . . . show someone . . . I wouldn't know how. I try to tell this to Aaron.

"What am I gonna do, Aaron? Just show up one day on the track and challenge Eliza Thompson to a race?"

"This is track and field, Wing. Not drag racing."

I poke Aaron in the side and he gives a gratifying wiggle. He's been ticklish since he was little.

"Ticklish?" I ask, because I don't want him to know I remember.

He snorts. "You know I am! You and Marcus used to corner me and tickle me all the time. No mercy. The two of you, man, when you decided to go up against someone, usually me . . ."

I laugh and shake my head. "What are you talking about? The two of you were always ganging up on me. Or totally ignoring me, off doing 'boy things.'"

Aaron flips over on his side in one fluid motion so he's facing me and his chest is just a few inches away. "If I remember correctly . . . ," he says, and his voice is soft and slow and then his hand darts out and he's tickling me and I'm squealing and wriggling and rolling away from him. Which feels completely counterintuitive, so I roll right back.

"Truce," I say, and now I've got the hiccups from laughing so hard.

"Truce," says Aaron with a grin. Then his voice goes low, goes serious. "Wing, you've got to show someone. Hell, you've got to show everyone. This is . . . it's incredible."

"It's my own thing," I say. I start thinking of people watching me run, people other than Aaron or Marcus, because oh, how I want my brother to see me run, but the thought of anyone else watching me makes my stomach twist into a pit of wrestling snakes. "It helps me relax. Takes my mind off . . . things."

Aaron blows out a long breath, his lips perfectly pursed, and I let myself imagine what it would be like to lean over him, my hair bouncing across his chest, against his collarbone, and press my lips against his. What he tastes like. If his lips are as soft as they look. How they would fit against my own.

"I get that." He rolls up so he's sitting next to me and I don't have as good a vantage point to admire him, but now he's sitting closer to me, so this new position has its perks. "What do you think I was doing out here in the middle of the night?" He adds, "I couldn't sleep," answering his own question. "My mom was asleep in front of the television, neighbors were shouting, I just wanted to get away. Get somewhere quiet. Be alone."

"Oh." The syllable falls out of my mouth like a pit in the middle of a plum. Sharp and awkward all at once. Something I can't swallow.

"Aw, Wing, girl, you know what I mean. Being with you is like being alone."

I frown, not sure how to take this.

"But better. I guess." He laughs softly. "If that makes sense."

He turns my face toward his, his fingers soft on my cheeks. "I'm glad you were here," he says, and I've never been so close to him and he's looking at me like he's never seen me before and I close my eyes because I am sure, absolutely sure that he is going to lean forward and kiss me.

"Wing," he says. His voice is soft and so close to me that I feel his breath on my cheek. "I gotta get home. And I bet you do too. You don't want your mama wakin' up and finding your bed empty, do you?"

I shake my head away from him, furious at myself for thinking he was going to kiss me. Just because he said that being with me is like being alone. Being with a tree is like being alone too. It doesn't mean you want to make out with a tree.

"Let me drive you home," he says.

His car is small; he looks like he won't fit in it. I realize I've never been in his car. When I mention this he shrugs.

"Marcus likes to drive."

I roll down the window to say goodbye to the night, but the sky is lighter than it should be. Where has the night gone? I think of Monica asleep in my room, waking up alone, wondering where I am. . . .

"What time is it?"

Aaron looks at the green clock on the dash. "Almost five."

How have I been at the track for so long?

I know the answer. Because Aaron was there with me.

"This isn't over," he says, and I feel my heart leap. Does he feel it?

"What?"

"I'm not going to let you hide . . . whatever this is."

"Are you sure?" Is he saying what I think he is, that he doesn't want to hide . . . us?

"You are good, Wing. And I think you could be great. You've got to show someone."

My heart stops its leaping and lies down. It tries to curl up into a ball, and I press my palm against my chest to comfort it. It's impossible for Aaron to know what my heart is doing, but still, it hurts when he goes on in the same excited voice.

"But you're right. You can't just show up at track. We've got to wait for the right moment." He looks over at my battered Converse. "Get you the right shoes. The right form."

"What's wrong with my form?" I frown. "I run just fine."

"Yeah, you do." He taps his hands on the steering wheel in a staccato beat. "But I could help you run better than just fine. You could be perfect."

His words echo in my ears the rest of the way home. They're still echoing when we pull up in front of my darkened house.

"Tonight wasn't what I was expecting," says Aaron. "I'm glad you were out there, Wing-a-ling-ring."

The childish nickname doesn't bother me the way it usually does. Instead, it reminds me how long Aaron's known me.

"You won't tell anyone?"

He shakes his head. "Nah."

"And you'll be out there tomorrow night? I mean, tonight?"

"Yeah," he says. "I've been sitting around every Saturday night, worrying over Marcus. I'm not gonna stop worrying over him now. But it'll be nice to have something else to do. I don't wanna party, but I don't wanna stay home either. This might be just what I need."

CHAPTER 19

I'm on the porch, putting my key in the lock, when the front door opens from the inside. I bite back a yell.

"So. Where the hell have you been?"

Monica is standing in front of me, arms crossed, eyes blazing.

She looks over my shoulder, eyes narrowing as she sees Aaron's taillights fade away down the street. She grabs my arm and pulls me into the living room. I can feel her fingers digging into my skin. She points at the couch.

"Sit," she says.

"Shhh! You'll wake up my mom!" There's no way she could wake up LaoLao or Granny Dee. LaoLao sleeps through anything and snores, so Granny Dee wears earplugs. And an eye mask. And sleeps with a hot water bottle, no matter how hot it is outside.

Monica sits next to me and leans very close to my face, so close I can smell her morning breath. Or middle-of-the-night breath. Whatever it's called at five a.m. I wrinkle my nose and she frowns.

"What?"

"Your breath stinks," I say, like it's an apology.

"Wing, were you and Aaron visiting Marcus? Without me?"

"What? No! Of course not!" I pause. "Monica, you know I've been to see Marcus, right? Without you?" Family only, the doctors say, but I bet if Monica came with us, she could charm her way in there, the way she charms herself into anywhere. But she hasn't been by to see us to ask to come with us, and I wonder if it's because she doesn't want to intrude. Monica should know that she can't intrude on us; if anything, sometimes it feels like our whole family is intruding on her and Marcus, the way they look at each other like there is no one else, and I mean no one else, in the room, in the house, in the whole world. She could never intrude. She shoulda known that and come round before tonight. But she's here now and I guess that's what matters.

"And how would Aaron and I sneak into the hospital at five a.m.?" I smile a little, trying to show her how ridiculous she's being.

She raises an eyebrow. "Well, you are certainly sneaking around doing something. . . ." She pulls back and looks me up and down, her eyes darting over the football jersey and the running shorts and back up to my hair, which has poufed out to almost twice its normal size since I didn't have a rubber band to tie it up. "Wing. What the hell is going on?"

I tell her the truth. Or at least, as much of the truth as I can. I don't tell her that I've got a dragon and a lion waking me up every night, or about my feelings for Aaron, but I do tell her that since the accident I haven't been able to sleep and I've been running at night.

Monica is less skeptical about the running bit than Aaron was. Maybe because she hasn't seen it. Doesn't know just how fast I go.

Or maybe it's because she's a better friend and believes I'm capable of doing something like running at night.

She is, however, *highly* skeptical of the fact that I just *happened* to run into Aaron on the field. Her line of questioning starts to make me think that she suspects my whole running thing is about seeing him.

"Wing, honey, didn't you know that Aaron likes to go running at night?" she says, and there's a touch of pity in her voice, like a pat of butter scraped over burnt toast. Like she knows what she's saying is going to make me feel like crap but maybe if she says it in a nice way it won't.

I think you shouldn't serve burnt toast at all, but that's just my opinion.

"I didn't know," I say, even as a memory of him mentioning it slots into my brain. "But, Mon, it isn't about Aaron. I like it. The running. And I think . . . I think I might be good at it."

"I'm sure you are, sweetie. But you can't go out running in the middle of the night." A slow smile spreads over her face. "Even if you know that Aaron'll be around to be your knight in shining armor."

"I don't need no knight in shining armor," I snap back. My exhaustion is finally catching up with me, making me lazy with my language. "I've got a dragon!" Apparently I'm also sloppy about what secrets I tell.

"Wing, honey, you know I don't always get your metaphors." Monica has that same slow smile on, the one I can picture her using on her kids someday when they've done something stupid or silly and she has to chastise them but doesn't want to make them feel bad. Like "Oh, Marcus Junior, sweetie, you can't eat a whole tub of peanut butter all by yourself." Or "Little Monica, don't you know that Santa only comes if you've been good?"

Thinking about Marcus and Monica's children makes my heart hurt. Because I don't know if there will be a Mini Monica and a Marcus Junior. I lean toward Monica, and even though I'm all sweaty hair and sticky skin and smelly jersey, I hug her tightly around the shoulders.

"What was that for?" she asks, but she's grinning.

"I'm just happy you're here."

"So you really aren't going to tell me the truth about these nightly rendezvous with Aaron?"

"There aren't any nightly rendezvous!" I protest. "Seriously. Tonight was the first night I've seen him."

"All right," she says, but I can tell she doesn't believe me.

"I swear," I say. I think of something to swear on, something sacred enough, and she looks up at me and I know we're thinking the same thing.

Do you swear on Marcus's life?

"I swear," I repeat.

"Well," she says, and the word is heavy and light all at the same time. "I bet it won't be the last."

CHAPTER 20

A SECRET, I QUICKLY LEARN, IS MUCH MORE FUN IF YOU HAVE someone to share it with.

I thought I loved running before, but now ... it is about so much more than just the running.

I don't rely on my dragon and my lioness to wake me up anymore. I set an alarm so I'm ready to slip out and meet Aaron. My dragon and my lioness don't come to the track as much either. Sometimes I'll see the shadow of my dragon above me, or think I see my lioness ahead of me in the dark, but now that I've got Aaron running alongside me, I barely even miss them. And every time he drops me off home, one or both of them are waiting for me under the porch, their eyes glowing in the dark like the nightlight I used to have next to my bed.

Aaron picks me up in the middle of the night, at the end of my street. At first we don't talk much; we sit in a cocoon of silence, the only sounds the engine humming to itself, the tires grumbling along the uneven asphalt. I don't want to be the first one to talk. The first one to make it weird.

When the words do come, the third or fourth time I clamber into the front seat of his car, at first they're about Marcus. How much we wish he were with us. How much he'd love late-night runs. I tell Aaron how I was following him when I broke my ankle as a little girl. He laughs, but in a nice way.

I ask him how it was quitting football. He clenches the steering wheel, knuckles going white. "It isn't the same without him. No one can throw like him. I've been fumbling balls every practice."

"What does the rest of the team say about him?" I think about how I try to make myself invisible when one of Marcus's old teammates walks by. I don't look at them because I'm scared of what I'll see in their eyes. What my brother did to Michael and his family and to Oakie sticks to me like gum to the bottom of my shoe: no matter how much I scrape, it won't come off, and as time has gone by, it's started to just become part of the shoe, part of me, and I can't remember it not being there.

"Aw, they're torn up about the whole thing. Most of them were there that night, they were drinking just as much as Marcus. But it's easy to hate on someone when they're gone. All the little things everyone used to keep inside, the things that bothered them about Marcus, all that shit is coming out now. And he's not here to defend himself and I'm tired of defending him. I can't defend what he did that night . . . but the other shit they're saying . . . I couldn't handle it anymore. Anyway. The only reason I was a good wide receiver was because I'm a good runner. I was never good enough to play football in college, not like Marcus or some of the other guys. But with track . . ." He shrugs. "I've got a shot."

I always did think that Aaron stood out a little bit on the field, not just to me, but to everyone. All lean muscle, long limbs, I hated to see his body covered up under all that padding. Sure, it was glorious to see him play, the way he would leap up to grab the ball, and whatever it was between him and Marcus that made them work together like a seesaw, in perfect harmony, it was magical. But I'm glad Aaron's quit football. I'm selfish like that. Because now he has more time for running. Now he has more time for me.

When we run, he shows me how to use my arms to go even faster, and then after, he shows me how to cool down.

And then one day, he touches me.

It isn't sexual. Nothing like that. We've been running hard, harder than we usually do, and I gulp my water bottle all in one go.

"You should lie down." His tone is the same as when he tells me you should lengthen out, you should pump your arms, but now he's telling me I should lie down. Outside. In the middle of the track.

I pretend I don't hear him because I don't know what he's talking about.

"Wing. You gotta lie down. Let me look at your calves."

Hold up. Look at my calves? I don't ever even think about my calves and now Aaron is saying he wants to look at them? My calves? I look down, scared at what I'll see. They look normal to me. Maybe a little more muscular than they used to be. I notice, with increasing shame, that I've missed a spot shaving on the left one. . . . Maybe there's something wrong with them and I just can't tell because it's so dark out. . . .

"Wing, your calves are seizing up. I can tell from here."

Now that he mentions it, they are all trembly and shaky. I didn't notice.

"What are you going to do?"

He laughs, the sound buzzing through the night and straight into my heart. "You sound so suspicious. I just wanna make sure the muscles aren't too tight."

I'm not sure why this means I have to lie down but I do, tentatively, and the grass is scratchy under my neck.

"Now what?" I ask. He's kneeling next to me.

"Bend your knees up," he says. So I'm lying on the grass with my legs bent, feeling like I'm in the position a woman is when she has a baby, when Aaron reaches over and starts pummeling my calves like they're miniature punching bags until they're flapping around like elephant ears. He isn't just pummeling either, he's slapping my calves one at a time between his palms, and they're just bouncing back and forth and I can hear the sound of his hands against my skin and I'm so shocked that I don't say anything for a moment. Then my mouth finally remembers how to form words.

"What the hell?"

He pauses midslap. "Is this hurting?" His forehead wrinkles in concern.

"No," I say, because it isn't, "but ... um ... it is kind of weird."

"Oh," he says, quickly standing. "Sorry. I thought you'd like it." He holds out a hand to pull me up. "The guys on the team, we used to do that to each other all the time. After a race. Helps you loosen up."

I'm pretty sure it's had the exact opposite effect. My whole body is tense. My mind is reeling, doing somersaults. Was that just some kind of massage or did it mean something and I'm so inexperienced, so clueless, that I didn't realize it?

"It was nice," I say. "I just ... didn't know what you were doing."

His laugh buzzes again. "Next time I'll explain better."

I'm glad there is going to be a next time.

"Aaron?" I ask on one Wednesday night when we're on our cool-down lap. He hasn't ninja-sneak-attack-massage-pummeled my calves tonight, but he has shown me how to lengthen my stride, how to kick it in at the end of the lap and find that last burst of energy to push myself over the finish line.

He glances up at me, eyes bright and focused. "You all right? Something hurt? We go too hard?"

I shake my head. I'm sore, but it feels good, it feels right.

"Um. Do I look weird when I run?" I feel like I'm flying but I'm starting to wonder what I *look* like.

Aaron doesn't answer immediately, which makes me want to take off running as fast as I can and go far, far, far away. Although I'd probably have to blindfold him first so he couldn't watch me. Because clearly I look like some kind of freak.

"Not weird," he says, but his tone doesn't match the words.

"It's fine," I say quickly. "It isn't like anyone is going to see me anyway."

Aaron stops suddenly and reaches out to grab my arm and slow me down. "Wing! Everyone is going to see you. That's why we're doing this, why we're out running every night. Making you better. Making you the best!"

"You"—I narrow my eyes at him—"aren't *making* me anything. I was running just fine before you decided you needed to swoop in and improve me. *Fix* me."

"Wing." My name comes out all in one breath. "I want to help you. Support you. That's all I'm trying to do." He cocks his head to one side like a pigeon. "You don't run weird, but you don't run exactly normal either. You run . . . like no one else. You look a little different, that's for sure. But, Wing, it ain't anything to be embarrassed about. I love how you run. You look . . ." I tense, waiting for it. "You look beautiful."

Then he smiles at me and it's like I've been living in darkness and now there is light. I think I hear a growl behind me, I think I see a dragon wing in the sky, but I ignore them, because right now, all I want is to just be with Aaron.

They're waiting for me, both of them, under the porch, when he drops me off. I climb up the steps, knowing to skip over the second one because it creaks, and suddenly my lioness is in front of me, blocking the front door, teeth bared slightly, a low growl rumbling in her throat.

"Move!" I whisper, but she doesn't, just keeps staring at me, her tail swishing back and forth like a switch. My dragon is perched on the porch fence, her eyes glowing.

"What?" I say. "You should be glad I'm running with Aaron. I'm getting faster. I know you see me. I know you know. We're helping each other, all right? He's hurting too. It's good for us, both of us."

My lioness stops moving her tail and she steps aside, pushing her head against me as she does, her growl gone. I rub the back of her ears as I unlock the front door and creep into the kitchen.

My dragon and my lioness stay in my room a long time that night. I fall asleep to the sound of their breathing.

CHAPTER 21

It's getting colder. I'm still running at night, but I've started wearing long-sleeved shirts and bringing a sweatshirt. I wonder if Marcus feels the temperature changing. Can he feel anything at all?

Every time we visit him, he hasn't changed or moved. His hair is growing out, which is weird. He gets stubble on his cheeks and jaw. The nurses shave it. They asked my mom if she wanted to, but she burst into tears and said she wouldn't know how.

Monica comes with us now. Sometimes she goes on her own—my mom got special permission for her and Aaron to visit him without us. Monica visits a lot. More than I do. I can't just sit there and stare at him. It makes me angry. I feel like if he just tried a little harder he could wake up. . . . I take out my frustration toward him on the track. You'd think it would make it harder, wearing his guilt when I run, but something funny happens when

I start to pick up speed. All my frustration slips off like a coat that's too big, and I'm lighter than I was before.

Aaron is late tonight. I've been standing out on the sidewalk talking to the moon for the past ten minutes and I'm starting to get cold. I hug myself and wonder if he's forgotten or if something came up. Should I go back inside? But if he does come, I don't want him to think I've forgotten.

I'd never forget.

Finally I see his little silver car crawling toward me. I jog in place to warm up, waving as the car sidles up next to me.

"Hey," I say, settling into the front seat, the seat I'm starting to think of as mine.

"Hey," says Aaron, tapping his hands on the steering wheel. He's got music on tonight, something low in the background, with a pulsing beat.

"I thought maybe you weren't coming," I say. I click my seat belt in. I never used to be all that bothered about seat belts. Ever since the accident, though, I always, always wear one.

"Yeah," he says, sounding distracted and far away. Like a pre-recorded message. "Sorry."

"It's fine! Don't worry! I mean, I should be thanking you for coming to get me every night. I could always meet you at the track. Run down there on my own." I'm chirping like a baby bird.

Aaron glances over at me, and for the first time since I got in the car, he smiles. "Wing," he says, and I love how he says my name, he says my name in a way no one else does. "I like picking you up. And what kind of gentleman would I be if I let you go running down the streets of Atlanta in the middle of the night by yourself?"

"I was doing just that before you came along and was doing just fine," I say, but I'm grinning too.

"Ouch," he says, smile even broader. "How about this? I'll pretend I don't know you don't need me, and you can pretend you *do* need me to get to the track. Fair trade?"

"Sounds good to me," I say, even though it isn't true at all. Sure, I can get to the track without him . . . but whether or not I need him is a different story.

"I'm just doing it for Marcus, you know. He'd have my ass if he knew I was letting you run around at night all alone."

Of course. It's for Marcus. It isn't for me. He's being a good friend to Marcus. I force a smile and turn to look at the nighttime world whizzing by.

Aaron clears his throat. "I've got something for you," he says, voice overly casual. "Under the seat."

I reach under the seat and rummage around. My fingers brush against a small, smooth bottle. It rattles like a warning as I dislodge it from its hiding place.

It's a small prescription bottle. My eyes focus in on the small print. Antidepressants. I shake it experimentally, and the sound of the pills jumping in their bottle makes Aaron look over sharply. When he sees what I'm holding he swears under his breath.

"Oh. Not that. Not those. Sorry. I didn't know those were in my car. The other thing. Maybe it's stuck under the seat."

We're at a stoplight, and he leans over me and pops open his glove compartment. "Put those in there."

Aaron's name isn't on the bottle of pills. It's Annamarie. His mother's name.

Aaron drives on. We're almost at the track. "She's been trying to stop drinking? After what happened to Marcus? It scared her?"

His sentences come out full of question marks. He's unsure and nervous, and he's talking faster than I've ever heard him talk. "So she's trying those."

"I didn't know ... didn't know your mom was taking anti-depressants."

"She shoulda been taking them a long time ago. She should be taking them more regularly too. When she doesn't ... she likes to ... what they call 'self-medicate.'" His voice is false and tinny. "Her job, down at Kroger"—he mentions one of the grocery stores near his house, where his mom works as a cashier—"the pay is pretty shit, but she's got health insurance, and it covers this kind of stuff."

"That's lucky," I say, and I mean it's lucky that the insurance covers it, because ever since Marcus's accident I've learned that there are all sorts of things insurance doesn't cover.

We've been sitting in the track parking lot for the past few minutes, but neither of us makes a move to get out of the car.

"It's hereditary," he says, not looking at me, not looking at any-thing.

"What is?"

"All her shit. The depression. The drinking. Sure she's passed down some other treats that haven't shown their ugly faces yet."

"There's nothing wrong with taking antidepress—" I start, but he cuts me off.

"I know that. But there is something wrong with not pay-ing attention to how many you're supposed to take. And chasing them with vodka."

"Maybe she should talk to somebody," I say.

"She's got nothing to say to anybody."

The air in the car is warm; we've heated it with our words. I wonder if Aaron used to talk to Marcus about this. I knew . . . I knew a little bit about his mom, but I didn't know it was like this.

He lets out a big whoosh, like a whale blowing air out its blowhole.

"That isn't what I had for you," he says, gesturing at the now closed glove compartment. He leans toward me, making me go still in anticipation. In the small, hot car I'm very aware of his smell, part boy musk and part clean clothes and part deodorant, it's a smell I like very much, and the closer he leans the more I can smell it. He reaches under the seat, his arm brushing against my legs as he does and his head is practically in my lap and I sit as still as I can, staring straight ahead. Does he realize how close his face is to my thighs?

"Ah, here we go. They were stuck."

He tugs on something and his arm comes up and out, between my legs (I feel like I might pass out from how close and almost tangled our limbs are), followed by a pair of gray and blue running shoes.

Women's running shoes.

The laces are a bit frayed and the heels a little worn down, but they aren't in bad shape.

"My mom got these at a sale a couple years ago and doesn't use them, so I thought you could. I think you guys have the same size feet."

The shoes grin up at me, begging me to try them on. I pull back their tongues to look at the label underneath and see that he's right, I do have the same size shoe as his mom. For the first time, I'm grateful to have feet that are the size they are.

"You don't have to take them. I know they're just a ratty pair of old shoes. But I thought they might be more comfortable than those." He nods at my worn-out Converse. They've done just fine for now, but the thought of wearing real running shoes . . .

"Does this make you my fairy godmother?" I ask as I take off my Converse and slide my feet into the cushiony comfort of the new old shoes.

"What?"

"You know . . . in Cinderella? The fairy godmother gives her glass slippers? Not that you look like a fairy . . . or a godmother . . ."

Aaron grins. "I can be a fairy godmother," he says, his voice rumbling through me. "But maybe I'm more like that cricket in *Pinocchio*."

I laugh, my feather giggles filling up the car. First time I've laughed like this since we went to Gladys's. "You mean Jiminy Cricket? The one that shows him right from wrong? His conscience?"

Aaron shrugs, a feather giggle falling off his shoulder. "He's got a dope hat. And what are you saying? That I don't know right from wrong?"

"Jiminy Cricket never gave Pinocchio any shoes."

"All right, all right. I'm not the cricket. I don't know how I feel about being the fairy godmother either."

"Yeah, you're much more of a Prince Charming," I say, and then snap my mouth shut. Stupid. I'm stupid.

"You think I'm charming?" He's grinning at me, grinning his grin that I can't help but beam back at.

"You know what? You can be the cricket," I say as I open the door and step into the night. My feet are so cushioned in my new shoes that I don't walk so much as bounce, like I'm walking on clouds.

CHAPTER 22

SCHOOL DOESN'T SEEM THAT IMPORTANT ANYMORE, NOT WITH Marcus still in the hospital and me running every night with Aaron. But my mom says I've got to go. So I do. The pain hasn't gone away, and it hurts, but it's a pain I know. One that's just *there*. Like a cut that can't close, a broken bone that won't mend. At least now I've gotten over that first slice, that first break.

I've started sitting with Monica and Tash at lunch. Aaron still sits where he's always sat, at the football table, but I see him watching us, and I wonder if he wants to sit with us. I didn't think Tash liked me very much, but she's nice. Nicer than I expected her to be. She's good with Mon too. When Mon starts crying out of nowhere, her tears falling into her french fries, getting them soggy and saltier, Tash will rub her back and position herself so people can't really see that Monica is crying, and she'll kinda croon to her like Mon is a baby who doesn't know any words yet. This happens at least three times a week. Whenever it does I stare down at my sandwich till Monica's breathing gets back to normal and she blows her nose and then she starts talking about something totally random like did we see that there's a new baby elephant at the Atlanta Zoo or did we know that in England the Thames River is pronounced "Tems."

Today is a crying day. Monica's sniffling, Tash is rubbing her back, and I'm staring down at my peanut butter sandwich. I've been bringing peanut butter sandwiches because money is so tight I can't afford to buy lunch. No jelly, no honey, just peanut butter on plain bread.

"Wing?" I look up and wonder what Marcus would say if he could see Monica's puffy eyes and red nose. He'd kiss her and make it better, I know he would.

"It's apple-picking time," she says, and I nod, even though I don't know what the hell she's talking about, because this is the kind of thing she says after she cries.

"Marcus and I used to go apple picking," she says, and Tash's eyebrows shoot up under her thick bangs. This isn't how after-crying conversation goes, we don't start talking about Marcus again, and she glares at me like it's my fault, like I brought him up, when all I've been doing is sitting staring at my peanut butter sandwich and thinking about running. And Aaron. Aaron and running. One thought always leads to the other and back again and round and round until I remember Marcus and that thought stops all my other thoughts.

Monica is still talking. "Marcus and I would bring back apples for Granny Dee and she'd make pie. I was thinking, maybe we should go? You and me? And maybe Aaron?" She turns to Tash, whose eyebrows are still hidden. "You can come too, of course," she offers, but Tash is shaking her head already, shaking her eyebrows back down to their normal place on her face.

"Just y'all should go," she says. "It'll be good for all y'all."

On Saturday, we end up going in Aaron's car. Monica's car is bigger, but she doesn't want to drive that far. She doesn't want to drive at all now unless she has to.

The leaves in the trees along the road are fluttering in the wind. I'd say they are straight up showing off, making themselves look like red and orange and yellow butterflies. We drive and drive, and I don't know who does it first, it might have even been me, but we start singing Marcus's favorite songs.

By the time we get to the apple farm, we've been singing for over an hour, and my face feels funny from smiling so much, like my face muscles forgot what it felt like. We tumble out of the car, and I stretch my legs, which are tense from sitting so long. Monica is staring out at the fields and trees of Whistle Apple Farms, and she's biting her lip as the wind whips her long hair all around her. I grab her hand and squeeze. She squeezes back. Aaron is next to me, holding my other hand, and I know we probably look like we're on a poster for superheroes, but standing there, all together, it makes me feel good. It makes me feel strong.

"Welcome to Whistle Apple Farms," says an apple-cheeked old woman from inside the squat red farmhouse. "Y'all been here before?"

Monica swallows and nods. "I have," she says in a fragile voice.

The old woman looks at me and Aaron, eyes resting on me

for just a moment longer, trying to figure out what kind of box I go in. "First time for you two?" We nod. She smiles at us as she hands us our wooden basket, telling us that we can pay for what we pick when we're on our way out. She also gives us a map that explains where all the different kinds of apples grow and what they're good for.

"Some are good for pies, others for juicin', and some . . ." She leans toward me, eyes sparkling in her wrinkled face. "Some are best right then and there."

It's hard to know where to start. The orchards go on and on and there are too many trees to count, each one bejeweled with fat, shiny apples. All different shades of red and green and yellow. I didn't know apples come in so many colors.

"I've never picked apples," I admit as I tug on an especially shiny red one hanging low on the nearest tree.

"Me neither," says Aaron. He's on the other side of the tree, reaching up as high as he can. "Reckon they taste sweeter at the top," he says, jumping a bit to pull one down. He's so graceful in everything he does. Even jumping up to grab an apple. I bet he'd be good at ballet. He's elegant in a way that it isn't fair for a boy to be; it's a fierce elegance, like he's a leopard or an eagle. I could watch him jump and run and just move all day long. I like to watch him when he's still too. I like to watch him all the time.

He lopes around the tree to where I'm standing and presents me with his apple.

"This apple," he says, bowing a bit, "is a perfect apple. I'm sure of it. Best apple in the whole damn orchard."

I don't know if he wants me to take it from him or take a bite while it's in his hand. The thought of eating it while it's nestled between his fingers sends shivers from my lips to my toes, but then he straightens himself up and takes a bite himself, giving an exaggerated moan of pleasure.

"A perfect apple! I knew it! I told you, best ones come from the top. The best ones, you have to work for." He takes another bite and it makes a satisfying crunch.

"Since when are you such an apple expert? I thought this was your first time picking apples," I say as I toss my own apple into the basket, trying to play it cool. "Monica, we're relying on you to be the real expert. . . . Monica?" I can't see her. "Mon?" I peer down the row of trees next to us and glimpse the back of her blond head just before she disappears behind another tree.

"Mon!" I drop the basket, not caring that my specially picked apple is probably bruised, and dash after her. I almost miss her. She's sitting slumped under an apple tree, tears trailing down her cheeks.

I sit next to her and try to rub her back like Tash does. "Mon?"

"Marc—" She hiccups. "Marcus was the one who picked all the apples last year. I'd point out which one I wanted and he'd pull it off for me, and he'd be stupid about it, you know him, he'd juggle some or try to put the whole thing in his mouth or put them down his shirt like apple boobs."

"Apple boobs?"

Monica chokes out a short laugh, snot bubbling out her nose. She wipes her nose with the back of her hand and takes a deep shuddery breath, so full of tears and snot it sounds like she's drowning from the inside.

"He's everywhere, Wing. Everything I do makes me think of him. And the thing is, I don't want to make new memories without him. I want to hold on to everything that makes me think of him. Is that wrong? Is that sick? What if . . . what if he doesn't wake up? What if the last time I saw him I was drunk and he was drunk and our last kiss tasted like beer and I forgot to tell him that I loved him before he got in that car? What if I never move on? If I can't move on, how can Michael or that woman's family move on?"

I flinch. We never say her name, the mother who Marcus killed.

"I can't stop thinking about them, Wing. I can't stop thinking about if it had been the other way." Monica's eyes are wide, so wide I can see the whites all the way around. She's staring at me without blinking, eyes getting wider with every word she says. "What if one of them had been driving and it was their fault? What would I think? Would I have moved on? Would I hate them more than I hate Marcus for what he did? If he had died too, would I hate him? Would they hate him? But he's alive, and I'm glad, so glad, and it is the most selfish feeling I've ever had, but I'm stuck. Stuck still loving him and still so angry at him, but if loving him and being angry at him were on a scale it would be no competition. Even if I wanted to stop loving him, and sometimes I wish I could, because it would be easier, you know? And sometimes I don't even think he deserves my love. Or your love. He doesn't deserve any kind of love after what he did. But I can't help it, I can't turn it off. I can't turn off loving Marcus and I'm scared I'll never be able to, and what will I be then? I don't wanna be a girl in love with the wrong kind of guy, but I don't want to ever stop loving him either."

At some point her tears stop and her snot dries up and her voice gets louder and louder and pitched higher and higher. The sun is starting to set over the hills and it's turning the air gold, and in the golden light, Monica looks like some kind of broken doll.

"I can't stop loving him either," I say softly. I know my love is a different kind of love, just like Aaron's love is different, and my mom's, and I don't want her to think I'm trying to take away from her pain. But even though we love him differently, I think the hurt is the same.

There's a light cough from behind us and then Aaron crouches down beside her. "You guys doin' okay?"

I wait for Monica to reply, and when she nods slowly, I know that we are.

"I got us some more apples," says Aaron, gesturing behind him at the basket. It's filled to the brim.

"From the tops?" I can't see Monica's expression in the fading light but can hear her smile.

"From the tops. We need some extra-special apples today."

On the drive back home, Monica and I both sit in the backseat, her in the middle, right next to me, and she falls asleep on my shoulder. Occasionally, Aaron catches my eye in the rearview mirror, and I smile at him. We don't talk, because we don't want to wake Monica. Instead, we sit quietly and breathe in air that tastes like apples.

CHAPTER 23

MONICA AND AARON TAKE SOME OF THE APPLES HOME BUT
leave most of them in our kitchen for Granny Dee. She goes
through them one by one, smelling them, inspecting them, sepa-
rating them out.

And then she starts to bake apple pies. She bakes and bakes
and bakes, and every time I come into the kitchen she's in there,
slicing apples or rolling out pie crust or putting in the filling until
our whole house smells like the inside of an apple pie.

She won't let us eat any, though. She bakes pies and says that
she'll make us our own pie but these are special pies, special pies
for special people.

I don't know what she's talking about.

Then, after the last pie has been baked, she takes off her apron,
wraps the pies in tinfoil, and puts a bow on each one. "I need you
to drive me somewhere," she says.

"I don't have my license," I say. "I only have my permit, you know that. I'm not supposed to drive without another licensed driver. Can't Mom drive you?"

She shakes her head. "It can't be your mama. It'll be too hard for her. And I'm a licensed driver."

"Are not. You haven't had your license for years!"

"Well, no one needs to know that. Now help me carry some of these pies to the car."

She doesn't tell me where we're going, she just directs. I don't know how she knows where she's going. We don't go far, only about fifteen minutes from our house, but it's far enough that the houses start to look a lot bigger, a lot nicer.

"Number thirty-two," Granny Dee says, and the pie she's holding is trembling a little. "Least I can do, the very least," she mumbles to herself.

"What?"

"Number thirty-two!" she snaps, and I manage to park in front of the big brick house.

We sit in silence, Granny Dee staring at the house, her eyes welling up.

"What are we doing?" I whisper, because it feels like we're sneaking around.

Granny Dee turns to me, eyes magnified behind her spectacles. "Listen to me. Here is what you are gonna do. You are gonna take these pies up to the door, ring the doorbell, and run back down here as fast as you can and get in the car and get out of here before anyone sees you. You got that?"

"You want me to ding-dong-ditch this house?"

"I want you to leave them apple pies! I'm too old to get up there and back down here without them seeing me. Now scoot!"

She thrusts a stack of pies in my hands and I look up at the house again. And I see the name on the mailbox.

Bell.

This is the family of the woman Marcus killed. Sophie Bell. Granny Dee wants to bring them apple pies. Like how people brought us casseroles and cookies when my daddy, her son, died. And that food we got, it was made with love, and I know she made these apple pies with love, but the food didn't make it better. And we sure as hell didn't get any pies from the family of the drug dealer who killed my daddy.

I don't think Granny Dee would have wanted that. So I don't know why she thinks dropping off anonymous apple pies is a good idea. Even I know this is a horrible idea. Because an apple pie won't make up for what Marcus did.

"Granny . . . ," I say slowly, "we can't do this."

She starts to cry. "I've got to do something. We've got to do something. They've got to know we're good people. We're good people, Wing. It was an accident. Marcus is a good boy. His daddy was a good man."

I reach over and hold her hand. "I know, Granny."

"I keep thinking about them. I keep thinking how the grief is never gonna go away. Because it doesn't. No parent should have to bury their child. I've got to do something."

"We can't do anything," I say, because I'm starting to realize that there's nothing we can do to fix what Marcus did.

She looks down at the apple pie in her lap. "I just thought . . . it might help."

"An apple pie isn't gonna bring their daughter back," I say, squeezing her hand.

She nods. "What are we gonna do with all these pies?"

We end up taking them to the hospital and leaving them at the nurses' station. As a thank-you for taking such good care of Marcus.

"That is so sweet of y'all!" one of them says, and Granny Dee looks away. Because these pies aren't sweet; they are full of sadness.

"I hope y'all enjoy them" is all she says.

After we get home, I give Granny Dee a big hug and hold her trembling frame, and then we both put on aprons and together we make one more apple pie. For us.

CHAPTER 24

I SHOULD HAVE RUN THE SECOND I SAW HEATHER PARKER sauntering toward me, a trio of girls trailing behind her. She has that smile on her face, the one she wears when she's going in for the kill. But I don't run. Instead, I back into the corner, wishing I were so small that all you could see of me was the tuft of my hair and it was so small you'd mistake it for a dust ball. That's how small I'm trying to make myself.

But for all my wishing, I stay the same size, and when I open my eyes they're all there, staring at me, like they know I tried and failed to make myself disappear.

"I'm surprised you're still here. Being the sister of a murderer and everything." Heather sounds gleeful. I've never heard anyone say the word *murderer* with so much pep. "Everyone hates him— you know that, right? Everyone thinks he should have been the one who died."

She's so close to me now I can smell her breath. It smells like ranch dressing. I can see every freckle across her nose. She's so close she could kiss me. Or bite me. "What's that old saying? An eye for an eye? Aren't you scared someone's gonna run you down to get back at Marcus for what he did? I'd be scared."

"Knock it off," says a voice, a low, strong voice that I feel all through my bones, like I've got radio receptors wired inside me and I'm tuned in to his channel.

"You playing big brother now that Marcus isn't around?" Heather laughs. "Isn't that sweet?" But there's nothing sweet about her tone of voice. "You gonna start dating . . . what's her name? That blond girl with a thing for black guys? Oh, wait. Not black guys. Black Chinese guys. Pretty particular taste, right, Rhonda?"

"Very particular," Rhonda chirps, tossing her blond ponytail.

"I'd say she has a thing for freaks."

"Shut up," Aaron growls. His jaw is so tight I'm sure it'll snap if he tries to say anything else.

Heather's eyes widen for a minute. But she stands her ground.

Bile is rising in my throat.

She lowers her voice to a hiss and leans toward me. "I hope he dies and then I hope you kill yourself so I don't have to see your freakish face anymore."

All the air leaves my body in one whoosh, like a balloon that's just been untied, because Heather Parker has said a lot of things over the years but she's never said anything like this. And nobody has said they hope Marcus dies. It feels like because she's said it out loud, maybe it'll happen. Like she's cursed him.

I can't handle it. I don't know what to do. So I do the only thing I can do.

I run. I push past her, leaving her wide-eyed and jeering.

I hear Aaron shouting after me. I don't slow down.

I speed up. I run down the hall and out of the building and I keep going until I'm at my front door, heart beating so fast and lungs working so hard that I don't realize tears are streaming down my face until there is a river of them at my feet and I'm drowning.

Strong arms pull me up out of my river of tears. For a second I think these arms that I know so well, that I want to know better, are going to wrap around me and hold me close until my racing heart calms down. But they don't. Instead, Aaron pulls me to my feet and lifts my chin up.

"I've never seen you go so fast," he says. "Let's get you some water or something." He pulls out a key and unlocks my front door.

"You have a key?" Part of me is astonished; part of me isn't surprised at all.

"Yep. I've had it for years. Marcus was always losing his or forgetting it or something."

I follow Aaron into my house. The hall is dark and quiet and distinctly unwelcoming. We go into the kitchen and I switch on the fluorescent lights and they hesitantly flicker to life. A cold cup of coffee sits on the table.

"Where are Granny Dee and LaoLao?" Aaron asks.

I shrug. LaoLao started working at the restaurant with my mom a few weeks ago. Hoping the minimum wage she'll make will help stanch the ever-widening hole of debt we're falling into. She didn't want to go back to work, she's old now, but I don't think we had much choice. I don't know where Granny Dee might be. Even though she can't drive, she'll take the bus sometimes, if she needs to get somewhere. I say as much. Then it hits me.

"Granny Dee is with Marcus."

She has to be. Where else would she be in the middle of the afternoon? I wonder why she hasn't told us. Probably because there's nothing to tell. It's not like he's woken up. I picture the scene: Him lying there, a lump on the hospital bed. Her sitting in a chair, watching his every breath, waiting for him to open his eyes. Not wanting him to be alone if he does.

When he does.

I should be the one visiting him. Spending my afternoons by his side. Standing guard. Waiting. Watching. I should be able to hold his hand by now; I should be able to touch his face, be able to pretend that he's just sleeping. But I can't. I can't. And the guilt I feel about not visiting him more, not being able to stomach it, not just what he looks like but what he did, has buried itself inside me like a tick. It was small at first, but then it gorged on my blood and just grew and grew, burrowing deeper. I've tried to brush it off, but it's far too deep. Did you know that if you don't properly remove a tick the head will stay in your body and infect you? My guilt is spreading and I can't stop it.

"I don't know if I've ever been here without him," says Aaron. He's poured himself a glass of milk, and after he takes a sip he has a milk mustache. I want to point it out but I don't want him to wipe it away. He looks so much like he did when he was younger. Softer. More innocent.

Then he frowns and the image is spoiled.

"I'm sorry, Wing. About Heather. The things she was saying . . ."

"It's fine." I open the refrigerator door and pretend to look for something to drink so Aaron can't see my face. I don't want him to rehash what she was saying. I don't want to relive it. I want to forget about it as fast as I can. I grab a jug of sweet tea that Granny Dee made last night and pour myself a glass.

"I wish Marcus was here," he says. He's wiped off his milk mustache.

"Me too."

We sit in silence at the table, him with his milk, me with my glass of watered-down sweet tea. It isn't a comfortable silence. It's thick, the kind that makes you choke when you breathe it in.

Aaron suddenly slams his fist on our table, making the glasses jump. It makes me jump too. I'm up and backing away before I even realize what I'm doing.

"God damn it!" he shouts, punching the table again. This is too much for the glass of milk. It topples over and lands on the ground, shattering and spilling milk everywhere. Neither of us moves to clean it up.

"Why, Wing? Why'd he go and do that? I told him . . ." Aaron's voice breaks as he stands and goes to lean against the fridge, his forehead pressed against it. "I told him he'd had too much and that we could sleep at Trey's place or we could even spring for a cab or go with someone else, but he said he was fine, he said he could drive, and I didn't argue with him! But I didn't go with him either. I don't even remember why now. I lay back down on the couch and closed my eyes, and the next thing I knew everyone was screaming that there'd been an accident and I sat up and I knew. Wing, I knew."

I want to tell him that it isn't his fault, but my mouth feels like it's filled with cotton balls and my tongue feels fat and I struggle to say the words. I don't know if I believe them.

Aaron looks up at me, his eyes fierce. "I was drinking with him that night, Wing. I did shots with him. Hell, I even held him up to do a keg stand." He shakes his head. "The goddamn keg stand."

I'm not exactly sure what a keg stand is, but I've seen enough teen movies to have a basic idea. Thinking of Marcus, my Marcus, upside down, guzzling beer, makes my stomach churn.

"What about Monica?" I say. The other person complicit in all this.

"Mon? She was trying to get him to stop. She always does. But after a while she started drinking too. Girly shit. Kahlua and flavored Smirnoff. Started flirting with some of the other guys, trying to get Marcus riled, get him jealous, get him to notice her. But Marcus was so gone he barely noticed. He'd just pull her in for a kiss every time he went by her, and after a while she got bored with flirting and was hanging over him like she does. Everyone was going to go get some food or something. Two different cars. Mon went in Roddy's car with Tash. Tash was drunk and crying and Mon was trying to be a good friend. Trying to be there for Tash. Thank God," he says, shaking his head again.

"Why didn't you stop him?" I say, finally voicing what I've thought since that night. "You or Monica. Someone should have stopped him!"

Aaron moves away from his position by the fridge and sits down next to me, hand raised as if he wants to stroke my back, but then he puts it in his lap.

"It's no one's fault," he says, and his voice is just as much of a dead thing as my own. "Wing. It isn't our fault."

"If there hadn't been that other car," I say in a whisper, and immediately feel ashamed for even whispering it. Because the other car wasn't in the wrong. The other car didn't run the red light.

The woman in the other car died. And no matter what Aaron says, it was someone's fault.

It was Marcus's fault.

He'll have to live with that. Two people are dead. He'll have that on his conscience forever.

If he ever wakes up.

CHAPTER 25

I DIDN'T RUN LAST NIGHT. AFTER WE CLEANED UP THE MILK and broken glass, Aaron and I came to some unspoken agreement that we weren't going to run. I thought about going on my own, but then I forgot to set my alarm, and for the first time in over two months, I slept through the night. But I'm paying for it this morning. My blood is sizzling in protest at missing the run and my whole body is thrumming with energy. I feel restless, wild; every step is a challenge. I feel like the whole world is going too slow.

At breakfast I slosh milk into my cereal bowl and it spills over the edge, pooling on the table, reminding me of the milk Aaron spilled yesterday.

"Careful," snaps Granny Dee. She's next to the coffeemaker. "Don't you know milk is expensive? Don't be wasteful. And clean that up quick. Don't dawdle like you always do."

If Marcus were here, he'd look at me and roll his eyes and make me feel better.

But he's not here.

I shouldn't care. I know Granny Dee is feeling tense because her and LaoLao got in another fight this morning. Right before my mom and LaoLao left to go to the Chinese grocery store down Buford Highway to get some kind of sauce they ran out of at the restaurant.

Granny Dee's been waking up early every morning, at the same time as LaoLao, and making LaoLao and my mom congee for breakfast. LaoLao's favorite. I know it's Granny Dee's way of trying to make up for the fact that LaoLao's working at the restaurant and Granny Dee isn't . . . but it doesn't stop LaoLao from calling Granny Dee lazy.

"You make congee and go back to bed! That not work! I'm on my feet all day. What do you do?"

Granny Dee will bluster, and then after LaoLao leaves, she'll look at newspaper ads, searching for something she can do. I've heard her calling a few places, but she hasn't even gotten an interview.

"Nobody wants to hire an old woman," she tells me.

So I should be nice to her this morning. But something about her tone, and her words, grates at my insides.

"I don't dawdle," I mutter.

"Since when?" says Granny Dee.

"You don't know everything."

"You keepin' secrets, Wing? From your Granny? From your mama? We got enough goin' on without any secrets." Granny Dee holds her coffee cup up to her thin lips, eyebrows cocked suspiciously.

"I don't dawdle," I repeat, frustration making me fierce.

Granny Dee's eyes widen till they're round as pennies. "Sugar,

I wasn't trying to hurt your feelings," she says carefully. "I was just sayin' you aren't the speediest little bird in the sky."

"You don't know anything!"

"Honey, what has gotten into you this morning?"

I don't answer. I go to the door and yank on my sneakers. I'm not even dressed yet, still in my bunny pajama bottoms and a ratty tank top. I pull my curls up into a ponytail on top of my head.

"Watch," I say to Granny Dee. She doesn't move, she's just staring at the sneakers on my feet. The ones Aaron gave me.

"I've never seen those before," she murmurs to herself.

"Granny!" I shout, and she jumps a bit, coffee spilling out of her mug. I watch it drip down the side and splash onto the linoleum, as if in slow motion. I'm sure I can hear the drops as they hit the ground.

"Watch what?" she asks. She sounds nervous now.

"Watch *me*."

The cracked and bumpy asphalt doesn't feel as good under my feet as the track does, but in moments I'm going so fast I barely notice what's under my feet. I run up the street, not so far that Granny Dee can't see me, and back again, not caring that Mrs. Swanson has stopped her gardening to gawp at me or that seven-year-old Jonny Bilt from next door is pointing and shouting. At the end of our street, a car slows down as I approach, a blue station wagon I think I recognize, I can't be sure, but I'm not going to slow down now to inspect it. I do two laps of the street and I'm not even winded. The sun is pouring gold down on me, drenching me in it, and I breathe it in with every step I take. I know I'm shining.

Granny Dee is standing on the edge of the front porch, gripping the rail.

"I told you!" I shout triumphantly as I swing up our driveway, feeling like the ground should be smoking in my wake.

Granny Dee sits down, heavily for such a frail old woman, hand on her heart. I wonder if she can see that I'm dripping sunshine. Maybe that's why she's so shocked.

"Granny Dee! What's wrong?"

Granny Dee is breathing so hard you'd think she was the one who just ran up and down the street. I go sit next to her, and even with the state she's in, I can't keep the smile off my face. Can't keep the gold from spilling out of me and all over her.

"I can be speedy," I say, my voice quiet in our buzzing street.

Granny Dee looks at me like she's never seen me before. Like I've just sprung out of the ground fully grown, the way Athena popped out of the head of Zeus. Like I'm someone she doesn't know at all.

"Granny Dee?"

"What . . . When . . . What . . ." She shakes her head as if she's shaking water out of her ears. I can tell she's underwater, that everything is murky and blurry for her and her information is coming in all garbled. But she'll come up soon.

I put my hand under her wrinkled elbow and help her up; the skin there is so loose it hangs like a pair of jeans on a washing line. She's still gawping at me.

"Wing . . . ," she says, and I won't lie, I'm glad she knows who I am, because from the way she's eyeing me, I was starting to worry that the shock was too much for her and my attempt to impress my grandmother might have given her a stroke or a heart attack or something.

But before she can finish her sentence, a car, the same car I saw at the end of the street, pulls into our driveway. And now I know where I've seen this car. It belongs to Eliza Thompson.

Who is staring straight at me the same way my Granny Dee has been staring at me.

And like that, all the gold and sunshine on me melts into a puddle at my feet.

I'm starting to think that showing off what I can do might not have been the best idea I've ever had.

CHAPTER 26

I CAN FEEL AARON'S EYES ON THE BACK OF MY NECK. I CAN perfectly picture his lips moving in a silent whisper, encouraging me, telling me this is the right thing to do.

Coach Kerry appraises me like I'm a horse she's thinking of buying. Eyes up and down and up and down.

"Can I help you?"

I force myself to meet her gaze. Where is Eliza? The other girls are huddled around Coach Kerry, eyeing me warily. I wonder what Eliza has told them. I look at the ground and notice they're all wearing the same brand shoes. Riveos. I wish I had a pair of those, best running shoes you can get, but least I have Aaron's mom's old running shoes and not just my Converse.

"I'd like to try out for the team?" I mean to say it as a declaration, but it comes out like a question.

"Anyone can join the track team," says the coach, her voice weary now. "You don't need to see me for that." She turns away, back to her huddle of girls, and I know I am already forgotten. My shoulders slump.

"Coach!" a voice shouts from the other side of the track. "This is the girl I was telling you about! The one I saw tearing down the street. I swear, this girl is faster than me."

Coach Kerry straightens up slowly and turns to face us. Eliza has jogged over and is standing next to me.

"Eliza." The coach's voice is sharp; it jabs through Eliza's excitement like a prong going through a gooey marshmallow. But Eliza's excitement is sticky, and it's spreading.

"You've got to see her."

"She looks a little . . . big to be a runner. Maybe she should go for the football team, take her brother's place," someone says in a stage whisper, and hushed giggles rise into the air like a flock of startled birds, getting louder the higher they get, the farther they fly. I swat one right out of my face, and just like that, they all stop flapping and fall back down to earth, silent again. Then I drop my bag and walk over to the starting line.

"You can do this," Aaron says. The coach's head snaps up at the sound of his voice.

"Aaron, what are you doing here?"

"I'm her coach," he says, and his chest swells up so big I'm worried he won't be able to see past it.

"Her coach," says Coach Kerry, her face stony-still.

"Maybe he gets community service for it." The same person who said I was too big to be a runner speaks out again, and this time when the giggles start I don't just swat at them, I run straight through them, scattering them in every direction, and I'm running so fast they can't catch me.

When I circle back around again, Aaron and Eliza are wearing matching smug expressions. The other girls are staring at me like I've just grown snakes for hair, and Coach Kerry's mouth is wide open like she's trying to catch flies for breakfast.

"Told you she was fast," says Eliza as I pull up next to her and pause to catch my breath.

Things move pretty quickly after that. Aaron asks Coach Kerry if he can be assistant coach but still train for his own races, and she has to get some kind of permission from administration, but not only is he still going to be my coach, he is going to get credits for it.

Coach Kerry makes me run over and over. I run alone. I run with the rest of the team. I run short distances. I run long distances. Coach stands with her stopwatch, eyes frantically darting back and forth between me and the time. Me and the time.

I never thought about trying to figure out how fast I was really going. I was just running. But now all anyone can talk about is my time. I've never thought of time like this. Like something you want to beat. My dragon and my lioness haven't run with me in a while, but sometimes when I'm out on the track with Coach Kerry and the others, I'll think I see my lioness tearing around a corner in front of me. I think she and my dragon are happy that I'm running more, running faster, running better. They still wait for me at night, under the porch or under my bed.

Eliza is the only one on the team who can keep up with me. During our warm-up and cool-down laps, I pull back to match her pace. She'll look over at me, shake her head, and grin so wide it's like the crescent moon is trying to imitate her smile.

"Damn, girl," she says, and she's laughing but it isn't a mean laugh, it's a laugh full of awe and happiness. "Where you been hiding all that speed?"

Everyone wants to know where my "new" speed came from. They don't know what I know, that it was always there, simmering under the surface, waiting for me to figure it out. I just needed something to run for, something to flip the switch inside me, so that my dragon and my lioness could lead me outside and show me how to run.

My steps are in time with Marcus's heartbeat, and even though I can't stand to be close to him at the hospital, what I'm doing is helping him. I don't think anyone would understand. Not even Aaron. Only my dragon and my lioness understand what running really is for me. Only they hear the beat of my feet. Only they know that every breath I take when I'm running is a breath for him and that as long as I keep running he'll keep breathing.

Now I practice in the afternoon, out in the open, under the sun—no more late-night moonlit runs for me—and it takes a while for me to get used to it. It's strange running with anyone but Aaron and my dragon and my lioness. I can't get used to people watching me, judging me, questioning me. Like one afternoon Coach Kerry pulls me aside after practice and says in a low voice that when the season officially starts I might want to have a doctor prove I'm clean.

"Clean?" I ask, not sure what she's saying.

"You know, that you aren't taking anything to help your performance."

My shock and offense must show on my face, because she holds her hands up and shakes her head. "Wing. Wing." She says my name twice in such quick succession that it sounds like she's a small child imitating a telephone.

"Wing," she says again, "*I* don't think that. Of course *I* don't. But I know what the other schools will say. Maybe even some of the other students or faculty here. It's a good idea."

"Does anyone else on the team have to get tested?" I spit.

I've never spoken to Coach Kerry, or any other teacher, like this. She frowns, her weathered face morphing right before my eyes. Switching from supportive coach to irritated disciplinarian. She takes her sunglasses off, eyes narrowed.

"No one else is as fast as you," she says. "And with you just coming out of nowhere, no training, never been on the team before, Wing, you've got to know that this whole thing is gonna look suspicious. You know I'm not the bad guy. Stop trying to make me out to be. I'm sure Aaron has been coddling you."

"Aaron does not coddle me."

"I'm not blind," she says. Then she sighs, long and loud, as if she's exhaling this whole conversation, getting it out of her system. "But maybe you're right." I start to relax. "Maybe it isn't fair to ask you to get tested and none of the other girls. How about this? I'll ask the whole team to get tested."

We all test clean. It turns out that Vanessa, the girl who has been the least welcoming, the one who was laughing the loudest and saying that I was some kind of community service project for Aaron, is pregnant. She didn't know. Doesn't know who the daddy is either.

It makes me wonder about Monica. If she's ever had a pregnancy scare. I might have put her and Marcus up on their pedestal, thought they were perfect, but even I'm not *that* naive.

Coach Kerry doesn't drop Vanessa from the team. She tells her she can let the team know whether she'll still be with us in

January. "Take the holidays to think it over," she says. Later, in the bathroom, I ask Eliza what "it" is.

"The baby," says Eliza, looking at me like I'm an idiot. "She'll get rid of it." She says it so nonchalantly. Like it's no big deal. "What the hell is Vanessa gonna do with a baby?"

I wonder what Monica would do. What would she have done if she'd found out, after the accident, that she was pregnant with Marcus's baby? Would she have had the baby by herself? She wouldn't have been by herself, though. We would all have been with her. I imagine Monica moving into our house of women. That baby would have had five mamas looking out for it.

I wonder what I would do. Not that I've ever had the chance to have anything close to a pregnancy scare. I've never even been kissed.

Closest I've come is sharing mac 'n' cheese with Aaron.

CHAPTER 27

I LIKE RUNNING WITH THE GIRLS ON THE TRACK TEAM, BUT
sometimes I miss my moonlit, star-chaperoned runs with Aaron.
I don't know how to tell him that. Don't know if I should. I've
never been so aware of a person before. He's usually running close
to me, watching, advising, but so is Coach Kerry and so is Eliza,
and I couldn't tell you how many breaths they took in a minute
or what their eyes look like when I beat my best time or what the
sun does to their smile. Even when Aaron's not near me, I know
exactly where he is. And when he leaves early or is off helping
someone else or doing his own training . . . I know that too.

At least I still get an occasional afternoon in the car with him
when he drives me home after practice. But today he has to run
an errand for his mom. I ask Eliza for a ride, but she's got a dentist
appointment, so I decide to run home. I leave my backpack in
my locker since I don't have any homework tonight. I'm about to

start jogging down the street when something in the sky catches my eye. A flash of gold and green. My dragon is high above me, so high she might be a plane, but I can tell it's her. I look around, knowing that my lioness can't be far behind. They're always together. And then, around the corner, I see it. My lioness's tail. I chase after it, glancing overhead to make sure my dragon is still above me, and she is. She's soaring lower now, looping around the clouds, making figure eights. She's flying like I run, with pure joy.

My lioness leads me down an unfamiliar street, but I'm not scared, I trust her, and then suddenly we're in front of a building I know all too well.

Grady Memorial Hospital. My heart hiccups and I look up for my dragon but she's gone behind a cloud or flown somewhere else I can't follow. I never visit Marcus during the week. Not because I don't want to . . .

I'm scared. Scared to go in on my own. What if he dies while I'm in there?

My lioness wants me to go in. I feel her behind my knees, pressing me forward, nudging me toward the building I've come to despise.

At the visitors' desk, the receptionist who was so rude to us the first time we came smiles at me. She recognizes us now. And ever since that time, she goes out of her way to be extra friendly. "Miss Jones! Lovely to see you. Just in time too. Visiting hours are over in thirty minutes. Your grandmother is inside already."

I knew it. I knew Granny Dee was visiting Marcus and not telling us. It is a miracle she's been able to keep quiet about it, especially with LaoLao always yammering about how all Granny Dee does is sit around the house. LaoLao might be working at the restaurant, but visiting Marcus is its own kind of work. Maybe I shouldn't intrude. Maybe she hasn't told us because she wants her own time with him. Not that he's any kind of company.

A familiar laugh, a laugh I love, a laugh I'll do almost anything to hear, buzzes down the hall.

Aaron. Aaron is here?

I nod at the nurse and walk as quickly as I can without running to room 304. Marcus's room.

The door is ajar, and inside I see Granny Dee and Aaron sitting on either side of the bed. Granny Dee is in the more comfortable chair, the one by the window, facing me. Aaron's back is to me and he's sitting on one of the low stools the doctors use when they come in to take Marcus's vitals.

Granny Dee doesn't even notice me when I open the door. Her eyes are on Marcus's unmoving face, but she's not crying, she's laughing. She's holding one of Marcus's hands and Aaron is holding her other one, making a little triangle.

"And then, Granny Dee, you won't believe what Marcus did next," Aaron is saying between bursts of laughter.

"He was only ten," says Granny Dee, wiping her eyes as she laughs.

"He dyed the neighborhood pool green! With fifteen bottles of green food coloring! And he didn't even get in trouble for it. You know who did?"

"I can guess," says Granny Dee with an indulgent smile.

"Because where do you think he got the food coloring? Of course I had asked my mom to get it, told her we needed it for a school project. I didn't know Marcus wanted to celebrate St. Patrick's Day in style."

"You boys certainly kept things interesting."

"Oh, and don't forget when he bleached my hair," says Aaron, shaking his head. "That stuff burned!"

I can't remember the last time I saw Granny Dee laugh so hard. Marcus lies between them, and both of them are laughing so hard their shoulders are shaking, and I wonder if he can feel the happiness the way I can. If it is seeping into his skin, into his bones. I hope it is. If anything is going to heal him, this is.

I sneeze.

Granny Dee looks up and smiles. "What are you doing lurking in the doorway? Get in here, Wing."

Aaron turns around and smiles too, but his eyebrows are raised. He's surprised to see me. I can't tell if it's happy surprised or unhappy surprised.

"I *knew* you were coming here," I say. I look hard at Granny Dee. "Why didn't you tell us?"

Her smile falters. "There's nothing to tell. I don't got much to do in the afternoon, and your mom's mother, she's helping at the restaurant. . . . I figured I could help here."

"And you?" I turn my gaze on Aaron.

"I thought Granny Dee might like some company," he says, voice soft.

I want to ask him why he didn't tell me, but I don't. Marcus is his best friend. He doesn't owe me any explanation. I would have gone with you, I want to say, but it shouldn't have taken Aaron coming to get me to visit. I should have come anyway. I should have been here this whole time. But then the hospital air starts to clog my throat like it always does, filling my nostrils with its stale sickly and simultaneously medicinal smell. I try to calm my breathing, but it's too late. I have to get out of here. I have to get outside.

I shift on my feet. "Well . . . it's good that you're both here."

The bitterness comes out stronger than I mean it to, like tea that's been left steeping far too long.

"Wing, honey, you can sit down," says Granny Dee. "This isn't a private party. You are always invited."

"I know," I snap. "I, um . . . I've got to get going."

"Get going where?"

"I've just got to go," I say as the hospital walls start to close in on me. I can't get enough air in my lungs.

"Aren't you even gonna say hello to your brother?"

I force myself to take in as much air as I can, as stale and sickly as it is, and take a step closer to the hospital bed.

"Hi, Marcus," I say, my voice coming out all plastic-like. "I miss you."

"Tell him about the running," prompts Granny Dee. Aaron looks up at her, a question in his eyes. "Oh, Wing showed me what she can do. Lord, you coulda knocked me over. I can't imagine what Marcus is gonna say when he wakes up and sees how fast she is. Heck, I can't even imagine what her mama and other grandma are gonna say." She narrows her eyes at me. "You are gonna show them, aren't you?"

I shrug. "I guess," I say. "But we can talk about that later. Not—"

"I'm sure your secrets are safe with him," says Aaron as he squeezes Marcus's shoulder. It's more than I can do. I can barely force myself to hold his hand. "I've been telling him all kinds of things."

"You've been telling him your secrets your whole life," I say. "Y'all don't have any secrets from each other."

"Well, maybe I've got some new ones," says Aaron with a look I don't quite understand but that makes me hot all over.

Granny Dee cackles. "Well, this has been a much more delightful afternoon than I was anticipating. You two should join me more often. I'm sure Marcus would appreciate it too."

Aaron drives us both home. Granny Dee sits in the front and chatters the whole way about how all she really wants is for someone to clear out the weeds in the pathetic patch of grass in front of our house she calls a garden so she can plant some roses. Aaron, of course, says he'll come by this weekend to do it.

We're home before my mom and LaoLao. Mom calls from the restaurant and says they're both working late tonight and Granny Dee and I are on our own for dinner. Granny Dee gives me a wicked smile and orders a pizza. I don't know where she got the money. We never have money for ordering takeout. Especially not now. But I don't ask any questions, I just tell her that I want half pepperoni and half Hawaiian.

After we eat, Granny Dee makes me take the empty box to the Dumpster at the end of the street. "Our little secret, Wing."

I know she isn't just talking about the pizza. She isn't ready for my mom and LaoLao to know about her visiting Marcus.

CHAPTER 28

It's been a week since I joined the track team, and I haven't told my mom or LaoLao about the running. They both work in the afternoons now, usually later, so they don't know when I get home. Granny Dee made jollof rice tonight. I don't even know what kind of meat she put in it. Guessing it's whatever was on sale. She made a big batch too, so I know this is what we'll be having for the next few days. No more secret pizza deliveries for me.

I spoon the rice into my mouth fast as I can. I've been so hungry ever since I started running.

"Wing," my mom says lightly. "Slow down, you'll choke. And please, get your hair out of your face."

"Mmm-hmm," agrees Granny Dee.

"Mmm-hmm," echoes LaoLao, her intonation exactly the same. The two old ladies stare at each other over the dining room table.

Granny Dee swings the lazy Susan toward me. "Eat more rice," she says.

"Why you want her to be fat?" says LaoLao.

"Wing." Granny Dee pauses, looks at me, a small smile in her eyes. "Wing is a growing girl. A growing girl who needs lots of energy."

"She almost sixteen! She already done growing. She grow too much too fast. She so tall! So big! Too big for a girl," LaoLao retorts, spooning up more rice for herself.

"Mother," says my mom, her exasperated tone as familiar to me as my own breathing, "I love how tall she is. I wish I was as tall as Wing." She smiles at me, but LaoLao's frown deepens.

She unleashes a torrent of Mandarin on my mother, who sits placidly sipping her tea, until LaoLao has seemingly run out of words. She looks expectantly at Mom, waiting for a response.

"Mama," says my mother, her voice on the knife edge of patience. "You know the rule. If you have something to say at the dinner table, you say it in English."

I'm not sure what the desired effect of that statement is, but my LaoLao launches into another verbal attack, still in Mandarin. Granny Dee leans back in her chair, eyebrows raised. "She sure got a set of pipes on her," she says. She holds her cup out to me. "Now get your Granny some more tea."

LaoLao passes me her cup without pausing in her diatribe. When I don't immediately take it, she pauses and looks at me. "Tea," she says, in English. "For me too."

Considering how similar they are, it really is astounding that my grandmothers don't get along better.

After dinner, I'm in my room, stretching on the floor. Eliza showed me some new stretches and I'm trying to figure out how to do them without looking stupid. Everything Eliza does looks effortless. She's flexible and thin and could probably be a gymnast if she weren't a runner.

I don't think I could do anything else but run.

My door opens without anyone knocking. Granny Dee steps into the room, her head cocked to the side as she stares at me on the floor.

"What exactly are you supposed to be doing?"

"I'm stretching," I say, keeping my voice low. "Now close the door. I don't want anyone else to see."

"Please," says Granny Dee. "Close the door, *please*." But she closes the door and then comes and sits on the edge of my bed. Her eyes are so bright and mischievous they practically sparkle.

"Here," she says, pushing on my back, her small hands firm and strong against me, so I'm stretching farther than I was on my own. "I know a thing or two about stretchin'."

"How?"

She laughs a little, the sound creaky and unused, like a door being opened that hasn't been opened in a long time. "Just because I move the way I do now doesn't mean I wasn't ever young like you, Wing."

I pull myself up and look at her. Try to imagine what she would have looked like when she was fifteen. There aren't many pictures of her when she was young; not many of LaoLao either. Granny Dee was born in Ghana and moved here when she was a little girl. She's never been back to Ghana. I wonder if she remembers it.

"I used to run too, you know. Not like you, I was never as fast as you, but I loved running when I could. Wasn't considered very ladylike, so I couldn't do it much, but I loved it, the feel of the wind on my face, the sun on my back, feeling like I could go anywhere. Feeling free."

I didn't know running made other people feel like that. I definitely didn't know that it made my Granny Dee feel like that. I can't picture her running any more than I can picture her taking flight. I don't say that, though. I want her to keep talking.

"That day you showed me what you could do, I saw me in you, Wing. But I feel like I was seein' you, really seein' you, for the first time. I remember the first time I saw Marcus throw a ball. He was an itty-bitty thing, maybe four, and he was in the backyard with your daddy, and they were playing catch. Marcus, even then, he was good. He had aim, he had style. It filled my heart to see him. I saw him and I said to your mama, I said, that boy is gonna be an athlete. I wish that I had seen it in you too, because I think you've got something just as special as what Marcus has. Not everyone can move like that, Wing. And watching you running on that street like your feet were on fire, I coulda watched you all day long."

She coughs and looks away. "Well, I got a little carried away there, didn't I? But you gotta show your mama. And your grandma. You've just gotta. I just wish your daddy, rest his soul, was here to see what I saw. He'd be so happy. But I'm sure he's watching you from heaven." Her voice cracks and she swallows, taking off her spectacles to rub her eyes. "Your mama could use some good news."

My mom doesn't understand why I've asked her to come to the track. Or why I've asked her to bring LaoLao and Granny Dee. Granny Dee was insufferable in the car, smiling her know-it-all smile and dropping so many hints I was sure my mom would know what was happening.

Eliza is here, like I asked her to be. So is Coach Kerry. I need my mom to know that this isn't just me, running crazy. That I'm going to be part of the team.

Aaron is here too. He comes over and gives my mom a hug, but I can tell he's distracted. He rocks back and forth on his heels. He knows that to me, this is a bigger deal than when I ran for Coach Kerry. He wants me to impress them.

Eliza gives me a hug before we run, and then we line up at the starting line, like it's a real race, and when Aaron blows the whistle, we take off. She's next to me for a second, and then I push forward, and then I'm running faster than I've ever run before. I know this, even though Coach Kerry isn't timing me. I can feel it.

My dragon and my lioness appear by my side, even though it's daylight; they're helping me go as fast as I can to show my mom and LaoLao that I'm good at something. That maybe I was born to do something too.

My mama can't believe it. She's hugging me and kissing me and holding me, not caring that I'm sweaty and smelly, and Granny Dee is hollerin' "I told you so! I told you!" like she had anything to do with this at all, and LaoLao is hopping up and down, which is a sight to see, grinning like I haven't seen her grin in a long time, not since before Marcus was in the accident, and she's stroking my head like I'm a prizewinning pup.

"Why didn't you tell us?" says my mom once all the hullabaloo has calmed down.

"I didn't know how."

My mom smiles and holds me again. "Wait until Marcus wakes up. He won't believe it!"

CHAPTER 29

I KNOW WHICH ROOM IS HIS. I STARE UP AT IT FROM THE OUT-side. It's two a.m. and I'm back outside Grady Memorial Hospital. It's infamous for the number of gunshot wounds they treat.

I guess I should be grateful that my brother killed someone in a drunk driving accident and not with a gun, and that he's being charged with vehicular manslaughter and not manslaughter. Guess I should also be grateful he's still breathing, even if it isn't on his own.

I ran all the way to Grady by myself in the middle of the night, but I don't know why. I can't get in. This isn't the movies, where I can pop into the supply closet, find an extra pair of scrubs, and masquerade as a nurse.

VISITING HOURS ARE OVER says the sign, and the nurses and receptionists will say the same thing.

It's funny, not ha-ha funny, but sad funny, because if Marcus were under eighteen, he'd be in the children's section. And in there, they let family visit anytime. You can't keep a mother away from her sick child.

I don't know why they don't get that even though Marcus is eighteen, he's still someone's child. He's still my brother. I still want to see him.

Sort of.

I'm about to turn away to start the long run home when something catches my eye. Something no one else can see. A dragon's tail, slipping around the corner, through the glass front doors. She isn't even trying to hide, and I know she wants me to go after her. It isn't the first time she's led me to my brother.

I follow her. Walking quickly, not running, because I'm trying to look like I'm meant to be at the hospital in the middle of the night. I keep my eye on the dragon's tail. She wouldn't lead me into trouble.

The reception area is empty. A TV is on in the corner, showing a fuzzy rerun. I could walk to his room with my eyes closed. I keep them open, though, just in case I do run into anyone. I slip along through the corridors. The lights are dim this time of night, and when I hear a voice, I open the nearest door and step inside before closing the door gently behind me.

There's a man sitting in the bed. He's wrinkly and older than LaoLao and Granny Dee. Maybe older than them combined. You know the phrase "older than God"? I never understood that phrase till I saw this old, old, old white man.

"What the hell?" he says, but he is more curious than concerned. "You one of them girlies selling lollipops? Visiting the old?"

I shake my head. "No, sir, I'm visiting my brother."

"At this time of night? I should ring my bell. Sound the alarm!

We can't have riffraff running through the hospital like it's some kind of back alley."

"Do you get many visitors, sir?"

He blinks at me, his old watery eyes narrowing. "That is a rude question, young lady."

"No offense meant, I'm just curious."

"Well, as a matter of fact, I don't. No one comes to visit me. You know why?"

"Why, sir?"

"Because I'm mean." He says this matter-of-factly, and I see his hand hovering over the red call button next to his bed.

"Sir," I say quickly, "my grandmother comes to this hospital every day to visit my brother. Now, my brother is in a coma and he can't talk, so he isn't very good company either. I'm sure my grandmother would rather talk to someone old and cranky than someone who can't talk at all. So how about, how about you don't hit that call button, and I'll ask my grandma to visit you sometimes? How does that sound to you, sir?"

He pauses, stroking his chin. "Is she a looker?"

I picture Granny Dee, and then try to see her through the old man's eyes. Compared to him, she's practically young.

"Yes, sir. And she's mean too, so she won't mind you a bit. But I think, sir, I think you don't seem all that mean."

"That's what happens when nobody visits you, you get soft. Forget how to be mean. Now go see your brother. I won't tell anyone. Not this time."

"Good night, sir." I smile and step out into the hall just in time to see a dragon's tail go around the corner. She must have been waiting for me.

I hope Granny Dee doesn't mind visiting that old man. I'd feel bad promising him she'll visit if she won't.

Marcus's room is different at night. All the machines beeping and bleeping are brighter in the darkness. It looks like he's being tucked into bed by a family of robots. Maybe they talk to him in robot language when we aren't here. Maybe he can understand them, even if he can't understand us.

My lioness is under his bed. I reach down and pat her head. "I'm glad you're here," I whisper. She purrs in response and stretches out on her side.

"Marcus," I whisper, "Marcus, if you wake up right now, you'll see my lioness. Remember? I told you I had a lion? She's here, watching you. She'll stay with you as long as you need."

I glance down at the lioness. "Right?" She nods in response, and I look back up at my brother's unchanging face.

"Marcus," I say, careful to keep my voice quiet, "when you wake up, I have something to show you. I'm a runner now. A real runner. Aaron is training me and everything." I tell him all about our training sessions. I leave out the parts about how I get shivers whenever Aaron accidentally brushes against me, or the time he massaged my calves. I lie and tell him that Monica is doing great and looking beautiful and that she visits lots and lots. I wonder what lies Granny Dee is telling him.

After a while, it starts to feel normal. Like I really am talking to my brother. At one point I even pause, waiting for him to respond. When the only reply is the whirr of the machines keeping him alive, I stop.

"I should have brought a recorder," I say. "So when you wake up I can play this back for you and you'll be all caught up on everything that's happening."

He stays silent. My lioness has gone wherever it is she goes when I can't see her. "I should get going too," I tell Marcus. I take a step closer to his bed and pause, looking down at the boy who was once my brother and supposedly still is, and, swallowing my repulsion and reminding myself that this is my brother, this is Marcus. I kiss his forehead, like he did to me when I broke my ankle as a little girl. A kiss to make it better.

CHAPTER 30

My grades have been slipping ever since the accident. Some of my teachers have been understanding, but it isn't like I can just stop going to class. We've got finals coming up, the last hurdle before winter break. In January I'll drop ceramics and take track instead. Because I'll really be on the team. Like a real athlete. Instead of just tagging along after school, when the rest of the team has already been stretching and warming up.

Tonight I stay up late studying in my room, listening to a classical music station on the radio, because Eliza says classical music helps you focus and she's a straight-A student, so she knows what she's talking about.

Even before the accident, I was never a straight-A student, not even a straight-B student. I'm a bit of a crooked student. I don't mean crooked like I'm cheating, I mean crooked like my grades jump around. I get some As (math, ceramics), some Bs (English, Spanish, history), and usually a C (science). Tonight I'm studying for my history final. History is just remembering facts. I could probably get an A in it, but that's the class I have with Heather Parker, and even though the stuff she says doesn't bother me the way it used to, I still can't ever fully relax when she's nearby. So 80 percent of me can listen to our teacher, but 20 percent of me is on red alert, ready for anything. But even that has improved recently because Andy Binder just dumped Heather, and he did it in spectacular fashion, right out in the parking lot. They both yelled a lot, and he said she was a psycho, and she kinda proved him right by getting out her keys and keying his car in front of everyone, but because she's Heather Parker nobody stopped her and she didn't even get in trouble, and now it looks like he's hooking up with this real pretty freshman girl named Shannon Tully, so Heather is preoccupied trying to make both their lives a living hell. And even Heather Parker can only torment so many people at once. If I were Shannon Tully, I'd probably switch schools. Or maybe join the witness protection program.

I'm almost done making my history flash cards, one side with a date or a place and the other side saying what happened and why it's important, but I've got a tickle in my throat that won't go away and it's distracting. So I pad into the kitchen, thinking about how maybe I'll start running at night again over winter break. I miss running at night.

My mom is standing in the corner of the kitchen, the cord of the phone wrapped around her like a snake slowly strangling her to death. Her back is to me, so she doesn't know I'm here.

"I understand," she says, her voice cracking like someone has taken a sledgehammer to it. "But we need to take out another loan. My son . . ." A sharp intake of breath. "Yes, that is my son. You know that. Just like you know that we need this loan."

A pause. I can just barely make out the tone of the scratchy voice on the other end of the line. It isn't a nice tone.

My mom pulls the cord tighter around her; it digs into her flesh. "No, please ... How about I come in tomorrow? To talk to your manager in person? There has to be some other option. Some other way ..."

I take the tiniest of steps back, begging the ancient floorboards to stay quiet, just this once. And they do. Another step, another, another, until I'm at the front door.

Her voice follows me. "There has to be something else we can do. Someone else I can speak to ..."

The slamming of the receiver makes me jump, but not as much as the howl that comes after. I look over my shoulder and see my mom hunched over the table, shaking, shaking, shaking as that inhuman sound comes pouring out of her. All I want is to comfort her, but I don't know how. I feel like I've just walked in on her in the shower and I should avert my eyes.

I take one more step toward the door, and this time the house isn't quiet. The creak is loud enough that my mother's head snaps up.

The noise she's making cuts off. "Wing," she says, voice not just cracked now but crushed to bits. "I ... I didn't see you there."

She wants something from me but I don't know what. I don't know how to make this better. I don't know how to fix Marcus, I don't know how to fix my mom, I don't know how to fix my family, I don't know how to fix any of it.

"Are ... you ... are you ... okay?" My words are so small, I wonder if they will even reach her.

She starts to nod; I see her cheeks try to go up in a forced smile, but it's too much, and the nod turns into a head shake and her lips quiver and I hate myself for being afraid, for not being good enough.

I take a tentative step toward her, needing some kind of sign that I'm doing the right thing. She takes a shuddering breath and blows her nose in a paper towel.

"I'm fine," she says, even as her chin wobbles. "Really. I don't want you to worry. Everything is under control."

My mother always flushes when she lies.

After I've gone back up to my room, I try to study some more, but the facts don't stay in my head, the dates are confusing, and I can't remember who fought who and when and where, and more than that, I can't figure out why it matters.

CHAPTER 31

IT'S CHRISTMAS EVE AND WE'RE SPENDING IT IN THE HOSPITAL. It is just me, Mom, LaoLao, and Granny Dee. Aaron and Monica are with their families. I brought some tinsel and wrapped it around Marcus's bed but Granny Dee made me take it down. She said it wasn't dignified. I wanted to shout at her that getting in a drunk driving accident isn't very dignified either, but instead I shrugged and took it down.

Between track practice and studying for finals, I've been managing to visit Marcus a few times a week. I wish it could be more, but at the same time . . . it never feels like him I'm visiting. It's just a body lying there. The nurses say he knows when we visit, that it will help make him better . . . and sometimes I believe them. And sometimes I think they might as well be telling me Santa Claus is real.

His bruises are all gone. And his ribs have almost healed. But his leg is still shattered and he hasn't woken up or given any sign that he's going to. I wonder how long he'll be like this. Suspended in a false sleep.

When we arrive, my mother smooths his hair, kisses him on his head, and wishes him Merry Christmas. Granny Dee sings a Christmas hymn. LaoLao holds his hand and whispers to him in Mandarin.

I stare at his face, willing him to open his eyes. But they stay shut. His chest rises and falls, the machines around us hum, and on he sleeps.

Our own Sleeping Beauty. Snow White. Rip Van Winkle. Marcus. My brother.

Leaving him is always hard, but tonight I feel like my intestines have unraveled and are wrapped around his hospital bed, and as I walk away they stretch and stretch and drag behind me and who knew that my insides could stretch this far without breaking, and I wonder how nobody else can see that I'm unraveling from the inside out and it hurts like hell.

The next morning I'm sitting in our living room watching some dumb Christmas movie when the door opens. It's Aaron and he's carrying a wrapped present.

"Hey," he says. He puts the present down in front of me. "Merry Christmas."

I haven't gotten dressed yet and am wrapped in a ratty red robe. I tighten it around me.

My mom bustles in from the kitchen, face flushed from cooking Christmas dinner. "Aaron! Merry Christmas! What a wonderful surprise! Do you want to stay for dinner?"

He smiles and shakes his head. "No thank you, ma'am. I just

came by to wish you all a Merry Christmas. How's Marcus?" Behind his words I hear that he's hoping for a Christmas miracle like we all were yesterday.

"He's ... fine. No change. But he's hanging on, and that's something," says my mom. She spies the present. "What's this?"

Aaron rubs the back of his neck. "Aw, it's nothing, really. Just something for Wing."

We didn't do presents this year. Couldn't afford to, what with Marcus's hospital bills. We did do stockings, but they were mostly stuffed with things we need, not things we want. Socks, toothpaste, that kind of thing.

"A present for Wing?" My mom's face is puzzled. "That is kind of you, Aaron. You've always been so good to Wing."

Like he's nice to me out of the goodness of his heart. Just because I'm his best friend's little sister. Not because he wants to be. Not because he really cares about me. Not because of *me*.

"Thanks," I say, keeping my eyes on the television. My mom mutes the Christmas movie and sits down next to me on the couch, both her and the couch sighing as she settles into it.

"Wing, aren't you going to open your present?"

Aaron hasn't sat down. He's standing over us, a shy, expectant smile on his face. A smile that makes me smile back without even realizing it. I take the present, a rectangular box, and gently tear off the shiny wrapping paper. And gasp.

It's a shoe box. Not just any shoe box. A Riveo shoe box. I whip my head up and stare at Aaron, who's looking both pleased with himself and anxious.

"Riveo? You can't afford Riveo shoes."

He shrugs. "You haven't even seen them yet. For all you know it's just a shoe box."

I open it, not knowing what to expect. Nestled inside, like kittens in a basket, are the most beautiful shoes I've ever seen. They're red and gold and perfect.

Riveo running shoes.

"Do you like them?" Aaron's voice is shot through with expectation and anxiety, and I look up from the shoes to his face. I've never seen him like this. He's like a puppy hoping someone will take him home. My heart does a backflip into my stomach at the sight of him—but I can't keep the shoes.

"Aaron," I say, holding the box back out to him. "I can't take these, and I . . ." My mom takes the box out of my hands, and I desperately wish she weren't here. "I don't have anything for you!"

"She's right, Aaron," says my mom. "We can't accept this. It's too much. You should return the shoes."

Aarons smiles a crooked smile. "I got a Christmas job," he says, shrugging like it's no big deal. "Just for December. Down at Lenox Square Mall. At the Riveo store. I got a staff discount."

Even with a staff discount, I know these shoes must have cost him half his paycheck. I hope he got himself a new pair too.

"Isn't it pretty tough to get a seasonal job at the mall?" I ask. Aaron shrugs. "Jasper helped me out. The store manager's brother owed him a favor or something." Or something. I don't want to know the details. And as much as I love the shoes, I hope this doesn't mean that now Aaron owes Jasper a favor.

"Jasper?" asks my mom. "Isn't he that boy who got into some trouble a few years ago?"

I'm surprised she remembers.

"Yeah, but he's an all right guy. I've known him my whole life," Aaron says with another shrug. "Plus, we are sort of related."

He's not an all right guy, I want to say, but then I remember that Jasper's never killed anyone. And Marcus has. So I'm not in any place to judge.

"Do you like the shoes?" Aaron's looking at me now. "If you don't, you can probably come in and exchange them."

"I love them." My voice is thick and sounds like it does when I have a cold. "They're perfect." I hug the shoes tightly to my chest. "Perfect."

CHAPTER 32

It's the new year, but LaoLao doesn't recognize that. "It is still Year of the Pig," she says. "Chinese New Year, that's when the new year will begin."

Right now she's sitting by herself in the living room, rubbing her left foot with an audible moan. Her eyes are closed, and she looks older than she usually does. The TV is on low, some soap opera. LaoLao loves her soap operas.

"LaoLao? Are you all right?"

She drops her foot and looks up at me. "My bones are too old," she says, shaking her head. "Too old."

I go over to her and sit cross-legged on the floor beneath her. "Did you have a long day?"

"So long. Too long. I forgot how when you are on your feet all day, the hours, they never end." The fatigue in her voice is matched only by the exhaustion in her eyes. "I never thought I would be back in a kitchen. Working, working all day. I am too old for this. Working is for the young."

"Do you want me to rub your feet?" I remember LaoLao rubbing my mom's feet when my mom would get home from work. It feels like a long time since I've done something nice for LaoLao.

"What's this? Wing acting like a proper granddaughter? Respecting her LaoLao?"

She's grinning at me like the Cheshire cat as she sticks out her foot in its polka-dot sock. I pull off her sock. The foot beneath it is as fleshy and plump as the rest of her. I massage the arch, and she settles farther back in her chair, content for once.

Until she wags her other foot at me. "This one too, and more pressure." I roll my eyes but take her foot.

"LaoLao?" I say slowly, quietly.

"Mmm?" she says without opening her eyes.

"Do you think Marcus is going to wake up?"

She stills and is quiet for several long moments.

"I hope so," she says, sounding unsure. Then her eyes fly open and she pins me with her gaze. "But even if he does not . . ."

I almost drop her foot. No one has ever admitted there is a chance he might not wake up.

"We will be okay. You will be okay. It will be hard." She takes a long, quavering breath. "So hard. But we will be okay. It is . . . life. Life . . . is hard."

I nod. I know.

She shakes her head as if shaking the conversation away and settles back into her chair.

"Other foot now," she says, and I massage my grandmother's feet in silence. I wonder if Marcus's shattered leg hurts, if his body hurts. Can he feel anything in his deep slumber?

"Wing." LaoLao's voice startles me from my thoughts.

"Other foot?" I ask, reaching for it.

Instead, she draws her feet in and leans toward me. "I do not like working," she says, slowly, "but for Marcus, it is nothing. For you too." She watches me carefully. "I would work. And it would be nothing."

I take her foot in my hands again, squeezing gently. I don't want her to have to work anymore. I want her to stay home and rest her old, tired bones. She might say it's nothing, but I know it's everything.

CHAPTER 33

·

THE PHONE RINGING IS LIKE AN ALARM IN OUR HOUSE. WE ALL jump, stare at each other, each of us scared to pick it up in case it's bad news. Bad news about Marcus. Bad news about the bank. Been a long time since anyone called our house with good news.

Which is why I'm so surprised when my mom tells me there's someone on the phone for me. It's Eliza.

"You got plans tonight?"

"Um, no. Why, do you want to go on a run or something?"

"Wing! Is running all you think about? Come on, girl."

No, I also think about Marcus. And Aaron. And running. But I don't tell Eliza that.

"We can hang out and not run, you know," she goes on. "I'm good for other stuff too. I don't know if you've noticed, but I'm pretty hilarious. And you haven't seen it yet, but I'm a hell of a dancer. And I play the piano."

"I can't play the piano," I say apologetically. "And I'm not a very good dancer."

"Well, we'll see about that. I'm coming to get you and you're coming over."

"Over? Over where?"

"To my house! My parents are at my cousin's wedding, so I've got the whole house to myself. I'm throwin' a party. You're invited."

"A party?" A party can be a whole lot of different types of things. The last time I heard the word *party*, it was Trey's party. It was the last party my brother went to. Possibly the last party he'll ever go to. So the thought of going to a party doesn't sound all that great to me.

"Yes, Wing. A party. But probably not like any kind of party you've ever been to before."

My silence speaks for me.

"Wing, don't worry. It isn't that kind of party."

That kind. The kind your brother went to. The kind where people get sloppy drunk and do things that ruin lives.

"Come on, Wing. It'll be fun. I promise. I'll pick you up in an hour? You can sleep over. All the rest of the girls on the team are coming." She pauses, and then the rest of her words come out real fast. "And Annie is coming too. I want you to get to know her a little bit better."

I think Annie is Eliza's girlfriend, but I'm not sure. She comes and watches us run sometimes, cheers us on, and after practice she gets into Eliza's blue car and they drive off together, laughing, always laughing, their heads close, Annie's braids falling over Eliza's shoulder. Annie goes to a different school, a fancy private high school. She's black, about five inches shorter than Eliza, and curvy, real curvy, and she's got a laugh I can hear all the way around the track. She's got a laugh you wish you could bottle up and wear like perfume whenever you're feeling sad because it would always cheer you up. Eliza looks at Annie the way Marcus has been looking at Monica since the seventh grade. Friends don't look at friends like that.

I wonder how I look at Aaron. If anyone can tell how I feel about him by the way I look at him.

I can't say no to the party. I want to be part of the team and do what the other girls are doing. And it is nice, really nice, that Eliza wants me to get to know Annie. It's like she cares about my opinion. Like she really does want to be my friend. And that kind of feeling is irresistible. I can't say no to that kind of feeling.

Eliza lives in a tractor factory out in Castleberry Hill, near the CNN Center. Or what was once a tractor factory but has now been converted into apartments. It doesn't feel like a factory, but it doesn't feel like an apartment either. It's right next to the train tracks, and every time a train goes by the whole building rattles. The floors are concrete, and the ceilings are so high that I wonder how the hell they ever change their lightbulbs. Her family's apartment unit is basically one giant room, the kitchen and living room and dining room all rolled into one, with two bedrooms and a bathroom tucked away in the back. The windows are so high they're practically skylights. No one can see in and all we can see is the sky.

In the middle of all the open space is a grand piano. I've never seen a grand piano before, and I've definitely never seen one at someone's house. There's art painted directly onto the walls and there are beanbags in one corner. It is the most ridiculous and the most amazing home I've ever been to.

When Eliza and I arrive, she struts (Eliza never walks) straight up to the piano, sits down, and starts to play Christmas carols. Some of the other girls on the team, including Vanessa (who didn't end up having a baby, not that she told me, but she's here and a baby isn't, so I think it's safe to assume), are already there, and they crowd around the piano and sing.

Annie, wearing a Santa hat, sits next to Eliza, laughing that laugh that makes everyone else laugh too. She whispers something in Eliza's ear and Eliza starts playing a different song, one that makes all the other girls clap their hands and belt as loud as they can. I want to crowd around the piano too, but it's like they all have a part and they know the words, and I don't.

Literally. I've never heard the Christmas song they're all singing.

So I perch on one of the beanbags and try to bob my head along. It's more of a pop song than a Christmas song. It feels a bit funny to be singing Christmas songs in January, but everyone else is loving it. Eliza's eyes land on me and she stops playing abruptly. It takes a few moments for the girls to stop warbling along.

"Do you not know this one?"

I shake my head, embarrassed. But it's more than that. I don't know how to act here; I don't know how to do anything but run in circles.

"How do you not know 'All I Want for Christmas'?" Vanessa asks, but not unkindly, just genuinely curious. "It is all that's on the radio, like, ever."

I shrug. I don't know how I don't know. And that's almost as embarrassing as the not knowing. I hate how they're all staring at me, I wonder if this is a trick, a mean trick, like in that horror movie where they invite that girl to prom just to throw pig's blood on her. I don't think Eliza would do that, but then I didn't think Heather Parker was going to dump a jug of sweet tea on me either.

"Well, get up here, you silly thing, and we'll teach you," says Eliza, grinning at me, asking me to trust her, and I'm filled with a certainty that this isn't a trick, that Eliza really is my friend, and the certainty is so snug and warm, it's like she's wrapped me up in a fluffy blanket.

It doesn't take long for me to learn the song. Soon I'm linking arms with the other girls and laughing so hard at one of Annie's stories that I fall into a heap on the beanbags with Vanessa, Vanessa who was so unwelcoming to me, and now the two of us are curled up next to each other, clutching our sides and shaking with laughter. And I've been missing this and I didn't know. Because I never had this with April. Never had this, not with Monica or Aaron or even Marcus.

Never been a part of something before.

Some of the other girls are drinking sparkling wine out of plastic champagne flutes, but I don't even try a sip of anything. Nobody pressures me. One of the girls gets out a deck of playing cards and they teach me to play a complicated game with hand slapping that I've never played. They say I need to learn all the card games before the training weekend in Hilton Head.

"What training weekend?" I ask.

"After the season officially kicks off and it gets warmer, Coach Kerry takes us all to Hilton Head and we camp out on the beach and run all day in the sand, and it's hard as hell but amazing at the same time, especially because we can go cool off in the ocean, and it's just the best weekend ever," Vanessa gushes as she refills her plastic flute, bubbles spilling out over the top.

"It really is," Eliza agrees, her arm around Annie's waist. No one here seems surprised about the two of them. They must already know. No one seems bothered. I'm starting to get the feeling that *team* trumps everything else. Doesn't matter who you're into or what you look like or how much money your family has. I think someone could show up with two heads, but if they could run fast and joined the team, they'd get along just fine.

Most of us stay up till the sun rises, and only then, when the light is starting to stream in the big windows, do I grab a couple of the beanbags and make myself a little nest. Eliza puts a blanket over me.

"Good night, Wing. I'm glad you came."

"Me too," I say, and I hope she knows what I'm really saying is thank you for inviting me. Thank you for making me feel like I'm a part of the team.

Like I'm a part of something. Like I belong.

CHAPTER 34

It's strange being back at school after Christmas break. I have a new routine with new friends and a new place to sit at lunch. I smile at Aaron in the halls, not shying away, and I can hear the whispers about me for the first time, ever, without caring. There are bigger things to worry about than what someone is whispering about you.

I'm finally getting used to Marcus not being here. I'm not expecting to see him come out of a classroom with his arm slung around Monica, laughing, smiling, glowing. Making everyone look at him without even trying.

The pain in my heart has started to scab over. It's still there, but duller now. Not screaming for my attention all the time. I guess it knows it doesn't need to; it knows I know it's always there.

I'm becoming someone else other than Marcus's little sister, and the strangest thing of all is that I want to.

We're in the locker room changing for the pep rally. Coach

Kerry said that since I'm now officially a part of the varsity track team, I have to go out with the rest of the team at the pep rally, which is when the kids on student council make announcements about all the "really fun activities" coming up, which never sound that fun, things like fund-raisers and themed dances and all sorts of stuff I never really pay attention to, and then the cheerleaders do a dance routine, and the marching band usually makes some noise, and the varsity sports teams are introduced and everyone's supposed to cheer (not just for the sports teams but for the cheerleaders and even the student council kids and the band). I've seen Marcus in the lineup so many times. I never thought it would be me. I don't have to say anything, I just have to stand in a row and smile. Not trip. Not make a fool of myself. Eliza will be introducing us. She's done it before.

We've been back at school over a month now, but this is the first time I've put on my track uniform. I've never had a uniform before, never had anything that declared to the world that I was a part of something, that I was good at something. It feels strange, like I'm putting on a costume. I tug at the bottom of my shorts. They seem way too small and insubstantial. My ass feels huge in them. Like it's going to burst free at any second. The jersey is a little snug on top too.

"Damn, girl." Eliza whistles. "You look good."

Eliza looks amazing in her uniform. She's all long and lean, like a supermodel. Her short hair is swept to the side, sleek and shiny.

"You all right, Wing?" she asks.

I nod, not trusting my voice to work.

"Then let's go."

The lights are brighter in the gym than they've ever been

before. When the pep rally commissioner, the master of ceremonies, some senior named Jill who loves the sound of her own voice, calls for us, for the varsity track team, we have to walk out in front of the whole school. My heart starts beating beating beating, so fast I'm sure it will pop out and fall to the floor for everyone to see and stomp on.

Jill passes the microphone to Eliza so she can introduce us all. I don't even hear what she's saying. All I see are all the eyes staring at me. And then.

Clapping. The noise rushes in my ears and I think it has to be a cruel joke, but then Eliza comes over to me and lifts my hand in the air like I'm a champion boxer and people start cheering even louder.

"I told them you were the fastest girl at our school in years . . . and that Olympic scouts are lookin' at you and you're gonna make our school famous," Eliza whispers in my ear.

"You said what?" I whisper back. I look over at where the teachers are and see Coach Kerry shaking her head but smiling. She knows Eliza is bullshitting everyone.

"Hey, it could be true. Who knows? Anyway, look at them, they love you. And now they'll come see you run. Everyone wants to say they were there before a star took off."

I grin, feeling ridiculous, feeling foolish, feeling adored, and loving every second.

I feel like Marcus. Like I'm the one people cheer for. I'm the one they watch. And for the first time, I kinda want people to watch me.

Someone catches my eye in the crowd, a face I immediately recognize. Oakie. The other guy in the car with Marcus. The guy who got out of the whole thing with just a badly broken leg. He's smiling, and when he sees me looking back at him, he gives me two thumbs up.

A feeling I can't place courses through me as we go back to our seats and Jill calls up the varsity basketball team. I don't think Oakie was making fun of me, but I don't know. He's never talked to me, not before the accident, not after. But his smile . . . it looked like he really was happy for me.

Maybe that means he doesn't blame me for what Marcus did.

Maybe it means he forgives Marcus.

I wonder if anyone else has.

CHAPTER 35

"You're still a freak."

I'm in the bathroom after the rally, washing my hands, when Heather Parker bursts in.

"Now you're just a freak that goes on parade."

I tense. Waiting for her words to burrow themselves deep inside me, the way they always do. But this time they slide right off and fall to the floor with a splat.

"Such a freak show."

I look into Heather's green eyes and notice a small trickle of blood coming from her left nostril.

"Heather?"

She blinks three times in rapid succession. I don't think I've ever called her by name, and it's throwing her. "What?"

"I think you have a nosebleed."

Heather raises her hand to her nose, looks at the blood and

back up at me. Her eyes go wide, wide, wider, and her face gets so pale I'm sure I can see her veins. "I don't like blood," she says. And then she slumps forward and before I realize what I'm doing I've stepped toward her, arms outstretched, and she collapses against me, head lolling to the side, blood still dripping out of her nose. More than dripping now, so much coming out that it gets on my new uniform.

I prop her up under the sink and put a damp paper towel on her forehead and hold another wad of tissues under her nose. The blood blooms like a peony. I'm not sure what to do. Only person I've ever seen faint was Monica in the hospital, that night, and there were doctors there who took care of her.

I pat Heather's cheek a few times, like they do in the movies. And then I slap her. Not a hard slap, not as hard as I would like to, but enough that my hand stings.

It does the trick. Her eyes flutter open.

"*Wing?*"

Just like she's never heard me call her by name, I've never heard her say my name. Never heard her refer to me like I'm a real person. "You got a nosebleed and passed out," I explain.

She tries to scramble up and nearly hits her head on the bottom of the sink. "Oh my God. Did anyone see me?"

"Just me. But, um . . . you should probably go to the nurse. Or something."

Heather shakes her head. "I'm fine." But her voice is weaker than I've ever heard it.

We stare at each other and I wait for it. The thank-you. The apology. This is our made-for-TV moment. We'll be braiding each other's hair and having sleepovers by the next episode.

CHAPTER 36

Aaron drives me home after practice today like he usually does, but this time instead of dropping me off at the curb he pulls into my driveway.

"Everything okay?" I ask, unsure why he's parked.

Aaron scratches his head. "I don't really know how to say this."

I swallow and try to keep my imagination from playing roulette with all the things he could say.

I'm madly in love with you.

I've got back together with Dionne and she doesn't want me spending time with you.

You know we're not really friends, right? I just wanted to be nice because of Marcus.

You really stink after practice and I don't want to drive you home anymore.

"Can I come in for a bit? It's just that ... I really miss your house. And your mom. And your grannies. I used to see them every day, you know?" He runs his hand over his short hair. "That probably sounds kind of weird."

I exhale. This is the best thing he could have said.

All right, fine. Other than telling me he's in love with me.

"That isn't weird at all. I'm sure they'd all love to see you. I mean, like to see you." My tongue is getting all twisted. "I should have invited you in before. I'm sorry."

"Nothing to be sorry about."

"You know you can come over whenever, right? You don't have to ask me."

He flashes me a smile that makes my heart do a somersault. "Thanks, Wing," he says. "I really appreciate it."

We walk into the living room to find Granny Dee and LaoLao facing each other in some kind of standoff. Granny Dee is shaking what looks like a child's sweater in LaoLao's face, and LaoLao looks both guilty and enraged at the same time. And I can tell you from experience, that is not a good combination.

"You shrunk my favorite sweater!" Granny Dee hollers. "Didn't you read the wash instructions?"

I take a closer look at the sweater she's holding. It's green with yellow stripes, and I've never seen her wear it before. I'm certain it isn't her "favorite sweater."

There's no denying it's shrunk, though. It looks like it might fit a toddler.

"It is just a sweater! Here. Take mine." LaoLao takes off her own blue sweater, huffing as she does, and pushes it at Granny Dee.

Granny Dee holds it with two fingers and wrinkles her nose. "And drown in it? You could fit about five of me in this big ol' thing."

LaoLao puffs up like a rooster before a cockfight. "What you saying? That I'm fat?"

"We all know you understand English, even if you can't read the laundry label," Granny Dee retorts. "You know exactly what I'm saying!"

"I am not fat!" roars LaoLao, which is a blatant lie, because LaoLao *is* fat. "You just too skinny! Look like starving person. Like starving . . ." She pauses, and I can tell she's trying to come up with a really good comeback.

"Like starving duck!" she says, and Granny Dee's mouth actually drops open. She knows that "duck" is one of LaoLao's worst insults.

"You take that back!"

"What? It is true," says LaoLao, looking smug.

Aaron makes this snorting sound that could be a laugh and turns it into a cough. It would be funny to me too, watching them go after each other like this, if it didn't hurt my heart, and my head, so much.

"LaoLao." I go to her and rest my hand on her back. "That wasn't nice."

"She wasn't nice first!"

"You shrunk my sweater first!"

"You broke my jade bracelet!"

"That was an accident! And it was five years ago!"

"Yes, five years ago. Plenty of time to get me a new jade bracelet." LaoLao crosses her arms.

Granny Dee throws her hands up in the air. "And tell me where I'm going to find a jade bracelet in Atlanta!"

"Exactly! Impossible! I cannot replace jade bracelet. You can replace ugly sweater."

"It is not ugly! I've had that sweater for eighteen years!"

Aaron whistles and it makes both my grannies look up.

"What?" snaps Granny Dee.

"Yeah, what?" says LaoLao. She's moved closer to Granny Dee, and the two of them are giving him matching glares.

Aaron shrugs. "That sweater is older than me. Pretty crazy to think about."

Granny Dee rolls her eyes. "A whole lot of things are older than you! What are you? Seventeen? Do you want me to go around this whole house pointing out all the things that are older than you?"

"No, ma'am," says Aaron politely, but I can tell he's trying not to laugh. "Unless you want to?"

LaoLao marches over to him and thrusts her sweater, the one Granny Dee said was too big for her, into Aaron's arms. "How old you think my sweater is?"

Aaron looks at me, eyes dancing with repressed laughter. "I don't know, LaoLao. Maybe . . . ten years?"

LaoLao snatches her sweater back. "Ten years! This sweater only two years old! Practically brand-new!"

Granny Dee's eyeing the sweater now. "Just two years old?"

"I only wear it a few times," LaoLao says, sounding like a used-car salesman. "Are you sure you don't want it?"

"Maybe I can alter it," says Granny Dee, taking the blue wool sweater from LaoLao. "If you really are giving it to me?"

"Of course I'm giving it to you. I shrunk your sweater, so now I give you new one."

"This isn't gonna be like that time you gave me that lotion and then got angry when I used it all?"

"You said your hands were dry, so I gave you my special lotion to be nice, and what happens? Next day it is all used up!"

"I didn't know you wanted it back!"

"Of course I wanted it back! If you were going to use the whole thing, you should have asked!" LaoLao sniffs. "It would have been polite thing to do."

"Well, you know I was sorry. And didn't I get you a whole new bottle for Christmas that year?"

LaoLao gives a grudging nod. "You did. But that same year I give you fancy bubble bath."

"That was a good Christmas," says Granny Dee.

LaoLao nods again. "Maybe this year you can give me jade bracelet," she says with a sly smile.

Granny Dee chuckles. "You stayin' for dinner, Aaron? This one's cookin', so I can't promise it'll be any good. . . ."

"Everything I make tastes good!"

"All right, all right." Granny Dee holds up her palms in surrender. "You make some okay dishes. I like those spicy green beans. Are you making those?"

"Maybe," says LaoLao, waddling into the kitchen. "But only if you cut and wash them."

Aaron ends up staying for dinner—he doesn't have much choice after both my grannies insist—and now we're in the living room, pretending to watch TV. I'm in the armchair in the corner and Aaron's on the couch. Everyone else is getting ready for bed. I keep waiting for my mom to come down and tell Aaron it's time for him to go home, but she doesn't. I guess, now that I think about it, she's never told him to go home before.

"Sorry about my grandmas," I say, tugging on a stray curl.

"Don't worry about it. Man, your grandmothers crack me up," Aaron says, smiling and shaking his head. "I don't know anyone like them."

"Nobody knows anybody like them," I grumble, but I'm smiling too. "They fight less now, though, with Marcus being in the hospital."

Aaron nods. "Makes sense."

"I'm sure when he wakes up they'll be back to arguing all the time over every little thing."

Aaron doesn't correct me, doesn't tell me that there's nothing to be sure about when it comes to Marcus. Instead, he pats the spot on the couch next to him. "Come here," he says. "This show is about to start and you can't see from where you're sitting."

I can see just fine, but I don't tell him that. I just grin and go sit next to him.

CHAPTER 37

I NEVER USED TO THINK ABOUT GETTING BETTER AT RUNNING.
I just did it, I just ran, and then I got faster, and then I pushed further, and that seemed to be all there was to it. I figured that training with Coach Kerry and the rest of the team would be more of
that.

Coach Kerry has different ideas. She has us doing all kinds of
crazy stuff that she claims will make us faster. Make us stronger.
Make us better.

I'm not running with Aaron as much now; he's training with
the boys' team, same track as us, but on the other side. Feels farther
than that, though. Still, when we go round and round that track,
I can feel his eyes on me. I know he's watching.

I hope he's not watching right now. Coach Kerry has me and
Eliza in some kind of harness, the kind Santa would use for his
reindeer, and we're pulling weights, actual weights. Usually running makes me feel light and free, but this, this isn't running. I'm

sweating so much I can barely see, and I can hear Eliza panting as we both try to drag these dumb weights around the track.

"Again," says Coach Kerry after we get around. "I know you girls can be faster."

"Why we gotta do this?" says Eliza, and it's the closest I've ever heard her come to whining.

"You've got to do this because I'm the coach and I told you so, and because it's going to make you faster. Once you take these things off, you'll fly. Trust me."

"I already do fly," Eliza grumbles, but we push off again, and this time, it is a little easier.

Between training, visiting Marcus, and hanging out with the team, time flies by. It's only two weeks till my first official race. Two weeks till all this dream running, all this, becomes real. I can't help hoping that maybe Marcus will wake up by then. That he'll be there, cheering for me, the way I always always cheer for him.

I'm still cheering for him. I'm still hoping he'll defeat everything and everyone, to prove that Marcus Jones can't stay down, that Marcus Jones always gets up.

Maybe we're more similar than I ever knew.

Finally, it comes. My first official race day. I wake up with my blood singing, my heart jumping, my feet kicking. Every part of me is ready to go.

It's also my sixteenth birthday. When I get to breakfast, my mom, LaoLao, and Granny Dee are sitting around the table, a small cake in the center.

"Cake for breakfast!" Granny Dee declares.

"And noodles for dinner," says LaoLao. I've been having

noodles for dinner on my birthday for as long as I can remember, and before that. Long noodles to represent a long life. Every year my LaoLao makes the noodles from scratch.

I wish, like I wish every morning, but especially on this morning, that Marcus were here. I've never had a birthday without him. I try to remind myself that he's had longevity noodles every year for his birthday too, and that has to count for something. He's gonna live a long life. He's just taking a little break right now, a little halftime. He'll wake up. And until he does, I'll keep wishing, wishing as hard as I can.

And maybe, today, because today is my birthday, my wish will count for something. Maybe my wish will come true. And maybe by the time it is Marcus's birthday, in August, he'll be eating his own birthday noodles and making his own wishes.

Another wish, a secret one, flutters by, and it has Aaron's name on it. I watch it for a moment, fluttering, floating, and then I grab it tight and crush it before anyone else can see it. I can feel the remnants of the mothy wish wings on my skin.

"Wing? Did you hear me? Are Aaron and Monica coming tonight?"

I look up. "What? Why would they come?"

My mom gives me a bemused smile. "Because they always come to your birthday dinner. I just assumed . . ." When I don't say anything she goes on. "Of course, it's fine if you want it to be just family too."

But it isn't just family. Because half our family isn't here. And it hurts that my mom thinks I don't have any friends of my own and the only people who would come to a birthday dinner at my house aren't even really my friends.

Two new wishes flutter next to me.

Aaron is your friend! says one.

Another wish pops up next to it. *Aaron is more than your friend!* it says.

I bat the errant wishes away and smile at my mom.

"I'll ask Monica if she can come over." I pause. "And Aaron." And then. Because now I have friends too. My own. "And Eliza? You met her the day you saw me run?"

My mom smiles. "Of course! Whatever you want."

"Now eat some of that breakfast cake before it gets cold," chides Granny Dee. "And what time did you say we had to be at that race today?"

I'm smiling so big you could probably sink an ice cream cone in each of my dimples.

"Three," I say as I cut into the cake. No frosting, just the way I like it. We'll have a proper birthday cake later, with whipped cream and berries, but birthday breakfast cake is always buttery pound cake.

"We get there at two," states LaoLao with authority. "So we not late."

"We wouldn't miss it for anything," says my mom. "I just wish . . . I wish Marcus could be here. He'd be so proud. And your daddy. I wish he was here too." She's still smiling, but her eyes are suspiciously overbright. A familiar cloud follows her words, a big dark cloud I know all too well but don't want around on my birthday. Maybe that makes me selfish.

Granny Dee takes a bite of cake. "Well, I know that I for one am going to tell Marcus every last detail when he wakes up," she says, her mouth full. "And I know your daddy will be watching. Don't you worry about that."

And just like that, the cloud floats out the window and far, far away.

I'm nervous all day. I'm nervous warming up, stretching, putting my shoes on, waiting at the starting line, nervous even as Eliza squeezes my hand for luck, nervous even as I see my dragon and my lioness a little ahead of me, ahead of the starting line. I'm nervous right up until the starting shot goes off with a bang, and then . . .

I'm running and everything disappears except me, the track, and the sky. I tear around the corner and fly across the finish line. I almost don't stop.

My first race and I shatter the school record for the 400-meter.

And twenty minutes later, I almost, almost beat the record for the 200-meter.

I've never seen someone so happy to lose as Eliza. She's crowing, strutting, grinning like she won. Aaron too. I didn't see his race, but I heard he won, and the two of them . . . I might not have understood that feeling, of awe and pride in someone else, someone you care about, except I've been feeling like that my whole life about my brother.

It feels pretty good to have someone else feeling that way about me.

I don't know if my daddy was watching, but a hell of a lot of other people were. News has gotten out about me. Apparently, I'm a "human interest" story because of everything that's happened with Marcus. And maybe because of that little lie Eliza told at the pep rally about me qualifying for the Olympics. And breaking that record, well, that put a whole ton of kerosene on Eliza's little flame of a lie. A local reporter comes up to me after the race.

"Miss Jones! That was impressive. Do you have a minute? Is it true that you just started running this year?" I nod, nervous again. "Athleticism seems to run in your family. Wasn't your brother quite the star? Before his drunk driving accident?" The world bottoms out and I sway, sure I'll fall over, but then Eliza is there and she grabs my hand and pulls me away.

"Don't talk to anyone you don't want to, Wing. You don't know what they'll say." Then she gives me a big Eliza smile. "I'm proud of you, girl."

As we walk off, I hear the reporter shout, "Miss Jones! Wing Jones! What about your brother? Do you wish he were here to see you run? Do you know if the family of the woman he killed has forgiven him? Does your running have anything to do with him?"

My sky-high joy from winning my races starts to fade and is replaced by a pounding anxiety, hammering away at my skull and my heart. After the accident, the story was in the paper for weeks, and then it fizzled out. I don't want it coming back.

Eliza glares over her shoulder at the reporter. "Come on, Wing. We got more important things to do right now. Like celebrating." She squeezes my hand and I squeeze back, because she's right. We do.

CHAPTER 38

Even a nosy reporter bringing up the accident and Marcus and the bad things (I hate, I hate, hate how now my brother and "bad things" belong in the same thought) can't stop me from having a good birthday. We go to the Chinese restaurant my mom manages, the one LaoLao now works at, down Buford Highway. We have a private room and everything. LaoLao makes the noodles herself; she says the younger cooks don't know how to make noodles right for her granddaughter. I don't know about the other cooks' noodles, but hers are perfect. Long and springy and chewy and endless.

Eliza brings Annie to the restaurant. When Eliza introduces her as her girlfriend, LaoLao nearly falls over.

"Girlfriend? Friend who is girl or girlfriend like Monica is Marcus's girlfriend?"

"LaoLao!" I exclaim.

Eliza smiles. "Girlfriend like romantic girlfriend, ma'am."

"My word," says Granny Dee not quite under her breath. "Well, I say that it takes all kinds and the Lord loves us all." She squints. "Now, is one of you meant to look like a boy?"

"This is, what you call it, lesbian?" LaoLao says in between slurping noodles.

"Why don't we talk about something else?" Monica interjects. "Like how proud we all are of our little Wing for winning her first race today?"

As everyone raises their teacups to me, smiles stretched wide across their faces, I try to smile back but can't help but think that Marcus should be here. He's never missed one of my birthdays. We're going to see him tomorrow. I hope he knows it's my birthday.

We eat noodles until we're all fit to burst, and Eliza and Annie heap so many compliments on LaoLao, telling her over and over how they're the best noodles they've ever tasted and she should probably go on a cooking show or at least enter some kind of competition, and on and on, that I'm surprised she doesn't fall over. She hugs both of them on their way out, telling them she'll make noodles for them on their birthdays, and they need to try her dumplings next, and asking is there anything lesbians don't eat? Because she remembers that I had a friend once, April, who didn't eat pork (LaoLao could not get over this, could not fathom someone not eating pork), and I have to interrupt her at this point.

"LaoLao! April didn't eat pork because she was Jewish."

LaoLao shrugs, unfazed by our giggles. "Well, maybe lesbians also don't eat pork. I don't know."

Eliza hugs her again. "I can eat just about anything, especially if you've made it," she says, and LaoLao beams back at her.

Granny Dee hobbles over, not to be outdone. "You want to

have some good cookin', you should try my apple pie. Monica, tell them!" It's a while before Eliza and Annie and Monica are able to get out the door.

Aaron stays the latest, even helping carry dishes to the kitchen. We've stayed so late that my mom sent the waitstaff home, so it's just me and Aaron loading the bowls into the industrial dishwasher.

"I'm sorry I don't have a present for you." Aaron looks down at the bowl in his hands.

"My Riveo shoes were a good enough present for Christmas and my birthday! And I didn't want you to get me a birthday present. I just wanted—"

I stop. The word want has come out of my mouth in big neon letters. WANT WANT WANT. I want so much. I hope Aaron can't see all my want. Although he'd have to be blind not to.

"What do you want?" he asks, looking up at me, and it's like there's a little thread inside me that I didn't know was there, and he has the other end, and I don't know how that happened, and it is fragile and thin, but when he tugs, I feel it, and I feel like I shouldn't have to tell him what I want, that he should already know.

"Wing?"

"I . . . I wanted you to come to my birthday dinner." I drop my end of the thread. "Because you do every year. I thought . . . I thought it would make it less hard. Having you here."

He nods, and I know he's dropped the thread too. It lies between us, unbroken, but with no one to pick it up, it's limp and sad on the floor.

"I'm glad I got to be here," he says. "Happy birthday, Wing." He leans toward me so slowly, oh so slowly, and presses his lips against my face. It isn't quite my cheek. It isn't quite my mouth. It's the corner of my lips, where lip meets cheek. He pulls away far too quickly and I wonder how I'm supposed to restart my heart, how I'm supposed to teach my lungs to breathe again.

"Happy birthday," I say. He smiles, only one corner of his mouth going up, and oh, I want to kiss that corner the way he just kissed mine. Or was it my cheek and he made a mistake?

"My birthday isn't till August," he says, still smiling his one-corner smile, but as my brain processes his words, my brain that isn't really doing its job, I don't think any of my body parts are doing what they're supposed to be doing because lungs are supposed to be better at breathing and hearts are definitely not meant to beat this fast and lips aren't supposed to tingle, and brains are supposed to work . . . DID I JUST SAY HAPPY BIRTHDAY?

"I know!" My words sputter out of me. "I meant thank you. Thank you!"

He shakes his head, laughing softly, his bumblebee laughter surrounding me.

"Proud of you," he says, still smiling, "for today. You were great. Marcus would be proud too."

The mention of Marcus reboots my system. It reminds me that I shouldn't be so giddy, because even though it's my birthday, even though I won all my races today, even though I think Aaron almost just kissed me (maybe), Marcus is still in the hospital. And happiness doesn't fit with that.

But my happiness is a squishy kind of happiness, squeezing itself in where it can fit, pushing around all the sadness and the stress and the pressure, finding any empty spot, any crevice, and filling it. *Don't mind me*, it says. *I won't bother anyone. I know this is a room for sadness, but I just need a little corner.* I try to kick it out, because it isn't welcome here, it didn't even come wearing black, but it won't go. It's a stubborn guest. One that I secretly want to stay.

"He'll be here for your next birthday," Aaron goes on. "Hell, maybe even your next race. He won't wanna miss his baby sister kicking so much ass."

CHAPTER 39

I don't remember the last time I went to the mall. I hate the way the mannequins stare at me. I feel like they're judging. Telling me I won't fit into what they're wearing, and even if I could, it wouldn't look good. Not that I can afford to buy any of it.

But Eliza wanted to go today to look at prom dresses. Three months before prom. When I pointed this out and told her I didn't think I'd be going to prom, she just laughed and told me to get in the car. I guess it doesn't cost anything to look. And it'll be fun helping Eliza pick something out.

We're on our way to the dress store Eliza wants to go to, Trumpet Gowns, when we pass the Riveo store. We both stop, lingering by the doorway.

"Everything in this store is so damn beautiful," says Eliza.

"I thought we were here to look for dresses," I say, nudging her with my shoulder.

"We are! We are! Can't a girl appreciate some fine running shoes and some satin and tulle?"

"I bet you would wear a ball gown with Riveos," I say.

"Hell yes, I would. And you know what? I'd match the dress to the shoes, not the other way around. Come on, let's go look at some of these beauties before we go to Trumpet."

"What does Annie think of that? Of wearing Riveos under your dress?" I ask as we step into the brightly lit Riveo store. The whole place is practically pulsating with color. Shoes resplendent in yellow and oranges and hot pinks line one wall. And in case anyone wants to match the Olympic team this summer in their patriotic finery, the other wall is a sea of red, white, and blue. Everyone's got Olympics on the brain, what with it only a few months away, and gonna be here in Atlanta. Coach Kerry got tickets for us all to go to one of the track and field events. I don't know how she did it, but it's enough to make me forgive her for putting us through hell in training.

Eliza wrinkles her nose. "She likes heels," she says, gnawing on a hangnail. "Not that it matters. We couldn't go to prom together anyway."

"Why not?" I say, pausing at a pair of red and gold Riveos. I recognize them. They match the pair on my feet. The ones Aaron bought me. The price tag nearly makes me fall over.

"Because Heather Parker and her mother and their whole Southern confederacy of idiots would come down on us and cause a goddamn riot. I don't want to deal with that. I don't want Annie to deal with that." Eliza picks up a hot pink and bright orange shoe. "I like this color combination."

"So if you aren't going to prom, why are we looking for dresses?"

"We're looking at shoes right now," she says, and I roll my eyes and take the pink sneaker out of her hand and put it back on the shelf.

"We'll still go. Just not *together*. Won't dance together, not the way I want us to dance together. Won't take pictures. We'll just be two friends hanging out together at prom."

I frown. "Then why go at all?"

"I don't want to miss out on my prom just because of what some people think. Maybe ... maybe if things were different. Someday we're gonna move to New York or San Francisco or somewhere like that and then it won't matter."

I raise my eyebrows, both of them, since I don't know how to raise just one. "You sound like Marcus and Monica."

"Oh yeah, where they gonna go?" Eliza swallows audibly. "I mean, where were they gonna go? I mean, where are they gonna go when he wakes up? You know what I mean," she says, eyes screaming *Sorry!* and the shape of her mouth shouting *This is awkward!*

"Somewhere together," I say. "I think that's all they care about."

"Yeah, I get that." Eliza sighs. "Come on, let's get to Trumpet before I change my mind and decide I'd rather have a new pair of Riveos instead of a prom dress."

"I'd rather have a new pair of Riveos," I mumble. Then a poster by the door catches my eye. It's drenched in hot pink and bright orange, like the shoe Eliza was just holding up.

DO YOU HAVE WHAT IT TAKES TO BE THE NEW RIVEO RUNNING GIRL?

Underneath is a silhouette of a girl with a high ponytail, crouching at a starting line. On her feet are a pair of yellow Riveos. I go closer, wanting to see what that little print at the bottom says.

They're looking for a high school girl to be the face and the feet of their new brand to get more girls running.

"I don't get it." Eliza has slipped up next to me and is reading over my shoulder. "Are they looking for a runner to sponsor or for a model?"

"I think it's a way to get around the fact that high school students can't have sponsors," I say, because I know this from Marcus. "If they accept sponsorships from companies, they forfeit being able to compete at the collegiate level."

"Listen to you, all fancy. 'Collegiate level,'" says Eliza, laughing.

I've been hearing about competing at the "collegiate level" since Marcus picked up a ball. I just never imagined it would be something I'd have to think about.

I reread the small print, and then read it again. Riveo has found a nifty little loophole. They don't say that they're specifically targeting athletes, but the "audition" is the only kind of audition I would ever consider: a race.

The deadline to sign up is next month, and the race that'll determine the winner and the new Riveo Running Girl is the month after that.

They don't spell out the details about what being the Riveo Running Girl would mean, but I know what it means.

Money.

It isn't till we're in Trumpet Gowns, elbow-deep in taffeta dresses, that Eliza says what I'm thinking.

"You know you've got to go for it, right, Wing?"

Eliza is clutching a tangerine dress to her chest, I talked her out of hot pink; sunshine colors look good on her. Any color would look good against her dark brown skin, but I think yellow looks the best.

"Don't you wanna go for it?" I say.

Eliza shrugs. "Wing, you need this a lot more than me. Look, I know y'all got some serious money problems right now with Marcus in the hospital. And this Riveo thing, there's gotta be good money in it, right?" Her eyes are eagle bright. "Don't you see?"

I look down at the floor, unable to meet Eliza's bright eyes. How does she know my family needs money? Is it that obvious? We've never talked about it before. But I never accept Eliza's offers to join her and the other girls for burgers after practice . . . or to do anything else that costs money. She must have noticed.

"I can't go to that audition. You know I hate having people . . . watch me." The thought of it makes my stomach flip.

"It's not that kind of audition." Eliza pulls the tangerine dress over her head. "And you are gonna have to get over that particular little issue soon anyway, or did you not notice that our track meets are starting to be real popular?"

It's true. More and more people have started coming to our races to watch us run.

Coming to watch *me* run.

"It is too an audition," I say, ignoring the second part of her statement as I help tug the dress down over her shoulders.

"I read that fine print too, you know. They might be calling it an audition, but it's a race. If they just wanted a pretty face, they'd hire any old model. They want a real runner."

"They probably want a pretty face too," I mumble under my breath.

"Well, then you'll be perfect." Eliza grins at me. "Now stop fishing for compliments and zip me up. What do you think? Yellow or orange? Be honest."

CHAPTER 40

"WING, COME HERE. IN MY ROOM! I WANT TO SHOW YOU HOW to play mahjong. Time you learn." LaoLao is shouting, really shouting, even though I'm only a few feet away from her. It's four days after my birthday, so I guess LaoLao thinks I'm old enough to learn how to play mahjong.

"I thought you needed four people to play mahjong," I say, wincing at the volume of her voice. I follow her down the hall to the tiny room she shares with Granny Dee.

There's a small card table between their little twin beds that functions as a shared nightstand. LaoLao pushes the things on Granny Dee's side off and onto her bed before she carefully picks up the things on her own side and puts them on top of a dresser.

"You play with four," she says as she reaches under her bed and pulls out a dark wooden case. I can hear the tiles clacking around inside it. "But today I am just teaching. For teaching, you only need two. Once you know the rules, then we play with Dee Dee and your mama."

"Granny Dee knows how to play mahjong?" I'm astonished.

"Of course!" LaoLao sighs heavily as she settles herself on her bed, the springs groaning under her weight. "We spend so much time together, I have to teach her something. She teaches me things too. Checkers. Gin mummy."

"You mean gin rummy," I say. LaoLao shrugs and rolls her eyes.

"Name does not matter," she says. "I know how to play."

As she starts to explain the meaning of the tiles, I hear a sob from down the hall, in the kitchen where my mom and Granny Dee are. I look toward the door.

LaoLao doesn't respond at first, she acts like she didn't hear anything, but then she starts talking even louder. "This is pong! Three same tiles, you understand? What is it called?"

"I thought you said the names of things don't matter," I say sullenly.

LaoLao swats my hand. "What it called? When three tiles are same? I just told you, don't be stupid."

"Pong," I say, but I'm straining my ears. "I'm going to get some water. Do you want any?"

"No water, please. I am teaching you to play mahjong. We can have tea after."

"Okay, that sounds good, but I want water now," I say, moving quickly to the door and hurrying down the hall toward the kitchen.

I stop abruptly. My mom and Granny Dee aren't alone. A man in a suit is there too. An official-looking man.

Granny Dee is holding a tissue to her face and sobbing quietly at the table. There are documents strewn all around her. My mom's face is tight. The man is speaking in a low, serious voice.

"... you have ninety days or we will have to take the house."

"*What?*"

Everyone turns to look at me. LaoLao is waddling down the hall after me.

"She would not stay and play!" she says plaintively, sitting down next to Granny Dee and rubbing her back. "She don't listen."

"You should go back with LaoLao," says my mom without looking at me.

"I'm not hiding in LaoLao's room pretending to learn how to play mahjong while someone comes in and threatens to take the house! I live here too, you know!"

The man in the suit gives me an unfriendly smile. "Your mother is right. This isn't a conversation for children."

I hate him. I hate him so much that I could grab LaoLao's sharpest knife, the Chinese-style cleaver, and chop him open and watch his oily guts spill out. Money would probably pour out of him too.

"I'm not a child," I say, teeth clenched. My lioness has slipped into the room, but no one notices. Even as she growls at the man in the suit.

"Wing . . ." My mom's voice is heavy with warning.

"Oh, let her stay," says Granny Dee, and she sounds old, older than she is, so old. "It'll save us the trouble of having to explain it all to her later." She takes a long breath and looks down over her spectacles at me. "You do need to learn how to play mahjong at some point, though. Excellent game. Best thing this one"—she tilts her head toward LaoLao—"ever taught me."

I don't understand much of what the man in the suit says,

but I think I get the basics. The bills are too high. Something about credit. And a second mortgage. And not paying a loan back on time. Multiple loans. And if we don't pay back our debt in ninety days, they're taking our house. Our crappy little house that Granny Dee bought with my grandpa when she was pregnant with my daddy. The house my daddy grew up in, the house I grew up in, the only place I've ever lived. Sure, I was looking forward to when Marcus was playing for the NFL and bought us a mansion, but even then I never thought we'd sell this house. We'd keep it forever.

That's what I thought.

Ninety days.

It doesn't seem real. I don't know where we would go. I can't imagine Marcus waking up and us telling him his room is gone. The house is gone.

And that it's his fault.

My mom tells me there's nothing I can do, that it has nothing to do with me. They'll handle it, the man in the suit was using scare tactics, she's going to call another bank, get another loan, it's all going to be all right.

I don't believe her.

CHAPTER 41

I can't sleep. Not after seeing that man in our kitchen, not after hearing him say he's going to take everything we have left.

The poster I saw in the Riveo store is blinking in my head, all lit up in neon, like a fast-food sign you can see for miles and miles on the highway, in your front and rearview mirrors. There's no way I'm gonna be able to sleep with images of that Riveo poster and that awful man in the black suit playing through my head.

I slip outside and do what my body wants me to do, the only thing I can do now.

I run. So fast that even my dragon and my lioness can barely keep up.

But as I wait for the calm to come over me, and for everything to disappear except me and the sky, the way it usually does when I run, something else takes over. Anger.

I'm so angry that even running can't shut it out. I try to channel the rage to make myself faster, but I can't.

I can't outrun this anger.

I hear a clap of thunder, but I don't care. I keep running, not paying attention to where I'm going, not caring.

The rain starts as a drizzle, light and soft. But this is Georgia, and we don't just get drizzles. This is a weather warning; in a few minutes the rain will really start, but I don't stop running. I keep going. Not caring where.

When the rain comes, I welcome it. I lean my head back and howl at the sky, feeling the fat drops on my face and in my mouth and down my neck, drenching me.

I yell until I can't yell any more. I yell at the sky, at my dragon, at my lioness. I yell at the road. I yell and yell and yell at everything because I can't yell at the person I want to yell at the most.

I can't yell at him for everything he's done. For everything he's ruined. It's all his fault and he can't ever, ever, ever make it better.

Damn you, Marcus. For doing this to us. For doing this to Monica. For doing this to Michael and his family and that woman, Sophie Bell.

For doing this to yourself.

I've been running and yelling and yelling and running for what feels like hours. The rain drowns out my shouts so that no one hears me, and soon it starts to drown out my anger too. It's hard to stay angry when you've been running in the rain all night. Hard to stay anything but tired.

I recognize the intersection ahead of me and I push myself toward it, make myself keep running. My dragon and my lioness are still by my side, but I can tell my lioness doesn't like getting wet.

"Tough," I tell her, and turn down a street I've only been down a few times before. I'm soaked and feeling stupid but I don't want to go home just yet, I don't want to keep yelling at things that can't yell back.

I step in a puddle, soaking my shoes even more, not caring, and then go up the driveway, and knock on a window, hoping it's the right one.

No answer. I knock again, louder. Then a face appears at the glass and when the face sees my face, the window opens, letting rain in the room.

"Wing? What the hell?"

"Wanna go for a run?"

It's almost like when we first started running. When it was just the two of us and the track and the sky and my dragon and my lioness.

But we aren't on the track, we're tearing down some back alley behind Aaron's house and I can't see, am just chasing him blind, hoping I don't trip on something. His shape is a shadow in front of me, until lightning lights up the sky, turning him back into a person, a person I'm pushing myself to catch, and when I do, I scream at him and don't care that the wind is screaming at both of us and instead of screaming back at me, the way I want him to, he takes my hand, and when he does, the touch of his skin in the dark, the sense of his fingers intertwining with mine, does something to me. He pulls me toward him, out of the rain, into a covered doorway, and then he's holding me and letting me scream into his chest.

Scream until there is nothing left inside me.

"You all right?" he asks.

"Not really," I say. Because it's the truth.

"You will be," he says. Then he hugs me tight and his hug gives me hope that he's right, that it'll all be okay. And it gives me hope that maybe he'll still be hugging me when I stop crying, when I'm okay. That he isn't hugging me just because right now I'm a blubbering mess who happens to be his best friend's little sister.

I stomp on that stupid balloon of hope. It is pretty darn resilient, though, and won't pop. I can't bring myself to puncture it, so instead I cradle it against my heart and hope Aaron can't see it.

Three days later I come down with a cold, a real bad one that comes with shakes and shivers and a runny nose and a scratchy throat, and I can't go to school for a week, and no matter what I tell my mom about needing to stay in shape for track, she makes me miss practice and stay in bed. Granny Dee and LaoLao fuss over me, bringing me cups and cups of tea and soup and then more tea and more soup, and when I'm sure I couldn't swallow another drop, they bring me even more. So I drink it down, because Granny Dee and LaoLao have been looking after sick kids and sick grandkids for a long time and I trust them.

My dragon and my lioness glare at me at night, and I know they blame themselves for letting me go running that night in the rain.

But as much as I hate missing practice, and I really do, some part of me likes the attention I'm getting from Granny Dee and LaoLao.

It's been a long time since anyone has taken care of me like this.

But still, I have to get better fast. Next weekend is our training weekend in Hilton Head, and there's no way I'm gonna miss that.

CHAPTER 42

"You ready for this weekend?" Eliza is practically bouncing up and down next to me, grinning her mile-wide grin.

I nod and grin back at her. It's Friday afternoon after practice. I've been back at school a few days after being sick. There are vans in the parking lot, ready to drive us to Hilton Head. My mom almost didn't let me go, but yesterday Coach Kerry talked her into it. "We do it every year. It's good for the team. It'll be good for Wing," she said. Mama, I wanted to say, you've been letting Marcus run around with his friends, with his team, since he was twelve. But maybe she was thinking that she should have been a little more careful with Marcus.

We pile all our stuff into the backs of the vans. I only brought my duffel bag and a sleeping bag. Coach Kerry provides all the tents; she got 'em donated from a local business. Whole trip has been paid for, partly from donations and partly from a fund-raiser that the rest of the team held last summer.

As we head for one of the vans, Eliza tells me how much fun we'll have and how we'll make a campfire every night and how Hilton Head is the most beautiful place she's ever been, and I'm just grinning at her because I can't wait to see it for myself.

I'm expecting Aaron to ride in the van with the rest of the guys on the track team, guys I know by face but not by name, so I'm surprised when he jogs over to our van.

"Our van is full," he says. "Y'all got any space for me?"

"Yep, in the back next to Wing," Eliza chirps, before I've even gotten in.

There are a few giggles, but if Aaron hears them, he ignores them. "Cool," he says, and I try to look nonchalant, like it's no big deal that we're about to spend seven hours squished up next to each other.

There turns out to be plenty of room and there's an empty seat between us, the middle seat, and no one takes it, and I'm not going to scoot into it just so I can be closer to Aaron, even though that's what I want. At first we're quiet, but then, I don't know who goes first, we start talking and we don't stop.

We don't talk about running. We don't talk about Marcus. We talk about how Aaron wants to go to med school but is worried he won't be able to afford it. He's been trying to pull up his grades, he didn't do too hot freshman and sophomore years, and he's hoping his last two years will be enough to boost his GPA to get in somewhere with a good pre-med program. He wonders if he'll be able to run track, the only mention of running, and still be pre-med. How he'll balance it.

The van stops for gas and someone in the front hollers back to us and asks if we want to switch seats, but we don't.

"I'm good!" I call back.

"Me too," says Aaron, and again, that slight pause, as if everyone else in the van can feel whatever it is sizzling between us.

The van starts back up again, and the roar it makes as it hits the highway is a comfort. Between that and the music Eliza is blaring, no one can hear me and Aaron in the back.

We talk about how I want to travel. I want to go to Shanghai and see where LaoLao is from and where my mom was born. And to Ghana, to the village where my Granny Dee's parents lived. I tell him, smiling shyly, that I want to study both Chinese and Japanese when I get to university. I know a little bit of Mandarin from LaoLao, but I want to be fluent.

"I didn't know you were so interested in languages," he says. "Or so interested in Asia. I thought I knew you, Wing-a-ling, but I'm finding out new things about you every day."

"What do you know about me?" Our knees knock against each other in the small space behind the seat in front of us.

"I know that you love to sing. And that you're afraid of heights. And you like to go to the beach. I know that you watch old cartoons on weekend mornings. And you bake real good chocolate chip cookies. And you're messy. And you'd do anything for the people you love." He leans closer, voice low, eyes tight on mine. "I know that when you're happy, you shine. And I love it when you laugh, I love the sound, and I feel it." He sits back and gestures with his hands around his chest.

He *does* feel my feather giggles.

"I like getting to know you, Wing Jones."

"I like getting to know you too."

Aaron reaches over across the empty seat between us and puts the smallest amount of pressure on the back of my hand, sending shooting stars up my arm. My hand flips over, making its own decision, I sure as hell didn't tell it to do that, so our hands are lying palm to palm. That line from Romeo and Juliet, the one about the lips being palms, and palms kissing, flits through my mind. Then he squeezes my hand, and if the first touch sent shooting stars, this is a whole meteor shower, racing up my veins from my palm straight to my heart.

Hours later, we drive through a tunnel of green. I've never seen trees like this before. Trees with long, wispy branches that droop and drape over the road like velvet curtains. I push the window open and breathe in salty, unfamiliar air. The ocean lies ahead of us, beckoning with open arms.

Hilton Head, South Carolina.

Our van trundles along, getting closer and closer to the ocean, and I stare out the window like a little kid staring at a tiger at the zoo.

"You gotta watch out for alligators here," Aaron says, leaning over my shoulder, and I can feel his breath on my neck.

"I don't believe you," I say, sitting as still and stiff as I can, not wanting to lean into him, not wanting to lean away.

He leans closer; his face is right next to mine. "Look," he says, pushing the van window open as far as it'll go. "Do you see that right there? Up ahead, next to that lady in the blue dress. She hasn't even noticed there's an alligator right next to her!"

I squint, trying to see. "That thing? That's a log."

"Nope." Aaron shakes his head. "That's an alligator."

He's teasing me; he's got to be.

Then, just as we're passing by the thing, it moves up out of the water and onto the bank. It has eyes. And teeth. It definitely isn't a log. It definitely is an alligator.

"Ah!" I scoot back away from the window, but there isn't enough room, Aaron is right behind me, and I slam against him, my head knocking into his jaw.

"Sorry!" I try to scramble back into my seat.

"Told you so," he says with a smirk.

"We're camping with alligators nearby?"

He laughs, and his laugh buzzes through me. "They won't bother us. They stay in the creeks and we'll be down on the beach."

"That isn't very reassuring," I say, picturing an alligator chomping through our tents.

"Don't you trust me?" His question stops my heart.

I trusted Marcus more than I trusted anyone in my whole life and look what happened.

His smile fades. "Wing? You all right?"

I lean as close to the window as I can. "Just need a little air," I say. I keep an eye out for alligators the rest of the drive, but I don't see any. Doesn't mean they aren't there, lurking in the water. Waiting for the perfect moment to come out and strike.

CHAPTER 43

THE WHOLE TEAM SPILLS OUT OF THE VANS AND ONTO THE beach, and before we even set up our tents we're running down to the water, racing without even meaning to.

I get there first and I kick off my shoes and dip my toes in, yelping as the water comes up to my ankles. It's colder than I thought it would be.

Eliza is next to me, frolicking like a pony, kicking the water and sending the spray everywhere. "I told you! I told you it was the most beautiful place!"

And it is. The sand is white and soft and the water is a dark blue-green, not turquoise, not aqua, but darker than that, like a color that doesn't have a word yet, and I love it. If I were going to prom I would want a dress this exact color.

"Come on, ladies! We need to set up camp before the sun goes down!" Coach Kerry shouts down to us, and we pull our feet from the ocean's grasp and run, run, run back up to where the vans are.

Aaron has rejoined the boys. I'm aware of him the way I always am, and I wonder where his tent will be.

I've never put a tent up before, and it's harder than it looks. Eliza and I tussle with our tiny tent, pulling the slippery material this way, then that way, trying to get the poles to go in the right places, and she's telling me I'm doing it wrong, that I'm not paying attention, and will I stop looking around and focus, but I'm just doing what she's telling me to do, I assumed she'd know how to do this since she's done it before, and then finally, when I think we're going to have to give up and sleep in the van, our tent is standing.

Our tents are all in a row. Coach Kerry's is at one end, far from us, and then on our other side, dotted down the beach, with more room between us, are the boys' tents. Coach Wilson, who usually trains the boys, has his tent between the girls' and boys' tents.

Aaron's tent is the farthest. I know it's his because I watched him set it up when I should have been focusing on putting up my own, which is maybe why it took so long. Not that I'd admit that to Eliza.

We set up campfires right on the sand and put hot dogs on sticks and cook them over the open fire. Mine gets a little burnt, and a little sandy, but it's still the best hot dog I've ever had. I'm sitting squished between Eliza and Vanessa, watching Aaron through the flames. He's laughing, nudging the guy next to him, a guy I don't know, and I wonder what it's like for Aaron to have to make new friends now that Marcus isn't around.

After dinner, Coach Kerry and Coach Wilson make a big show of going into their tents and going to bed. Coach Kerry tells us she doesn't care how late we stay up (that isn't what she told my mom, but I'm not arguing with her), but that we better be up and ready to run by five a.m.

We toast marshmallows and everyone has their own strategy for getting the perfect roast. Eliza puts hers straight in the fire till it bursts into flame and then she waves it around till the fire goes out and she's left with burnt and blackened gooey mush that was once a marshmallow. She swears it's the only way to eat them. I like to put mine real close to the coals and let it turn golden on the outside and soft on the inside. Slower than Eliza's method—she gets through about four in the time it takes me to roast just one—but mine is perfect. Worth the effort.

When we're out of marshmallows and the fire is starting to die, we play cards by flashlight, our marshmallow-coated fingers making the cards almost too sticky to play with. I don't know who goes to bed first, but eventually someone does, and then someone else, until there are more people in tents than out around the dying fire. I've played more rounds of Egyptian Rat Screw, the card game with all the slapping, than I can count, and I'm hoarse from laughing so much.

I wave goodnight to Aaron and follow Eliza into our tent. I'm sure I won't be able to sleep, I've got too much happiness racing around inside me, too much sugar too, but as soon as I slide into my sleeping bag and close my eyes, exhaustion takes over and the waves sing me to sleep.

CHAPTER 44

THERE IS SOMETHING OUTSIDE OUR TENT. I CAN HEAR IT RUS-tling. I don't think it's an alligator, but oh my God, what if it is. I sit up, careful not to wake Eliza. If it is an alligator, there's nothing she can do about it. And if it isn't, well, there is nothing she can do about that either.

She's curled up in her sleeping bag next to me, breathing heavily. She fell asleep almost as soon as she slid inside it. "Coach isn't kidding about that five a.m. start," she said.

I wonder what time it is now. I wonder what this thing outside my tent is. Maybe it's my imagination. Or maybe my dragon or my lioness followed me all the way to South Carolina. Maybe it's the wind. Maybe it's a dog. Or maybe it's an alligator.

And then someone whispers, right up against the tent, so close that I bet if I put my mouth on my side of the tent my lips would touch theirs.

"Wing! You awake?" It's Aaron.

I unzip the tent as quietly as I can, watching Eliza the whole time. Aaron's face is right next to the tent. He's smiling, I can see that even in the dark.

"You gotta look at the ocean. It's glowing."

It's true. Every time a wave crashes, the ocean shines a bright, sparkling blue. Like there are Christmas lights strung in the surf.

"Wanna go see it up close?"

We walk way down, away from where everyone is camping, until it feels like it's just us on the beach. Like we've got the whole thing to ourselves. And now we're standing in the surf, and it's still glowing, but Aaron isn't even looking at the sparkling sea, he's looking at me. More than looking. He's staring at me. Staring like I'm a magical creature, like a unicorn or a Pegasus, and I might disappear if he looks away for even a second. I wish I were wearing something nicer than the oversized T-shirt I went to sleep in.

The wet sand beneath my toes is somehow both rough and soft at the same time, and it reminds me of Aaron's hands, which are strong and rough but soft between the fingers. This isn't something I should know about him; this isn't something you know about your older brother's best friend or about your assistant track coach. But I know it. I've known it for as long as I can remember. Anytime Aaron held his hand out to me to pull me up, or passed me a fork at the table, or gave me a high five, my hand was memorizing his hand, my skin was remembering his skin, even though my brain didn't know what was happening. And now it's all coming back to me. I take the tiniest of steps toward him.

I want to know what else my body remembers about him. All the little touches, glances, brushes, every laugh, every breath, one by one they've seeped into me and now I want more. I want to know what his chest feels like pressed up against my own. I want to know what those hands feel like entwined in mine, what they feel like on my skin.

He takes another step toward me and his foot sinks in the sand and he isn't smiling and I'm not smiling, the moment feels like it is drenched in honey, everything is going so slow and everything feels so heavy, and I know it's so much more than the humid South Carolina air. The surf crashes over my feet and it propels me forward, like the waves are pushing me toward him, and then, somehow, without me being aware of either of us taking another step, he's right there, so close I could touch him. His skin is darker in the moonlight, and more perfect, as if he's been carved from onyx, and my hand rises of its own volition and rests on his face, my palm on the chiseled curve where his cheek meets his jaw meets his lips and oh.

His lips are on my palm and it's not even a kiss because his lips aren't puckered but just resting, but still, it is as if the not-kiss is a plug and my palm is the socket and he has just sent sparks all through me. I am certain that I must be glowing. There is fire in my veins, fire that wasn't there before, and it is lighting me up on the inside, more than lighting me up, melting me, melting my bones, because I can feel them going soft and liquid, and I'm sure I'm going to dissolve into the sand and be taken away by the sea.

We haven't moved in a minute. Maybe more than a minute. Maybe an hour. Maybe several. Maybe all night. Time has lost all meaning. I've fallen into some sort of alternate reality where there is no time. Just the feeling of his mouth on my palm. Nothing else matters.

But then he moves and rests his hand on the small of my back, drawing me closer, and he brushes my hair out of my face with his other hand, but it's a futile attempt because the rebel curl springs back exactly where it was, exactly where it wants to be, and then he smiles, I can feel the muscles move in his cheek beneath where my hand still rests. We're standing in the surf now, because even if time stopped for him and me, it has gone on all around us and the tide has come in, and the sand that was once soft and rough is wet and our feet are sinking. I can't even see my toes and I wiggle them to make sure they're still there, and that slight movement is enough to make me lose my balance and I lean into Aaron, and he puts his other arm around me and my arms wrap around his neck and we aren't smiling anymore.

"Wing," he breathes, like a wish, like a prayer, and it's as if it is my heart's name and not my own because my heart flutters in my chest, desperate to get out to fly to him.

The best I can do for my poor heart is to press myself even closer to him and hope my heart will hear his, and that will calm it.

I don't know what my heart hears but whatever it is sends it into a frenzy, it's beating faster than when I run, and I feel each beat all throughout my body.

I sense a deep and building *something* low in my belly and I wonder if any part of my body is my own or if all the pieces will mutiny to get what they want.

I wouldn't mind. I want what they want.

The waves are coming up higher now, above my ankles, the stars singing over our heads, and the breeze is blowing against us. The night is warm and the breeze and the water offer a welcome relief.

"Wing," he says again, and it is less of a prayer and a wish and more of a plea and I tilt my head back and look at him, his eyes dark and infinite in the night, and I let my fingers splay on the back of his neck, up against his short, tight curls, and I lean up and press my lips to his.

I've never kissed anyone. And I'm not exactly sure what comes next.

Aaron makes a low sound in his throat or his chest or from somewhere deeper inside of him and wraps his arms around my waist and pulls me even closer and he opens his mouth, and I open mine, my eyes fluttering open in surprise, as if they're moving in accord with my mouth, and I can see the stars above our heads and in the distance the lighthouse, and the beach is still blessedly empty but keeping my eyes open is distracting and taking away from the kiss so I shut them, quickly, and lose myself in the kiss. Lose myself in Aaron.

Runner's high has nothing on kissing.

I feel like I've learned to fly. It's like when I started running, really running, for the first time and my body woke up and every part of me was in tune, and it was the most right thing in the world. Kissing Aaron feels like that.

But better.

Bubbles are popping all inside me but not soap bubbles, honeyed bubbles, and they're lifting me up but keeping me grounded all at the same time, and when they pop they're full of liquid gold that's pouring through me.

A wave splashes against the back of my legs, soaking my underwear, and I jump, breaking the kiss, but not breaking the moment.

Aaron is looking down at me with a smile on lips and in his eyes. "Wing," he says again, and this time it's like my name is his *everything*. My whole body responds, not just my heart, but everything inside me.

His hands have moved down from my back and rest on my hips. Another wave comes, and this time it nearly knocks me over. I giggle, suddenly shy.

Aaron takes my hand and pulls me up out of the surf, and with my wet legs and the wet hem of my T-shirt, I feel like a mermaid emerging from the sea. Now that we're out of the water and not pressed against each other, the breeze feels cold on my skin. The sand feels even rougher as it grips my legs and climbs over my feet and up my calves. The clouds are moving quickly across the sky, blocking the moon, and now that we aren't in it, the water isn't glowing anymore and looks dark and dangerous.

CHAPTER 45

WE SLOWLY, SLOWLY WALK BACK TO WHERE ALL THE TENTS are, our hands still locked together, and we pause outside a green one at the end of the row. Aaron's tent. His tent that he isn't sharing with anyone. "I could come hang out in your tent for a bit," I say, so nervous he'll say no that I can't look at him. He takes a deep breath, like he's preparing to say no, and I tense, waiting for it.

"It's okay with me if it's okay with you," he says. Is it okay? Because this is supposed to be a track training trip, and I'm definitely supposed to be in my own tent, not in Aaron's. Because we have to be up and running in about three hours. And because Marcus is my brother and Marcus is Aaron's best friend and Marcus is still in a coma and we should be doing everything we can to help him and instead we've been kissing on the beach. And I want more.

"It's okay," I say, and climb inside his tent.

I don't know if it is because Aaron is so much bigger than

Eliza or what, but we can't both be in his tent without touching. It's impossible.

He takes my hand, gently rubbing his thumb over my palm. All my sensations are centralized there, in the center of my palm, and I watch his thumb move, mesmerized by the movement. My head tips slowly over and finds a place on his shoulder. Our feet are still covered in sand, and I feel bad for getting his tent all sandy, but not that bad.

I never knew that wanting something could feel so good. Or that sitting next to someone, listening to them breathe, having my hand in their hand, could make me lose all sense. No one ever told me this. I think of all the times I've seen Marcus holding Monica's hand, brushing her hair off her neck, and wonder if it feels like this every time for them.

Thinking of Marcus sends a bullet of guilt straight into my stomach. Not just one bullet, a whole round of bullets, one for each of the different types of guilt I feel for being here with Aaron. Each one tears through my stomach lining and lodges deep inside. It must show on my face, because Aaron's thumb stops its rhythmic movements and I feel him still.

"Wing? Is something wrong?"

I turn toward him and scoot back, pulling up my legs to sit cross-legged on the sleeping bag. Aaron leans back on his side, curled toward me.

"I'm thinking about Marcus," I admit. And it's like Marcus is already a ghost and is there in the tent with us. Haunting us. He's sitting at the entrance, glaring at us with reproach.

Aaron rolls onto his back and closes his eyes. "I think about him all the time," he whispers. "He's never not in my head. But, Wing, we can't stop living just because he has."

"He's not dead," I say quickly, even as Ghost Marcus keeps staring at me. I scoot closer to Aaron.

"I know that," says Aaron, his eyes still closed. Then his voice goes very quiet. "But he isn't exactly living either."

And now Ghost Marcus has moved from the edge of the tent and is sitting between us. I swear I hear the sleeping bag crinkle under the extra weight.

"Wing?" says Aaron, his eyes fluttering open. I stare at him through the body of Ghost Marcus. Who isn't really a ghost. Because he isn't really dead. But still. He's here. Between us. "Don't you think Marcus might be happy for us? You know. Be glad that we have each other? That we can comfort each other and all that crap?"

I smile, and to my amazement, Ghost Marcus smiles back. Maybe Aaron's right.

"I mean, I know you're his baby sister," Aaron says. "You'll always be his baby sister. No matter how fine you get." He winks at me and I roll my eyes but can't stop grinning. "And, Wing, I know this is so hard for you. It's killing you. You have to know that I know. Because it's killing me too. Marcus is my brother, and he always will be. Nothing could change that. Nothing ever will. But just because he's like my brother . . . it doesn't make you my sister. It doesn't make you off-limits. Or it shouldn't." He sighs and closes his eyes again. "I don't know, man. It's so complicated."

I lie down too, my hair fluffing out all around my head like an electrocuted halo on the top of the sleeping bag.

My hand finds his and I lace my fingers through his and squeeze.

"I know," I say. "But it's more than that. It isn't just whatever . . .

this is. Whatever . . ." I stop and swallow, nervous about what I'm going to say next. "Whatever we are . . ." I stop again, waiting for him to clarify that regardless of everything that has been happening, we aren't a *we*. Not that kind of *we*. But he doesn't. He squeezes my hand and waits for me to go on. I take a deep breath. "How can I be so . . . happy? It doesn't feel right."

"It doesn't?" he asks, his voice like velvet.

"No," I admit, my own voice breathy, like an old-school film star's. "It does feel right. But it shouldn't."

"Why not?"

"Because how can I be happy when Marcus is in a coma? When we don't know if he'll wake up?"

Aaron turns toward me, and his hand that isn't holding mine comes and pushes my hair off my face, caresses my cheek. "Wing, Marcus will wake up," he says with such conviction that it must be true. "He has to. He will. And when he does, he wouldn't want to hear that you've been moping around, crying all day long. He'd want to know you've been living. Wing, all Marcus ever wanted was for you to be happy."

"Even if it's with you?"

Aaron's eyes are shining. "I hope so," he says. "Because I know Marcus wants me to be happy too. And hell, if we're happy together, well, that should, like . . . multiply the happiness."

Sometime in the past few moments Ghost Marcus has floated up above us. He's looking down at us with a smile on his face.

"What are you looking at?" says Aaron.

I smile at him and then up at Ghost Marcus, who is fading as quickly as he came, leaving us to be.

"You're right," I say. "He'd be happy for us. And he's going to wake up and he's going to be happy. I know it."

"He's lucky to have you as a sister." Aaron leans toward me, closing the gap between us.

"He's lucky to have you as a friend," I say, and the word *lucky* feels sour in my mouth, because even though everyone keeps using it about Marcus, saying that he's lucky to be alive, I still think it would have been luckier if he had never gone out that night at all.

"And I'm so lucky to be here right now," he says, his voice husky in my ear.

Me too, I'm about to say, but then his lips are on mine.

Our legs are tangled, the sleeping bag is tangled, my hair is tangled, everything is tangled up and still it's not close enough and I press myself against him and hold on to him like we're back in the ocean but the tide has come in and we're drowning and he's the only thing that will save me.

He's breathing heavily, like he's just run a race, and I wonder if I sound the same. He kisses my eyelids and runs his finger down my nose and over my lips and across my jaw and down my neck to my collarbone and then his finger dips lower beneath the loose collar of my sleeping shirt and I stop breathing.

So does he. I know because I can't feel his chest moving and the sudden silence echoes in my ears.

"Is this okay?" he whispers, so softly, so quietly. And I want it to be. I want it to be okay more than I want anything and my body is screaming *yes* but I tell it to shush and I blink and try to draw myself out of this fog that I'm in where nothing matters but him.

My pause is answer enough. He sighs, a rough sound edged with disappointment, and moves his hand up to cup my face and kiss my forehead.

"Let's get some sleep," he says, and we curl up together like kittens, his arms around me, our legs still tangled, his breath on the back of my neck, the skin on his stomach pressing against the skin on my lower back where my shirt has ridden up.

I want to tell him I love him. The words have almost bubbled out of my mouth before I can stop them, but something, some defense mechanism I didn't know I had, keeps my lips pressed closed and the words, poised on the tip of my tongue, so ready to dance out and declare themselves, are pushed back down, back into my heart instead. The whole effort almost makes me choke but I keep the words down. I shudder, once, and Aaron tightens his hold on me.

"Good night, Wing," he says, and his voice is like the sand earlier tonight, soft and rough at the same time.

"Good night," I whisper, only opening my lips a fraction, worried that if I say anything else, the words, those three traitorous words, will come bounding out and ruin everything.

CHAPTER 46

"WING! ARE YOU IN THERE? WAKE UP! WING!"

I'm dreaming that I'm wrapped in Aaron's arms and someone is trying to wake me up.

"You better not be naked! I'm coming in!"

My eyes fly open and I try to sit up but I wasn't dreaming, I really am wrapped in Aaron's arms and someone is unzipping the tent.

Eliza pushes her head inside and she's ferocious. "What. The. HELL! Wing! Come on! You're gonna miss our morning run and Coach Kerry is not going to be happy about it." She frowns at me. More than frowns, scowls. "I don't know how we are gonna get you out of this tent and back to our tent without anyone noticing. It's gonna be a goddamn sandy walk of shame, that is what it is gonna be."

"Morning, Eliza," mumbles Aaron without opening his eyes.

"And you!" Eliza reaches into the tent and smacks the bottom of the sleeping bag. I think she's aiming for Aaron's shin, but she gets my foot instead. "You shoulda known better! You know what camp is like. Don't 'morning, Eliza' me! You both get your asses up and out NOW. Coach asked me where you were, Wing, and I said you weren't feeling well so you'd gone on a morning walk. I already had to lie about where you were. Don't make me do it again."

"Eliza," I whisper as I crawl out of Aaron's sleeping bag. "I don't have any pants."

Her eyes nearly pop out of her head. "You don't have any pants! I want to hear about that later, but not right now. We don't have time for you not to have any pants!"

A whistle blows.

"Aaron, give her a pair of your running shorts." If I thought Eliza was bossy before, it's nothing like how she's being now. "I am all for some moonlit make-out sessions, but you go back to bed where you are supposed to! And if you don't do that, you wake up in time so you don't get caught!" She shakes her head as I yank on a pair of Aaron's running shorts and try to tamp down the thrill of wearing something of his.

Eliza straightens up. "Okay, Coach is looking the other way. You've got about thirty seconds to get out, go around the other side of the tent, and look like you're walking up toward us. Aaron, you better wait at least three minutes before you get out."

Eliza disappears back into the sunshine and I stagger out behind her, careful to follow her instructions and go out around the other side and come up from behind the tent.

By the time I've changed into my running clothes and put my sneakers on, everyone else has finished stretching and is lined up for the morning beach run.

"Feeling better?" Coach Kerry asks from behind me and I jump. "Eliza said you weren't feeling well. Are you sure you should be running?"

"I'm fine," I say, looking at my shoes.

"If you say so," she says, a frown creasing her face.

She blows her whistle to get our attention. "I've put cones on the other side of the beach. Now, I know some of you haven't run in sand before, so don't worry if your time is a little slower than you are used to. Ready, set, go!"

I take off, sand billowing out around my ankles. Someone comes up from behind me and passes me.

It's Eliza. She's faster than me. She's a lot faster than me. I stare at the back of her head and try to force myself to go faster and I'm pushing myself and . . .

Vanessa passes me too.

It's the sand, just the sand, I tell myself as I try to go faster. I'm not used to running on it. They are. That's why. It isn't because I'm tired. It isn't because I'm distracted. It isn't because I'm thinking about Aaron.

Right before I get to the finish line I trip and fall face-first into the sand. It coats my forearms and my shins like body paint and it stings.

The whistle blows and we run back to where we started. Again I fall farther and farther behind. Again I blame the sand.

It's the sand's fault. It isn't because I was up all night.

The rest of the day, no matter how hard I try to win, I come in third, fourth, fifth. Coach Kerry asks if I need to sit out. "You seem distracted," she says, and I see Eliza rolling her eyes. Aaron has been training with the boys' team all day; I've barely seen him, but he's all I've been thinking about.

When the sun sets again, everyone is too drained to stay up late playing games and making s'mores. We ran more today than we ever have in one day. Up and down the beach and back again. Again and again.

Before I go into my tent, I slide up next to Aaron.

"Hey," he says, and smiles. "How are you?"

"I'm good," I say, suddenly feeling shy, suddenly feeling nervous. "A little tired."

"Yeah, me too. I hope you didn't get in trouble."

"I didn't," I say. And then I hope and hope and hope he'll ask me if I want to go watch the ocean again tonight.

"Still," he says, "you should probably sleep in your own tent tonight . . . just in case."

I swallow and nod too enthusiastically. "Definitely," I say. "I was coming over to say just that." I stare at my feet. "So. Um. Good night?"

"Good night, Wing," he says before leaning down to press a kiss on my cheek. On my cheek. Nowhere close to my mouth.

"This is more than a crush, isn't it?" Eliza is already tucked into her sleeping bag.

"I don't know what you're talking about," I say, avoiding her wide-eyed gaze.

She sighs. "I thought you were gonna focus on training for that Riveo thing," she says. "The competition?"

I haven't thought about it all weekend.

"I don't even know if I'm gonna go for it," I admit.

"Wing! You've got to! I think you could win! Unless you start running like you ran today," she says, eyebrows raised.

"I'm not used to running in sand," I say, but even I don't believe the words.

"I think you're not used to running when you've been up all night and when you've got a boy on your mind." Eliza wiggles in her sleeping bag and I swat at her.

"Shhh!"

"And I didn't like that I had to lie to Coach Kerry this morning. Do whatever you wanna do, but if you aren't in this tent when I wake up tomorrow, I'm not gonna come find you."

"I'll be here," I say, but I'm hoping that maybe I won't be. That maybe Aaron'll change his mind and come back to my tent tonight.

He doesn't.

I don't fall asleep thinking about running or even thinking about Marcus. I go to sleep thinking about Aaron. And when I wake up, he's already on my mind.

I don't even want to run today. All I want to do is skip to the end of the day, when we can go in the ocean, when I can be close to Aaron. I can't stop thinking about him. About how I want more nights like the night in his tent.

The day goes even slower than I do, it feels like it drags on and on, and for the first time, I resent running. Eliza, Vanessa, or one of the other girls beats me every time. I can't focus. I keep looking over at where the boys are running. I keep watching Aaron and remembering what his lips felt like on mine. And by the time I've snapped my focus from my tingling lips back to my aching feet, I've fallen behind again. Finally, Coach blows her whistle for the last time and training is officially over and now our time is our own.

"Wing! Come on in! The water's great!" Aaron is already

splashing around in the ocean like some kind of god of the sea, or maybe a sun god who was dropped in the sea, shining and wet and glowing. He's beaming at me, and I swear he's the most beautiful thing I've ever seen.

I want Aaron so much that it scares me. I feel like it might take over, like I might drown in my wanting. Like I'll be nothing but want. Like I won't be able to think about anything or do anything but just want him.

Nobody ever told me it was like this. And even if they had, I wouldn't have believed them. I thought I wanted Aaron before, but now that I've kissed him, now that I've felt him against me . . . now that I know he might want me back . . .

I don't know if my heart is gonna be able to take it. Between being broken over Marcus and pumping so fast to keep up with me when I'm running and now all this wanting.

It isn't fair to my poor heart. It just isn't fair.

CHAPTER 47

It's the Tuesday night after we got back from Hilton Head and something is bothering LaoLao. I can't tell what it is. She's so sharp I'm surprised she isn't cutting herself straight open. And she's been glaring at Granny Dee all dinner. She's so focused on drilling holes into Granny Dee with her eyes that she hasn't looked down at her own plate once and is spilling food all over the table and down her front.

It takes Granny Dee a little while to notice. At first she ignores it. Then she tries to glare back at LaoLao, and Granny Dee's glares are nothing to trifle with, but she can't compete with LaoLao.

Finally, she puts down her fork. Keeps hold of her knife, though. Uses it to point at LaoLao across the table.

"Is there somethin' on my face?"

My mom looks up. If she's noticed the Olympic-level glaring going on, she's been ignoring it, which is a feat in itself.

"No. Nothing on your face," she says.

"Then could you please ask your mother why she is staring at me like that?" says Granny Dee primly.

This is all the encouragement LaoLao needs. She takes such a deep breath that I think I can see her lungs expanding, like she's an opera singer. I'm glad I'm not about to be on the receiving end of whatever she's about to unload on Granny Dee.

"You not doing anything for our family!" LaoLao puffs up like a rooster and she shakes her head at Granny Dee. "How come I the one who has to go work? Why not you? You could get work too!"

Granny Dee raises her hand to her chest and gasps, and I think I can hear the air rattling all the way down into her lungs.

"How dare you!" Her voice is shaky. "I might lose my house!"

"This not just your house. This my house too." LaoLao's tone is petulant. "I work, work, work all day. Work to save Marcus. Work to save house. What do you do?"

I remember rubbing LaoLao's feet in the living room when she said that work is nothing because it's for family. I know she meant it. I know she's tired today. She's had a long day. The head chef shouted at her and the line cooks make her feel stupid. She wants to sit at home and watch her soap operas. She's bitter that Granny Dee isn't working too.

Granny Dee turns to my mom. "You know I can't get work, Winnie. My vision . . . it isn't what it used to be . . . and my hearing . . ."

"I know, I know," my mom says soothingly, rubbing Granny Dee's back.

"Your hands! Your hands work. You could do something!" LaoLao snaps back. "My eyes no good! My ears no good! But I use my hands. All day."

The kitchen lights flicker, once, twice, and then the kitchen goes dark.

"Oh crap," my mom mutters. "They really did turn it off. Wing, can you get a flashlight from the drawer under the phone?"

"And now we so poor we can't even keep lights on!" LaoLao roars. Apparently even getting our electricity cut is not going to stop her.

"Mama." My own mom's voice is sharp. "Give it a rest, please, just while we get some light."

"Give what a rest? Give me a rest? I need a rest!"

"Ow!" I stub my toe trying to get to the drawer under the phone. There are two flashlights there. I turn on one and put it on my LaoLao like a spotlight. It's all the encouragement she needs.

"You do nothing," LaoLao hisses at Granny Dee.

"That's not true," I say, putting the flashlight in the middle of the table like a lantern. Granny Dee shakes her head at me even as her eyes fill with tears. She doesn't want them to know, but they need to.

"Granny Dee visits Marcus every day," I say, my voice rising with every word. "Every. Single. Day. That isn't nothing. I couldn't do it. Couldn't go and just . . . sit there. Watch him just . . . lying there. It doesn't even feel like it's him! It doesn't make me feel better. It makes me feel worse! I hate it. *I hate visiting him.* Because it isn't him. Not really. But Granny Dee sits and knits and watches and waits. Where do you think all the scarves have come from? The pot holders?"

"I would visit!" LaoLao's words are bigger than mine. She's standing, and I can tell I've upset her. "You think she so special? She making him better? Who is paying for him to be in hospital? Me! I want to visit him too." She's a shaking mountain, like a volcano about to burst. "I would visit him every day! If I could! But I work and then my bones are so tired."

Granny Dee turns to face LaoLao, and if LaoLao is a shaking mountain, Granny Dee is a tree blowing in the wind, bending this way and that, trembling, but never breaking.

"I would work! Don't you dare say that I wouldn't. But . . . no one will take me! I can't cook like you, at least not dumplings or noodles or any of that. And no one wants to hire me to make stew or any of the things I can make. What do you think I should do? So high and mighty! You been workin' just a few months. A few measly months! What about when you first moved in? You remember that? Who was workin' then?"

"I was taking care of Winnie! And the babies!"

"Well, now I'm taking care of the babies! They just ain't babies anymore."

The two women glare at each other, each one immovable, and I think we'll never leave the table, that Granny Dee and LaoLao will sit and stare at each other till Granny Dee sprouts roots and LaoLao turns to stone.

Then LaoLao looks away, puffing her cheeks up full of air, just as Granny Dee bites her own, making her face look sunken and older than it is, especially in the glow of the flashlight. LaoLao exhales, loud and long like a teakettle shooting out steam, and reaches out to pat Granny Dee's brittle branch of an arm.

"Next time," she says, her words coming out heavy, "next time you visit Marcus, I go too. I know is hard to go alone."

In my room, the Riveo Running Girl entry form shimmers and glows. Using a flashlight, I read and reread the terms and conditions. I read about the prize. The winner of the Riveo Running Girl race becomes the official Riveo Running Girl. She will be featured in Riveo ads across the country. On billboards. The Riveo Girl will be in a commercial. The Riveo Girl will be paid a lot of money.

I stare at myself in the mirror, at my face that doesn't look like any other face I've ever seen, and try to imagine it on a billboard, or in a commercial.

I can't.

I can't.

Winning the race is one thing. It's what comes after that scares me.

But for Marcus, for my family, maybe I can.

I have to.

The entry form asks for a parent's signature, but I can't ask for that, not with everything going on, so I forge my mama's signature. Not hard to do, I've seen it enough times. My lioness comes out from under my bed and nips at my ankles, but I ignore her. I can't risk asking my mom and having her say no. Or worrying about the pressure. I need this. Our family needs this.

I'll go to the Riveo store tomorrow and hand deliver it.

I think about what Eliza said at Hilton Head. How I won't be able to win if I run like I did that day. I can't be distracted. I'm gonna run harder, faster, better than I ever have. Than anyone else.

I can't afford not to.

And then when I win this thing and get the money, maybe my LaoLao and Granny Dee will laugh at the dinner table, my mom won't look so stressed, and maybe even Marcus will wake up. Because if I can become the Riveo Running Girl, maybe anything can happen.

CHAPTER 48

"WING! COLLEGE SCOUTS ARE COMIN' TO OUR RACES THE NEXT few weeks." I haven't seen Aaron much since Hilton Head. I've been scared that if I see him, that feeling I had on the beach, the feeling of drowning in him, will come back. And I'll be slow again. Because he turns my bones into honey, and I can't have that. No matter how much I want it. I've turned in my Riveo Running Girl form. It's official now; I'm going for it. And if I'm gonna win—and I've gotta win—it's gonna take all my focus. I can't afford to be thinking about Aaron.

I can't afford much of anything right now. The electricity only came back on yesterday, and that was after my mom finally got through to a nice person at Georgia Power and convinced them to extend our payment period. I don't know what she thinks is going to happen in the next three months, but at least we've got power again. Until we lose the house.

"Scouts? That's great," I say, looking down, worried that if I look too closely at him I won't be able to control myself and I'll jump on him like some kind of feral cat. "University of Georgia?"

That's where Aaron is hoping to get a scholarship. He's already been accepted, but his scholarship is dependent on his spring track performance. A bit like the Riveo competition.

Do I distract him? I wonder what I do to his bones. What I do to his heart. I don't want him slowing down either, not when he's got so much at stake.

Not when we've both got so much at stake.

"Yeah! And I hear you're going for this Riveo Running Girl thing?" He whistles low and long. "Gonna be tough, but I bet you can do it."

"Yeah, I've gotta be focused, though," I say, and the words come out sharp.

"You're the most focused person I know." Aaron smiles at me, and it's enough to make me wobbly on my feet.

"Anyway . . ." He smiles again, a different kind of smile. "I was hoping we could get together today, after practice."

Yes Yes Yes Yes Yes Yes Yes, screams my heart. Lucky for me, my heart doesn't have a mouth.

"I'm training late tonight," my mouth says. "You know, because of the Riveo thing."

He shakes his head, still smiling. "Man, you *are* focused. But don't put too much pressure on yourself, all right? I know you really want to win this thing, but you don't want to get burnt out.

"What about tomorrow? You can't be training late two days in a row. You've gotta take a break."

He doesn't get it. I can't take a break. Not right now. Not tomorrow. Not ever. The Riveo race is everything. I've got to train and I've got to win.

"Aaron . . ." His name tastes delicious on my lips. I could say it over and over again. I don't believe what I'm about to say, but I have to say it. "I think, right now, because we've both got so much goin' on, maybe, um, maybe we shouldn't . . . we shouldn't . . ." I don't know what to say. "I need some space."

The hurt flies across his face so fast that for a minute I think he's about to cry out, but then it's gone, like it was never there.

"What do you mean, Wing?"

"When I see you . . . all I think about is you."

"What's wrong with that?" His voice is gruff.

"Like I said, I need to focus. . . ." I look down again because I can't take the hurt in his eyes. "And so do you. You've got scouts looking at you. I don't want you losing out on anything because of me."

He sighs, and there are so many feelings in his one breath, it's more than one breath, it's an orchestra of breaths, each instrument saying something different, and then he puts his hand on my lower back, just for an instant, leans down, and kisses my cheek.

"If that's what you want, Wing."

And he jogs off. Leaving me alone.

Two weeks later Aaron gets a letter from the University of Georgia offering him a full scholarship. He comes by the house to tell my mom, but not me. I hear him in the kitchen, but I stay in my room.

Aaron still comes round to our house quite a lot now, to ask how Marcus is doing, to say hi to Granny Dee and LaoLao. If my mom thinks it's strange that I hide in my room every time, she doesn't say so. I've caught her watching me when she thinks

I'm not looking. But she doesn't say anything. And for that I'm grateful.

Just like I'm grateful that none of the girls on the team have said anything about how Aaron doesn't run with us anymore. Even Coach Kerry keeps her thoughts to herself.

I watch him at his next race. It's like watching a cheetah. Or a gazelle. Or some kind of hybrid of the two, so much grace and power and beauty, and it takes all my strength not to run after him.

All that matters now is winning that Riveo race. I'm not doing this for me, I want to tell Aaron; I'm not being selfish. I'm doing it for my family.

I'm doing it for Marcus.

Running used to make me feel weightless, like it set me free. But now . . . now it's something else. Something heavy. It doesn't matter if I love it. It doesn't matter how it makes me feel. Only thing that matters now is winning.

I'm not running for me.

I'm running because I'd give anything for my brother, and this is all I've got to give.

CHAPTER 49

"THIS GOOD FOR YOUR FEET, AND YOUR HEART," SAYS LaoLao, pushing a strand of gray hair behind her ear. She didn't used to have gray hairs.

I'm in the kitchen with my mom and LaoLao. My mom is doing the dishes and LaoLao is putting together some concoction that she claims will be good for my blisters. I want to tell her I can get something for my blisters at the drugstore, but she's sure her ancient remedies are better.

I don't remind her of the time she made me something to make my hair soft and it made my head stink for a week. After sixteen years, neither Granny Dee nor LaoLao know what to do with my hair.

"What's wrong with my heart?" I ask.

"It's broken! You don't have to tell me. I know."

I blink, wondering how she knows about Aaron.

Then I realize LaoLao is talking about Marcus.

I didn't know it was possible for a heart to break so many times and in so many ways.

The phone rings and my mom puts down the bowl she's rinsing and crosses the kitchen to pick it up, cradling it between her shoulder and jaw.

"Hello?"

LaoLao is humming tunelessly, pausing to ask me to pass her various ingredients. Garlic, lemon, vinegar . . . my feet are going to smell like something that needs to go in the oven for a few hours and be cooked on low heat.

"Of course," my mom says into the phone, and the words are innocuous but the way she says them makes my LaoLao stop mashing together her mixture, makes me look up from the fridge, even makes Granny Dee wander in from the living room.

"We'll be right there." Mom's breathless, like she's been running.

She clangs the phone down and turns to us, tears crinkling in the corners of her eyes.

"Marcus is awake."

Her words are a hot glue gun on my heart, sticking it back together again.

I've never seen Granny Dee or LaoLao move as quickly as they do after that. I didn't know they could move so fast.

Granny Dee rambles the whole way to the hospital that she should have been there, that she can't believe he woke up alone.

"He wasn't alone. The doctors were there," says my mom, merging lanes without signaling, making my newly mended heart speed up.

"Be careful, Mom!"

"I'm being careful," she says, right as she runs a red light.

"Mom!"

LaoLao takes my hand and holds it. "Don't be nervous," she says.

I wonder how she knows. If she's nervous too.

No one has said what I'm thinking. No one has said . . . what if he doesn't remember us?

What if it isn't him?

I close my eyes and lean my head on my LaoLao's shoulder. She's so round and well padded I can't even feel the bone; it's like snuggling a marshmallow. Soft and spongy and comforting.

"It will still be him," says LaoLao, like she's read my mind, stroking my head. "It will still be him."

CHAPTER 50

I'VE FORGOTTEN WHAT MY BROTHER'S EYES LOOK LIKE.

He's sitting up. *He's sitting up.* I haven't seen him in any position but horizontal in months and months and now he's sitting up.

And staring at us.

Smiling at us.

My mom is trying so hard not to cry. I can't see her face but I can tell by the set of her back and the trembling in her arms, and then when Marcus says, "Hi, Mama," it's as if he's opened the floodgates and my mom is shaking and sobbing so hard I think she's going to disintegrate right in front of us.

"It's okay," says Marcus softly. "I'm okay."

I step forward, nervous, shy—feelings I'm used to having but never with Marcus. I'm staring at him like he's not real, like he's going to disappear before I get to him.

"I'm glad you're back," I say, my voice hesitant and unsure as a kid on the high dive.

"I never went anywhere," he says, smiling the smile I know so well, and I can tell he's waiting for me to reassure him that everything is still the same.

"How are you?" I say instead.

He shrugs and winces. "All right. Been better."

"I missed you," I say, and he smiles again.

"I missed you too." He looks at me like I'm not quite real. Like I'm not who he remembers.

He isn't who I remember either.

"You got taller," he says. "And you look . . . older."

Now I shrug. I don't know if I'm any taller than I was seven months ago. It's possible. Anything's possible.

I want to ask him where he's been. If he knows we've been visiting. If he's seen my dragon or my lion. I want to ask him so many things.

"Wing is running." It's LaoLao; she's bustled forward and is clucking around his hospital bed like a mother hen. "You will not believe when you see. She so fast!"

Marcus looks at me, confusion scrawled across his face. "Fast? Wing? I guess I really was out for a long time."

"You're gonna be so proud," says my mom, her eyes still on Marcus. I don't think she's ever going to look away from him again. "She's on the track team and everything. She's been winning all her races."

Now Marcus looks at me like he definitely doesn't remember me.

"That's great . . . ," he says. Then he lies back down in his pillows. "I'm sorry I'm not more excited. I don't think my brain can keep up with everything."

He looks down at his inert body and raises a limp arm. "My

body sure as hell can't." Then he laughs, the sound a shadow of what it used to be. "Are y'all just gonna stare at me all day? I don't know if I'm gonna be able to go back to sleep with y'all watching me like that."

"You've been sleeping just fine for the past few months." The words spiral out of my mouth before I can stop them.

He shakes his head and then winces, because the movement was too quick and must have hurt him.

"Months," he says, disbelief woven through his words like a mismatched thread. "Months."

He remembers us.

But he's different. I knew he'd be different. But I wasn't expecting my brother to be gone.

My strong brother. My proud brother. My brave brother. He's gone. What is left is a boy who cries in pain, whimpers, who stares into space for hours.

This new Marcus doesn't remember what happened that night. Or a lot of what happened before. He doesn't remember taking me to Gladys's. He remembers Monica. Who won't leave his side even though finals are coming up and she needs to be studying. He remembers Aaron. Who I know is visiting because Monica tells me, but he's never there at the same time I am.

Marcus isn't proud of me. He pretends he is. But he isn't. I want to tell him that it is all for him, but I don't know how to make him understand.

I perch on the edge of his hospital bed, lap full of all his favorite treats. Snickerdoodle and chocolate chip cookies, beef jerky, sunflower seeds, Skittles. He's lost so much weight. We're trying to fatten him up, but the doctors say it will take time.

He didn't know, when he first woke up, about the accident.

He didn't know how bad it had been.

He didn't know that even if he could play football again, and he can't, no team would have him now.

He didn't know he killed two people.

"I'll never play football again," he says to the wall. "I'll never go pro."

I'm torn between wanting to hug him and wanting to slap him. I want to tell him that we don't care that he'll never go pro. He lived. He lived when two people died. I want to ask him why isn't life enough?

But the doctors and the psychologists say this kind of thing isn't helpful or healing. So instead I rub his back and make comforting sounds.

He doesn't ask me about my running. I don't think he really believes it. That I'm good at something.

I don't think he believes that this is his life now.

CHAPTER 51

"I KNOW SOME OF YOU HAVE ENTERED THE RIVEO RUNNING Girl competition," Coach Kerry says after practice one day. It's a Tuesday. Marcus has been awake for eight days. "It's a fantastic opportunity, and it would be wonderful if someone from our team won," Coach Kerry goes on.

There's a woman with her. It's Natalie, with the ice-blond hair and navy blazer and matching heels, who works at Riveo. She was the one I handed my entry form to at the shop. When I turned it in she looked at me like she knew me already. "You're that girl who's been in the local papers, the fast one, right? The one breaking all the records?" She smiled then, but it wasn't a friendly smile. "You look so . . . distinct. A hard face to forget. An unforgettable face is a good thing for a campaign. I hope you're as fast as they say you are." Her eyes are hungry today, like they were that day in the Riveo store. She looks at me like right now I'm just a rock but with enough pressure I'll turn into a diamond. One that she's gonna rip out of the ground herself.

Coach Kerry tells us that Natalie is here to check our times during the races leading up to the Riveo race. "They're going to other schools too. The decision is nothing to do with me," Coach says.

The next day at practice I force everything else out of my head. Even Aaron. Even Marcus. I run so fast and so hard that my body can barely keep up with my feet. My stomach sure can't. I barely make it into the nearest bathroom before I start puking, my whole body trembling as I heave.

I don't tell anyone I threw up. And I go even faster the next day.

The following Thursday I'm stretching before a race, a real one, a race that Riveo Natalie is gonna be at, when Eliza flutters close to me. My hair is pulled back tight; I had Granny Dee braid it as tight as she could.

"What's wrong, Wing? You look like you're gonna be sick." Eliza's face is scrunched in concern. "Are you sure you should be running? Maybe you need to take a few days off." I've told her that Marcus is awake but still needs a whole lot of medical care and she already knows how bad everything is at home. We still don't know how we're gonna pay for this never-ending and always-growing mountain of medical bills. Marcus woke up two weeks ago, and that's the best thing that ever could've happened, the very best thing, but it doesn't mean all our problems have gone away. He's still in the hospital. Plus now he's got physical therapists, special medicines, all sorts of stuff insurance doesn't cover. And we've only got six more weeks before we lose the house. And what are we gonna do then?

"The Riveo rep is here," I say. "Of course I've got to run."

"Wing, you won't be automatically disqualified for missing one race, you know. Why don't you sit this one out?"

I shake my head, my vision blurring a little bit. I'm just so tired. "I can't. I need her to see how fast I am. I can't stop."

Then I run like if I run fast enough I can turn back time and go back to before the accident, before the party, and stop Marcus from going. I run like all my nightmares are chasing me. I run like everything depends on me getting faster.

I win.

After the race, Natalie comes up to me, looking out of place as always in her blazer and heels, always navy. I don't know why she doesn't wear Riveo sneakers.

"You'll have to beat your last time to stay eligible," she says, and my stomach clenches like a fist full of nails. "We like what we see. You're good, Miss Jones, really good, and you've got the kind of . . . determination that we want to see in our Riveo Running Girl. But you do need to be faster."

"But I won," I say as sweat that has nothing to do with my just-finished race starts to gather at my temples.

"You won *this* race. There are a lot of girls who want to be the Riveo Running Girl. Each one is the fastest girl in her school. This is a nationwide competition, Miss Jones. If you want to win, you're going to have to get faster. Consider this a little tip from me. I like you, and I'd like to see you win."

My next race I shave off 3.2 seconds.

Just enough to stay eligible for the Riveo race.

Coach Kerry says I'm pushing myself too hard and that I can't maintain it. She tells me I'm by far the fastest girl in Atlanta. I tell her that I'm trying to beat my own times, that I'm my biggest competition. None of the other girls on the team who entered the contest are fast enough to be eligible for the final race.

It isn't running anymore. It isn't even racing. It's something else entirely. My footsteps used to run to the beat of Marcus's heart, but now that he's awake, I've lost that beat. There is no rhythm, only the jolt of my feet hitting the ground again and again. They shouldn't even be hitting the ground, because that means I'm going too slow. To win this, I'm gonna have to fly.

Running for Riveo is the same thing as running for Marcus, I tell myself. Because winning the Riveo deal would mean money, and Marcus needs money. We all need money. But even running for Marcus doesn't feel the same anymore. I used to think my running would wake him up, and now he's awake, and maybe my running was part of it, but he's not who I thought he was going to be. He's not himself. He's ungrateful. He doesn't know how hard I'm working for him.

Still.

It's worth it, I tell myself as I see my mom trying again and again to get another loan from the bank. It's worth it, I tell myself, when Marcus starts seeing a special physiotherapist insurance doesn't cover. It's worth it, I tell myself, when I cancel plans with Eliza to train harder. It's worth it, I tell myself as I glance at Aaron across the field. Looking so far away. Looking so small. Like he isn't a real person at all.

It's worth it.

It has to be.

CHAPTER 52

I CAN'T SLEEP, SO I'M IN THE LIVING ROOM, FLIPPING THROUGH an anime comic, when the phone rings. It startles me, and I answer right away. My palms have already started to sweat and I have a hard time gripping the receiver. I'm scared that it's about Marcus. Scared that he's slipped back into his coma or his heart has stopped. I'm scared the worst has happened.

It isn't about Marcus. A different voice, one I haven't heard in weeks but used to hear every day, slurs down the phone. "Wing? Wing? Are you there? Can you come get me? I'm, I'm at the Clermont Lounge."

In the background I hear shouts and jeers. I close my eyes and try to picture him. Standing outside the biggest strip club in Atlanta. No, not standing. If he is anything close to as drunk as he sounds, he's staggering, falling over.

I breathe into the phone, not sure what to say, not sure what to do.

"Wing? Can you come get me?"

A beat, and then he says the thing that would make me go anywhere, didn't matter if it was the Clermont Lounge or the Playboy Mansion or what.

"I don't think I should drive tonight."

I haven't driven since I took Granny Dee to drop off those apple pies. I know I shouldn't be driving after midnight with just my permit. I know I shouldn't be driving alone at all with just my permit. If my mom wakes up and I'm not home, and the car is gone, she'll freak out, but . . . I can't not go to Aaron. Not with the way he sounds.

I tiptoe down the hall, scrawl a note for my mom, just in case, and grab the keys to her car.

Driving puts all my senses on high alert. Every light and sound is amplified and I'm gripping the steering wheel with both hands, hoping I don't get pulled over, hoping that the other drivers out this late are being just as careful as me.

I pull into the Clermont Lounge parking lot and immediately spot Aaron.

He isn't alone. I don't know why I thought he would be. There's a group of three guys I don't recognize with him. I pull up next to them; my hands are slick with sweat on the steering wheel. I roll down the window.

"Aaron?" I say, my voice coming out louder than I mean it to. The three boys with him—men, now that I look at them—jump back as if my voice is a cattle prod and they are the steers.

Two of them are supporting Aaron, his arms around their shoulders; his head is lolling around. I've never seen him like this, never thought he got like this, and the sight makes me want to press on the gas and drive far, far away from here, as if it never happened. I think of all the times I've imagined Aaron reaching out to me, or me reaching out to him, all the times I've imagined how we'd fix what was once so good between us but that I broke because I was scared by how much I wanted him.

I never imagined it would be like this. Me coming to get him from the parking lot of Atlanta's most infamous strip club, with alcohol fumes coming so fast and strong off his breath that I can smell him from inside the car. I didn't think I'd have to find him in the company of three guys I don't recognize, guys who are leering at me through the open window, guys who are snickering and muttering under their breath, things I can't hear but I can guess from their eyes and their mouths. I wonder what Aaron is doing with them.

His eyes focus on me for a second, and he smiles, but it isn't his smile, it's a sloppy smile and it looks like it might slip off his face and fall on the ground.

"Wing!" he cries, and tries to step toward the car but he stumbles and the guy next to him catches him and holds him upright. The one not supporting him steps toward the car, his manner vaguely menacing. I grip the steering wheel harder and put on my best bitch face.

"You're the girl?" he says with a sneer. I don't give him the satisfaction of a reply; instead, I narrow my eyes just a tiny bit more and wish that I could shoot acid out of them that would melt a man. The streetlight behind him flickers, making his silhouette jump and grow. He's wearing an Atlanta Braves cap pulled down low, and it's shadowing his face. I'm surprised he isn't wearing sunglasses to complete the look.

"Yo," he says, now leaning into the window, and it takes all my resolve not to lean away from him. I sit still as a statue, my fingers glued to the steering wheel, my feet itching to run, itching to take me away from here because now I recognize him. It's Jasper. Aaron's somehow cousin. Recognizing him doesn't make me feel any better. It makes me feel worse.

I should never have come. It was stupid. But it doesn't matter that it was stupid or that I shouldn't have, because no matter how you look at it or tilt it or twist it, I will always come when Aaron calls. Jasper leans farther into the car and his breath smells like whiskey and cigarettes and it mixes with his cheap cologne and the whole stench of him makes me feel sick.

"Girl, I asked you a question."

I wish, for what feels like the millionth time, that Marcus were here. The way he used to be. Not as he is now, not in the hospital bed crying for more morphine, his limbs wasting away, glaring at me when he thinks I don't see, pretending to be happy about my running but not even managing a smile, moaning and being someone completely different from the big brother I remember. In the back of my brain a thought prickles and expands. There is a very good chance that if Marcus were here, he would have gone to the Clermont with these boys, but the only difference would be instead of Aaron being held up, he'd be the one holding Marcus up.

My continued silence is too much for Jasper, who makes a quick move, like a snake, and suddenly something hard and metallic slams against the back window of the car, making me jump.

It's a gun. This asshole has pulled a gun on me because I won't answer his question. I know I should be scared, but instead anger fills me like oxygen, expanding in my lungs, and when I exhale I'm surprised that smoke doesn't come out. No, not smoke. Fire.

My eyes are on his. Now that I look closer, I can see that his pupils are dilated and I know he's on something, and I wonder if Aaron is on something too, but I don't have time to dwell on that because if I do I know I won't be able to do anything else, and so with my eyes locked on the eyes of Jasper, the gun-wielding junkie, because that's what I've decided he is, I change gear and reverse. Just a bit. Enough to almost, almost run over his toes.

It has the desired effect. He jumps back as if he's been scalded, waving his gun.

"I'm here to pick up Aaron," I say, and my voice comes out stronger than I feel and I am sure this is because of the anger coursing through me. "Could you put him in the car?"

"Why?"

"Because he called me and I came to get him and if you don't stop waving that gun around like a damn lunatic I swear to God I will run you down right now and claim self-defense. Now put Aaron in the car." To prove my point I lean on the car horn, and it blares into the night.

Out of the corner of my eye I see a bouncer jogging over. Good.

Jasper the asshole blinks at me and doesn't move, but his friends do. They bring Aaron over and I unlock the doors and they slide him into the backseat, putting him on his side. Aaron moans but doesn't make a fuss. They curl his knees up so that they can shut the door. And then they stand there, staring at me, eyes wide, like baby birds waiting for something from their mama.

I sigh. The bouncer is almost here and I'd rather not have to talk to him, although I'm hoping he saw Jasper waving his gun around. Even though they don't deserve any help from me . . . I don't want them driving either. "Do y'all need a ride somewhere?"

"No," says the one closest to me. "We're gonna go back inside. We were just waiting for you to come get Aaron." The guy stares at me with a drunken solemnness. "Because you're his girl."

CHAPTER 53

I CAN'T TAKE AARON HOME. NOT LIKE THIS. I START DRIVING, not even sure where I'm going, trying to listen for his breathing so I know he hasn't gone and died on me. I drive until I find myself near Piedmont Park, and I manage to parallel park right on the street, which is a minor miracle in itself. I turn in my seat and reach back and jostle Aaron, a little less gently than I could.

"Aaron. Aaron. Wake up."

His eyes flutter open, and then when he sees me, I swear they light up. Even with the fog of booze and who-knows-what-else, his eyes light up when they land on my face.

"Wing!" he says, and I start to wonder if he's going to say anything other than my name for the rest of the night. Then he scrunches his face up and holds his stomach. "I'm gonna be sick," he says, and I get out and open the door just in time.

"Not in my mama's car," I say as he leans out and throws up on the sidewalk. Not sure if it's the right thing to do, I rub his neck and back while he pukes his guts out. When there's nothing coming up but sounds and air, I go back to the front seat and grab a half-empty water bottle.

"Sit up," I say, and he blinks and slowly pulls himself upright. I tilt the water into his mouth. A good bit dribbles out the side of his mouth and down his chin, but I think he's swallowing some of it and that's all I can ask.

I hold the bottle to his lips until it's empty. Then I tug on his arms. "Come on," I say. "Let's go for a walk."

I know that Piedmont Park isn't the safest of places at night, but I think Aaron needs the air. Anyway, I can outrun almost anyone if I need to. This knowledge makes me feel safe and strong until I loop Aaron's arm around my shoulders and my body buckles under his weight. So much for being able to outrun anyone.

But the park is empty. Or appears to be. I'm sure there's a bum or two or five sleeping in the bushes, but nobody bothers us as we make our slow, staggering way along the sidewalk.

It's a cool night; I'm glad I'm wearing my fleece. The dogwoods are in full bloom, and as we pass under one, the wind blows, scattering blossoms around us. A few petals land on my shoulder and in my hair.

We don't talk. Not because I don't want to—I want to talk so badly. I want to tell him how training is going and that I'm so stressed about getting the Riveo Girl contract and that it's making me sick but I can't stop training, can't slow down, not when I think I really have a shot at it. I want to tell him I don't remember how to run for me anymore. How it used to be.

And I want to shout at him for being out at Clermont Lounge. I want to ask him what the hell he was doing with Jasper. Is it my fault he's out with him, making bad decisions? Is it because of how far I've pushed him away? But Aaron's making me make bad decisions too, coming out late like this, driving when I shouldn't be. This is why I pushed him away in the first place, because I started to worry that maybe he was bad for me, because when I'm with him he's all that matters and I don't care about anything but him and I'd do anything for him and I want to tell him he makes me fearless and stronger and weaker all at the same time. And I miss him and dream of him and when I run I imagine him next to me, or behind me, or waiting for me at the finish line, cheering me on.

I want to tell him that I love him.

There's so much I want to tell him but I don't say a word. Partly because I'm waiting for him to speak first, because I'm a stubborn fool like that, and partly because I'm pretty sure he won't remember it tomorrow.

When he finally does speak, I'm not expecting it. Even though his mouth is right next to my ear, his words are so quiet that at first I don't realize he's talking at all.

"I didn't think you'd come," he says, and there's a sadness in his voice underneath the drunken slur, and that sadness cuts into me like a spear into a fish, it goes all the way through and out the other side, leaving me gasping for air.

"Of course I came," I say, stopping and turning so I can see his face. His beautiful face. "I'll always come."

"Then where ya been, Wing? Where ya been?" He's swaying, so I guide us to a bench under one of the dogwood trees and sit him down and then slide in next to him, as close as I dare, and not nearly as close as I want to be.

"Aaron," I say softly. "What happened tonight?" I'm not expecting a coherent answer, but I'm curious what he'll say.

"I miss you so damn much. It isn't fair. First I lost Marcus and now I lost you."

I lean closer to him and take his hand in mine. A spark erupts between our palms, and I feel it go straight into my heart, waking it up from a long sleep.

"You didn't lose me," I say. "I haven't gone anywhere."

"You're too fast now." Aaron squeezes my hand. "I can't keep up. I can't follow you. You're too fast for me, my Wing-a-ring-ling."

I know he's drunk and he's spouting nonsense, and that I shouldn't pay any attention, but there is a truth hidden in his words, a truth that tugs at me. Being fast is all that matters to me now. There is nothing I can say, so instead I squeeze his hand back.

He hiccups loudly. "I'm proud of you," he says. "I'm proud of you, but it hurts. It hurts that I'm not the one by your side anymore. You don't need me anymore. Nobody needs me anymore."

"Aaron!" I can't have him thinking that I don't need him. That I don't care about him. I let go of his hand and roughly pull his face toward my own and kiss him as hard as I can. I enjoy it, for a few luxurious moments. Then I wonder if I'm taking advantage of the situation. Taking advantage of him.

I pull back, quickly, so quickly that I leave his mouth still open, his arms stretching out to wrap around me.

"Wing, Wing," he says, his words still slurred. "Don't tease me like that."

"I'm not!" I say. "Are you going to remember this in the morning?"

"I hope so," he says, and then hiccups again.

I rest my forehead against his and our noses press together. Even our eyebrows are practically touching. If his could crawl like caterpillars, and they look like caterpillars, they could hop from his face to mine. "Aaron, I do need you. I need you to go be . . . a better you. The best you. Can you do that? For me?"

His head bobbles back and forth, gently knocking into my own. "I'd do anything for you, Wing. Anything. I didn't realize, I didn't realize . . . it was before the running. Did you know that? It was before the running."

"What? What was before the running? You aren't making any sense."

"My feelings! The feelings I had for you. They were there before the running. They were . . ." He looks down at his hands and opens and closes his fingers like he's counting. "I don't even know how long I've had them."

All the air has left my lungs. And I can't breathe any more in because I can't move. I'm sitting frozen on the bench, not quite believing what he's saying.

"Dionne . . . ," he says, and I frown.

"Dionne?" Is he calling me Dionne? Oh my God, what if he's so drunk he thinks I'm Dionne? That doesn't make any sense because he was just calling me Wing . . . but . . .

"Dionne used to say all the time, 'I know you've got a thing for Marcus's sister,' and I do," he says, grabbing my hands. "And you aren't his sister. I mean, you are, but to me you're just Wing."

I lean forward and press my lips against his again.

I can't not.

CHAPTER 54

At some point, we move from the bench to the back of my mom's car.

Aaron lies down, blinking and yawning, and puts his head in my lap. "I don't want to go home," he says, his words still blurry. "Can I stay with you?"

He closes his eyes and falls asleep before I answer. He looks soft in sleep, unguarded. His chest rises and falls in a slow, even rhythm. I match my breathing to his and lean my head back against the headrest, closing my eyes for just a few minutes.

A car alarm goes off, jarring me awake. My few minutes' rest have turned into an hour or more. The sky is waking up, changing color behind the trees.

My leg has fallen asleep beneath Aaron's head. I jostle him

awake, gently, and grin at how his eyes flutter open like he's a princess in a fairy tale.

"How are you feeling?"

He looks up at me, and then around the car, and for a moment I worry that he won't remember how he got here. He won't remember me picking him up from the Clermont Lounge.

He won't remember calling me.

Needing me.

"I thought I was dreaming," he says, his voice raspy with sleep. I love the sound. I want to take it and make a scarf out of it, so I can wrap it around myself and rub my face against it, soft and scratchy. Familiar and warm.

He slowly sits up, scrunching his eyes in the morning light. "This . . . this is embarrassing."

"It's fine," I say. And I mean it. It's more than fine. "I'm glad you called." I pause. "How much do you remember?"

He shrugs. "Bits and pieces. Calling you. Being in the park. Kissing you."

I swallow. "Um. That was more me . . . kissing you."

We stare at each other and then he looks away. "It wasn't my idea to go to Clermont. Jasper . . ."

"He had a gun. He pulled it out, was waving it around."

Aaron leans back, closing his eyes. "Shit. I'm sorry." He takes a long breath. "Not just for Jasper. I'm sorry for me, too. Sorry for calling—"

"No." I slide over, sitting closer to him. "I'm glad you did."

"Are you?"

I know he's asking me more.

"I mean . . . I don't want to make picking you up from a strip club parking lot a regular occurrence. . . ."

He snorts.

"But . . . I'm glad you called."

"How about I take you to breakfast to make up for it?"

I drive and Aaron directs, telling me he knows just the place. It's a little French bakery, tucked down a street lined with dogwood trees. It opens at five, but we're still a few minutes too early.

"Simone will open up," he says, rapping on the glass door.

Simone conjures up images of a leggy brunette with dark eyes and a mysterious smile. I'm not expecting a lady who is almost as wide as she is tall to open the door, hair tied up in a scarf.

I'm even less prepared for her to open her arms and scoop Aaron in for a hug, babbling in French.

And when Aaron replies, in *French,* I nearly fall over. I don't know what he says, but Simone lets him go and is suddenly hugging me.

I put my arms gingerly around her, patting her on the back. She's still speaking in French, the words pouring over me like some kind of exotic perfume. It smells delicious.

Not just the words. The bakery smells delicious too.

"I don't speak French," I blurt when Simone stops for a breath.

"Oh, no problem! Come, sit! The beignets are hot." Her accent isn't exactly French, but it isn't Southern either. She leans toward Aaron and sniffs loudly. "Woo, boy! You stink! I'm guessing you need a coffee too." She shakes her head, clucking to herself. "Silly boy!"

She bustles off into the kitchen, whistling as she goes. I sit in one of the tiny café chairs. It's so tiny I think I might break it, or at the very least spill off it.

Aaron looks like a giant sitting on dolls' furniture.

"Simone?" I say, eyebrows raised.

Aaron grins back at me. "Told you she'd open up early for us."

"Who is she?"

"She used to look after me. When I was little. Her and my mom used to be real close . . . but then . . . well . . . my mom said a bunch of real stupid crap. Crap she didn't mean. But she hasn't said sorry either."

"How does your mom know her?" My mind is whirling. I can't picture Aaron's sullen, mean mom being friends with this welcoming woman.

"They grew up together. In New Orleans. That's why Simone makes beignets."

"Your mom is from New Orleans?" I don't know why this surprises me so much.

"Yep. Taught me French when I was growing up. She doesn't speak it anymore, though."

I thought I knew all there was to know about Aaron. And here he is, like one of those Russian nesting dolls, holding all kinds of different Aarons inside him.

Simone comes back and puts the piping hot beignets down with a flourish. "Ta-da! Beignets to save the day. And hot coffee."

"I don't drink coffee. . . ."

"Oh, let me get you a hot chocolate, then. But this one"— she rolls her eyes in Aaron's direction—"this one needs coffee. He looks like the cats dragged him down the alley and back up again."

She goes back into the kitchen, leaving us alone with the smell of the beignets and the steaming coffee. Aaron takes a small sip, wincing at the heat.

I pick up a beignet and take a bite. It's fluffy and soft and perfect. Powdered sugar goes everywhere.

"Here," Aaron says, leaning toward me and wiping the corner

of my mouth with his thumb. He pauses, still close. "Wing," he says, and something in the way he says my name makes me stop chewing, stop breathing, it stops everything.

"Everything has gotten kinda crazy, huh? You and your running, the whole Riveo thing. Look, I'm supportive of it, I know what it means to you, I know what it could do for your family, but it hurt, it hurt a lot when you pushed me away. Hurt so much that I let Jasper and those guys talk me into a night out at the Clermont. And the hurt, it wasn't just because of how I feel about you, although that was most of it. I was ..." He pauses, and I can tell he's searching for the right word. "Offended. I thought ... I guess I thought I discovered you. Discovered what you could do. How talented you were. And then here you were, telling me you were better off without me." He holds his hands up. "I know, I know, that sounds ridiculous. But I mean, all these years, Marcus never knew you could run like that? At first I was doing it for him, you know, because I thought it was what he would have wanted. What he would have done. And then, then I was doing it for you, because I loved seeing you run, loved seeing how happy it made you. And then I think maybe I was giving myself too much credit for something that was just yours." He pauses again and takes another tentative sip of his coffee.

Maybe it's the coffee, maybe it's the conversation, but I feel more grown-up than I ever have in my whole life. I feel like we aren't high schoolers in Atlanta, wearing the same clothes we went to sleep in last night, but like ... like we're lovers (just thinking the word makes my face hot) in a sidewalk café in Paris.

"Wing, you're really good. You're better than good, you're great. And I wanna help you however I can," Aaron says. "If that means running with you, great. If that means backing off and letting you do your thing, hell, I can do that too. You let me know."

Aaron is watching me with so much hope shining out of his eyes I'm surprised it isn't blinding me. I smile a small smile back at him and take another bite of beignet. The second bite is just as good as the first. I take a third bite and chew as slow as I can, trying to figure out how to tell Aaron that right now, running is everything. Racing is everything. Riveo is everything. I don't have space in my heart for Aaron right now, because when he's in it, he takes up the whole thing.

"Thanks," I say eventually. "I think that's what I need at the moment. Just to focus. Just for a little longer."

Aaron grins behind his coffee mug. His smile is so big it peeks over the edges. The smile makes me think he doesn't quite understand what I'm saying.

"Can I still come cheer you on?"

"Sure. I'd like that," I say. Because surely there is no harm in him being a face in the crowd. "But, Aaron, I still can't see you. I have to focus. And when I'm with you . . ."

I shrug, not having the words to tell him what happens to me when I'm with him, how suddenly nothing else matters, and that scares me. It scares me how much my want overrides everything else.

His smile fades like a rainbow in too-bright sunshine. "I get it," he says, staring down into his mug.

"I've just got to win," I say, hating the defensive tone that creeps in uninvited. "You know?"

He squints at me, scrutinizing me, like my secrets are written on my bones. Like if he stares long and hard enough he'll be able

CHAPTER 55

I'M SITTING ON THE FLOOR SURROUNDED BY BALLOONS AND streamers and the cupcakes we stayed up all night baking. Our living room looks like a party for a four-year-old. Monica is pacing back and forth in front of me, and Granny Dee and LaoLao are on the couch, each of them sitting so tense and upright they look like sentries. They haven't said a thing since my mom left to go pick up Marcus from the hospital. Not even when I dropped not one but two cupcakes on the floor. Not even when I spilled tea. Not even when I hugged a balloon so tight to my chest it popped.

The front door swings open and I hear my mom chirp, "Welcome home!"

I can't make out my brother's reply as my mother wheels him in his wheelchair toward us. We've put boards down the front porch steps as a makeshift wheelchair ramp. Thank goodness his room is on the ground floor, we didn't have to move his things all around.

"Welcome home!" I try to shout, but he looks so sad, so lost, that my voice comes out feeble. Granny Dee and LaoLao stay silent.

"Come on, you two," my mom says to them, wheeling Marcus next to me. "Where's your festive spirit?"

"They're right," Marcus mutters, eyes downcast. "This ain't anything to celebrate."

"Aren't you happy to be home?" My mom's voice is small small small.

"I'm not happy . . . ," Marcus grunts as he starts to wheel himself down the hallway toward his bedroom. ". . . about anything."

The women he leaves in the living room, all the women in his life, stare at each other. Each one of us daring the other ones to go after him. Monica sighs and puts her determined face on. "I'll go," she says. She hasn't even stepped into his room when we hear his roar.

"Get out! Leave me alone!"

I've never heard Marcus shout at Monica before. It makes me angry.

Monica returns to the living room, cheeks pink with shame. She tugs down one of the streamers. "I think I better get going."

"No," I say, putting my hand on her arm to stop her from taking down any more decorations. "You stay. Please. Just a little longer."

Monica nods but doesn't meet my eye. A timer goes off in the kitchen and my mom jolts up as if she just sat on a tack.

"The casserole!" she says.

"I'll help," says Monica, and the two of them disappear into the kitchen, leaving me with my silent grandmothers.

A crash and a dull thud come from the direction of Marcus's room.

"You should talk to your brother," says Granny Dee.

"What?" I scoff. "You heard him. He said he wanted to be left alone. I'm not going in there."

"Dee Dee is right," says LaoLao. I'm surprised that Granny Dee doesn't have a heart attack right then and there—I've never heard LaoLao say Granny Dee was right about anything in my whole life. But Granny Dee just nods. "You are who he should talk to."

I approach his room slowly, cautiously, not knowing what I'll find inside.

Marcus is sitting in his wheelchair, his head in his hands. Scattered on the floor are almost all his trophies. Only the ones too high for him to reach still sit on their perch, looking down on him.

"Marcus."

"Go away," he says without looking up. "I don't want to talk to anyone."

"I don't care what you want."

"Wing. Leave me alone."

"You don't get to be left alone right now," I say. "You're being a big baby! Mom planned this little welcome home celebration for you and you are being so ungrateful. Come on."

"I already told you, there's nothing to celebrate."

"Um, what about the fact that you're alive? What about that?"

He mumbles something under his breath.

"What?"

"I said, I don't deserve to be alive. I wish I hadn't woken up. My life is ruined. I'd rather be dead."

His words take all my air.

"Don't say that." I'm so angry that my voice is shaking. "You know that two people *are* dead, right? That a little boy doesn't have a mother anymore? And you're going to sit here and tell me that you wish you hadn't woken up?"

"What do you want me to do? Go to their house and apologize? What is that going to do?"

"That would be a start! You're just being so selfish! Yours isn't the only life that was ruined that night, Marcus!" I'm shouting at my brother. I haven't shouted at him since we were little, fighting over toys. And even then, I always gave him what he wanted. "And you're lucky"—I fling the word at him like a weapon—"lucky to have a life at all!" I take a deep breath. "You haven't even thought about what these past few months have been like for the rest of us." How hard I've been training. How hard Mom and LaoLao have been working. How hard it's been for all of us. How running has turned into something else because I have to, have to, have to win that contract because otherwise I don't know what's gonna happen to our family. And how it's all for him. Because of him. His fault. "Maybe if you stopped thinking about yourself for one goddamn second and looked around you, you'd realize that we've all been suffering, we're all still suffering! Haven't you seen how stressed-out Mom is when we visit? How tired LaoLao is? Do you have any idea how hard I'm working, how much I'm pushing myself to win this stupid Riveo thing? For you? Don't you realize that everything everyone in this family is doing, everything we've given up, is for you? Because of what you did?" My shouting has gotten so loud I think it might blow the roof off our house.

"I'm sorry that my coma was such an inconvenience for you

all," he says, voice harsh and strange. "It sure as hell wasn't easy for me either."

"Well, it looked easy! It looked like you were just lying there doing nothing." The sharp snap of my words makes us both flinch. We stare at each other, and I feel so far from him but closer than we've ever been. I feel like his equal. Like his sibling, not just his little sister. He breaks eye contact first, turning away from me to stare at the wall.

"I'm sorry," he says to the wall. "Every second I've been awake I've spent wishing I could take it back. Wishing I could fix it. But I can't, Wing. I can't fix this. I'll never fix it."

I have no words of comfort. I have no lies to tell him. Instead, I put my hand on his shoulder, my anger giving way to sadness.

"I know," I say.

His sobs are violent and silent, his whole body shaking, his tears flowing fat and fast. I squeeze his shoulder and he reaches up and puts his hand on my own, so his arm is across his chest, over his heart. Finally, he looks up at me, eyes swollen.

"I keep thinking, what if Monica had been in the car? Or Aaron? I keep thinking about what if it had been Mom in the other car? Or you? And I'm so glad it wasn't, and I'm so ashamed of myself for being glad, you're right, I'm so goddamn selfish. I'm so selfish." His voice is splintering and I crouch down so we're at eye level.

"Monica wasn't in the car. Neither was Aaron. Or me. Or Mom. We're all okay." I pause, look hard at him. "You're okay." I take a deep breath. "And I'm selfish too. Because I'm glad, more than glad, there isn't even a word for how glad I am, that we're all okay. That you're okay."

"I'm scared, Wing." I've never in my whole life heard Marcus admit to being scared. "I'm scared about going to jail. I know I'm going to. And . . . I should. I deserve to. I deserve worse, but even though I know I deserve it, I'm scared."

"That's all right," I say. "It's okay that you're scared. And you're gonna be okay, I promise." I force a smile, fragile as chipped china. "Just stop being such an asshole, all right? It's hard enough as it is."

Marcus laughs, just a little, and it is wet and snotty and a shadow of what his laugh was, but hearing him laugh lights a little flame of hope deep inside my heart.

"I love you." I hug him and hold him tight. "No matter what, okay?" Because even though what he did can never be forgiven, I still love him. Irrevocably. Selfishly.

"I love you too," he says, his voice muffled in my hair.

The door opens and Monica steps in, her lips as tight as her jeans. "Hey," she says, tugging on her braid. "Are you okay?"

Marcus looks at me and smiles. "Yeah, I think I'm okay."

I smile back at him, really smile, and stand. "I'll let you guys talk." As I pass Monica in the doorway, I squeeze her hand.

I close the door behind me as gently as I can and go into the kitchen to help my mom set the table.

CHAPTER 56

It's hard, having Marcus back home. Harder than I thought it would be. I guess I couldn't think past him waking up, him coming home; that was the important thing. I thought everything else would just figure itself out.

And having him home is a million million million times better than the alternative. No matter how hard it is, it's worth it, and I'm so grateful. Grateful in a way that makes my skin tingle and my heart full; I've never been so grateful for anything. . . .

I'd be even more grateful if he weren't so sullen and sorry for himself all the time and if we didn't have the heavy, heavy cloud of debt hanging over our house, getting bigger and fatter and closer every day. Next month we'll lose the house, unless I win the Riveo Race. Just because Marcus is home doesn't mean the bills stop. He's got physical therapists and he's got psychiatrists, and he needs that, I know he does, and now that he's out his lawyer has been coming by, and who knows how much every minute of his time is costing. Marcus doesn't even want a lawyer, keeps saying that he knows what he did was wrong and he's guilty and he'll do whatever the judge says. The lawyer says that Marcus'll change his tune when he gets to jail and he'll wish the lawyer had pushed harder for a lighter sentence and Marcus'll close his eyes and say if he was making wishes what he'd be wishing for is that he never got behind the wheel of his car that night.

We all wish that.

The parents of the woman Marcus killed, Sophie Bell's mom and dad, they came by too. The mom, she was angry, I could tell, she could barely look at Marcus, and I don't blame her. I wouldn't have blamed her if she'd smacked him. And the dad, the dad looked sadder than anyone I've ever seen, and I've seen more than my fair share of sadness. He kept his hand on his wife's shoulder and spoke in a low voice. He told us that it was important for them to forgive so they could move on. When he said that, his wife's face got so tight, like a clenched fist. "We forgive you," she said, her voice creaky and cracked, "but you ruined our lives. Don't ever forget it." Then she got out a photo from her handbag, one that had been folded and creased, and handed it to him. "This was our daughter. This is her son. You took away his mother. You took away our daughter." Marcus held the photo with trembling hands and stared at it, really stared at it, for a long time. "I'm sorry," he said. "I'm sorry."

"We know," said the father. After they left Marcus locked himself in his room and cried so loud we could hear him in every corner of the house.

I ran from his tears; I couldn't stand to hear him. I ran out of the house and down the street and I ran and ran and ran and for the first time in a long time I didn't check my times. I didn't care.

But I can't afford not to care. The race is next week. Riveo somehow managed to get it set up so the race will be in the Olympic stadium. I'll be running in an Olympic stadium. Just that thought alone should be enough to get me pumped up, but all it does is remind me what a big deal this is, how much is riding on this race.

I'm so close.

CHAPTER 57

LaoLao is swearing up a storm in the kitchen. English swearwords, Mandarin swearwords, I even think I hear a French curse or two.

"LaoLao! What's wrong?" I've just gotten home from practice, one of the last practices before the big race on Saturday, and am dripping with sweat and don't really want to be in our stifling kitchen, but she seems upset. Really upset. "Where's Marcus?"

She ignores me and carries on swearing. And chopping.

"I make a mistake! One little mistake. One mistake and Mister Head Chef shout at me. At me! My daughter is his boss and he shouting at me." She clucks in disgust. "He say I am too slow, that I take too long. I show him. I can cut chicken faster than anyone!"

I smile, but her words sit uncomfortably in my brain. *Faster than anyone.* It's all I've been able to think about for weeks, and it sounds funny coming out of LaoLao's mouth.

She's got a whole chicken on the counter in front of her and she's hacking at it with a cleaver and rubbery bits of raw chicken are flying everywhere.

"Careful," I say, because it doesn't look like she's paying attention and I know that cleaver is the sharpest knife in the kitchen.

"I work every night! I never take breaks! I make noodles, I make chicken, I make dumplings, I never ask for rest! And then, today, today I forget to put chicken in *da pan ji* . . ."

"You forgot to put the chicken in the Big Plate Chicken dish?" *Da pan ji*, or Big Plate Chicken, is one of my favorite dishes LaoLao makes. A huge bowl of spicy stew with chopped chicken, on the bone, always on the bone, chunks of potatoes, and fresh noodles. I don't know how she could forget to put in the key ingredient.

The cleaver comes down on the counter with a *thwack* and I step away to avoid getting splattered with chicken bits.

"I have a lot on my mind! I think about Marcus and your mother, and you. And the house! And the money! Too much to think about. Chicken, chicken is least important."

Thwack.

The cleaver goes through the chicken's breastbone. LaoLao isn't really looking where she's cutting, she's just tearing the chicken apart.

"And Mister Head Chef pretend he being nice. He say, 'Oh, you so tired, go get rest,' like I have a choice. I know what he doing. He sending me home because I am old!" She thwacks off a leg.

"But, LaoLao . . . you *are* tired." I don't tell her she's old. We both know she's old.

"But we cannot afford for me to be tired!"

Again, her words send a tremor through me. That's how I feel.

I don't want LaoLao feeling like that. That's why it's so important for me to win on Saturday. My LaoLao shouldn't be feeling like this.

"It's okay," I say, stepping closer to her. "Here, why don't you go lie down?"

Thwack.

I see the cleaver going into the soft underside of her arm, below her elbow and above her wrist. A chunk of skin comes off with it; it looks alarmingly like the raw chicken. And then, blood.

For a second, I don't move. It looks unreal. Like I'm watching a movie. But then LaoLao gives a short, sharp shriek of pain and the cleaver clatters to the floor.

I don't know what to do. I don't know what to do. Blood is getting everywhere. LaoLao has slumped to the ground, she's trying to cover the gaping hole with her other hand, but blood is spurting out through her fingers.

"Wing . . . ," she says, her voice scared, "get Dee Dee."

I can't leave LaoLao. I grab a dish towel but then worry it's dirty and I don't want to put a dirty dish towel over an open wound, so I whip my shirt off and try to staunch the blood.

It keeps coming. Oh God, it keeps coming. She must have cut an artery.

"Granny Dee!" I scream as loud as I can. "Granny Dee!"

Granny Dee comes into the kitchen, rubbing her eyes. She must have been napping in her room.

"Oh my Lord! Mei!"

I've never heard my Granny Dee call LaoLao by her first name. By her Chinese name.

Granny Dee goes into action, hobbling around the kitchen

while I keep the soggy and bloodstained shirt pressed up against LaoLao's arm.

"Wing, call an ambulance," Granny Dee says. She's got the first-aid kit tucked under one arm and an armful of clean dish towels.

She takes my place next to LaoLao and I rush to the phone. Of course. An ambulance. I should have called an ambulance instead of shouting for Granny Dee. But I couldn't do that. I couldn't leave LaoLao on the floor by herself, bleeding all over the place.

The 911 operator has a calm voice. She asks me a few questions and says an ambulance will be here shortly.

Then I call the restaurant. Lisa, the girl who works at the hostess stand, answers. She's cheerful and says she doesn't know where my mom is but can she take a message?

"Just tell her to come home as soon as possible. Tell her LaoLao cut herself real bad and we had to call nine one one."

"Oh my goodness!" squeaks Lisa. "Is she okay?"

I can smell the blood now.

"I don't know. Just tell my mom to hurry," I say, and slam the phone back in its cradle.

Granny Dee is holding a bloodstained dish towel against LaoLao's arm, but the blood just keeps coming. LaoLao is getting paler and paler and she has her eyes tightly closed.

"Come on, Mei! Keep those eyes open and that head up. Can't have you dying on me now. Not after all we been through together. Not after Marcus has just woke up! Don't you leave me to look after this family all by myself."

LaoLao doesn't even smile. Granny Dee's voice is shaking but she keeps shouting. "Wing! Get more towels! I'll stay with LaoLao."

I run, really run, down the hall and into the bathroom, grabbing as many towels as I can, and sprint back to the kitchen.

There's more blood pooling on the linoleum floor. So much blood. I start to feel dizzy and I slump against the kitchen table. I don't want to look away from LaoLao, but I can't stand to watch all that blood draining out of her. How can my LaoLao be losing so much blood? She moans and her head lolls over on Granny Dee.

"Hold on, Mei, an ambulance is coming! You're gonna be all right."

The ambulance is taking too long. I should have driven them. Marcus should have been here. Where is he? Then I remember, it's Tuesday. He's at physiotherapy. He won't know what's happened till my mom goes to pick him up tonight.

Marcus would have known what to do. Or at least, the old Marcus would have known. I don't know what this new Marcus would have done. Still, a useless Marcus is better than no Marcus.

Where are my dragon and my lioness now? I need them. I need them.

LaoLao isn't responding to Granny Dee. Granny Dee is trying to support her, but she's so small and frail and LaoLao's so much heavier than her. I go behind LaoLao—at first I try to avoid stepping in the blood but it's impossible—and try to support her.

She's deadweight.

Granny Dee is crying but I don't thinks she knows it. She keeps crooning to LaoLao as she swaps out one blood-soaked dish towel for another.

Finally the ambulance arrives. The paramedics don't knock, they come straight in. They've got a stretcher. They get down low next to LaoLao and quickly tie a tourniquet above her elbow before carefully putting her on the stretcher.

"You did a good job," he says. "Keeping pressure on it like that."

"Is she going to be okay?" I ask. She looks so fragile lying on the stretcher.

"She's lost a lot of blood," he says. I already know that. That isn't answering my question. "Looks like she caught an artery. You two did the right thing."

That isn't exactly the reassuring answer I was hoping for, but I know he can't make any promises.

The paramedics hoist up the stretcher and carry LaoLao out on it and into the ambulance.

"I'll go with her," I say, even though I can't imagine anything worse than going to the hospital and not knowing if LaoLao will be all right, but Granny Dee steps in front of me and hugs me tight.

"You stay here. You gotta tell your mama and Marcus what happened. I'll go. LaoLao will be all right." But she won't look at me when she says that.

I watch the ambulance drive away.

The kitchen is a disaster.

There are bloody footprints everywhere. Bloody sneaker footprints. I look down at my shoes, my prized Riveos.

There's blood caked on the sole. I've been tracking it around the kitchen without realizing it. I don't want my mom to come home and see this. I can't run away from this. I take off my shoes and reach under the sink, where we keep the bleach and the cleaning supplies, and get out everything I need to clean. I fill a bucket with scalding hot water.

And I start to clean. I clean until the blood is gone, but even then I keep scrubbing. I scrub until my arms ache, and when my mom comes in the door I'm still on my hands and knees, scrubbing the floor like it'll never be clean again. I'm shaking so bad I can't even stand.

I don't know how I'm going to run on Saturday. Running, the thing that has been everything, more than everything, doesn't feel so important anymore.

CHAPTER 58

THE HOSPITAL PATCHED UP LAOLAO, GAVE HER A BLOOD transfusion, and sent her home with a stern lecture about being careful with knives. She won't be able to go back to the restaurant for a while. She's spent the past two days tucked up in bed with Granny Dee fussing over her. Even Marcus has been trying to take care of her, when he isn't in any kind of shape to be taking care of anyone but himself.

Last night I went into my grannies' room. Marcus was in there; his room and their room are both on the ground floor, so he can wheel himself back and forth pretty easily. LaoLao was propped up by so many pillows she looked like she was sitting on a pillow throne. Granny Dee sat on her bed.

"I'm sorry I can't come see you run tomorrow," she said. Because even though she's not bleeding anymore, she's weak, and the heat and the crowds wouldn't be good for her.

"It's all right," said Granny Dee, patting LaoLao's wrinkled hand with her own gnarled one. "I'll stay home with you tomorrow. Wouldn't be fair for me to go without you."

"I don't know if I want to go," I whispered.

"Not go? But, Wing, this is what you've been working so hard for. You've got to go." Granny Dee nodded so emphatically her glasses nearly bounced off her nose.

"I don't know if I can win. I'm scared I won't win and it will have all been for nothing."

"That's not true. Look at you! You're the fastest girl in your school. My goodness, you're the fastest girl in all of Atlanta!" Granny Dee said.

Marcus cleared his throat. "You know what, Wing? Remember all that crap I used to say about how I played football for the crowds? And because I wanted to go pro?"

I nodded.

"I'd give just about anything to be able to go out and just throw a ball around with Aaron. I know I don't have any right to miss anything, but I can't help it. I miss playing football so much. Just football. Not the winning. The game."

He looked at me. "Wing, just do what you do. Run."

Granny Dee took my hand. "You don't have to win, Wing. We're so proud of you. And if you don't win, we'll figure it out. You can't run with all this pressure weighing you down. Tomorrow, you run the way you did when you first showed me what you could do. Go on out there and be a show-off."

"I want to see you run like that," said Marcus. "I want to see you running for you."

* * *

And now it's finally here. The Riveo Running Girl Race.

The cheers are deafening.

The whole state has gone crazy for track and field with the Atlanta Olympics only weeks away, and it looks like all of Georgia has turned out for the Riveo Running Girl Race. Even Claire Gordon. Claire Gordon, a Georgia native and the fastest woman on the U.S. Olympic Team, is supposedly here. She said she wants to see "the next generation of great Georgia talent."

I'm stretching at the starting line when someone comes up behind me and wraps their arms around me tightly, fiercely. "You fly today, you hear me? You fly." It's Eliza. I hug her back and then she lets me go, turns to the crowd, and holds up my hand, like she did at the pep rally, and the crowd goes crazy.

"You're the fan favorite," she whispers in my ear. "Don't disappoint them. You can do this." I watch, eyes prickling with tears, as she jogs to the side of the track.

I repeat her words over and over again in my head. I can do this, I can do this, I can do this, I can do this, I can do this. . . .

But I don't know if I can. My stomach is in my throat, my heart is in my feet, none of my body parts are where they are meant to be, and I don't know if my legs are gonna know how to run when that starting shot goes off.

I look at the other girls staggered along the starting line. They are all fierce and focused. None of them look like they've been throwing up after races or like they really need this the way I do.

I need this.

I need it.

I scan the crowd, looking for my family. I can't make out any faces. From the track, everyone is a blur. The announcer is saying something, the race is about to start, and all I can think about is how much I need to see my family, to remind me what I'm running for. I wish my Granny Dee and LaoLao were here. Even though I wouldn't be able to see them, just knowing they were here would make it better.

They won't always be here, though.

I get into starting position, but when I close my eyes I see LaoLao slumping over in her own blood.

"On your marks!"

We crouch. I see Marcus crying in his wheelchair.

"Get set!"

I see my daddy kissing my mom for the last time in the kitchen, when none of us knew it was going to be the last time.

The starting gun goes off at the same time the announcer shouts "Go!"

My body shoots off at the sound, shoots off like a rocket that isn't ready. I careen into the next lane, losing precious seconds and nearly knocking into the girl next to me. She doesn't even blink, just pushes forward, leaving me behind.

These girls are faster than anyone I've ever run with before.

These girls are faster than me.

They can't be. I won't let them be. No one's ever been faster than me, and seeing the back of their legs, the soles of their feet, it wakes up this animal inside me, an animal that will do anything to catch the thing it is chasing. The drive to catch them, the need, takes over my body. Except I don't just want to catch them, I want to pass them. I have to. I need to. I grit my teeth and push as hard as I can and I fling myself forward, pumping my arms as fast as they'll go. I push harder, and I pass one girl and my lungs are on fire, every breath I take feels like swallowing a match, my lungs can't handle going this fast, I'm not made to go this fast, but now I'm passing another girl and I can't slow down now, I can't, and I lengthen out as much as I can, and my left thigh is too tight, like my thigh is a violin and one of the strings just snapped, and I stumble, just for an instant, but I won't stop, I can't stop, even though sharp pain is shooting through my leg every time my foot hits the ground. Why isn't the race over yet? I just want it to be over. I just want it to end.

A roar. My lioness is next to me and she's going fast, faster than me, and now she is just ahead of me with my dragon flying above her, they're both just out of reach. Wait! I try to scream, but I don't have enough air. The lioness looks over her shoulder at me, just once, and then she leaps into the air, away from me, and my dragon is next to her, they're flying away. I have to catch them. They can't leave me. They are getting farther and farther away and smaller and smaller until I can't see them at all.

Then all I can see is the finish line. While I was chasing my dragon and my lioness, I must have passed the other girls and now nothing is between me and winning.

I hurl myself over the finish line.

CHAPTER 59

I COLLAPSE ON THE HARD TRACK, SCRAPING MY KNEES AND barely feeling it because my whole body has gone numb.

Eliza rushes at me from the sidelines and picks me up. I'm shaking all over, but she's got me, and we embrace in a sweaty tangle of arms and I lean on her and I'm crying, I can't stop crying, and she's laughing and telling me that I did it and I want to tell her that my dragon and my lioness are really gone now, I know they are, but I can't, because I still haven't caught my breath, I still can't talk.

I hear the announcer saying "And the very first Riveo Running Girl is WING JONES!" and the crowd starts chanting my name.

I did it.

"They love you," Eliza says, beaming at me. And it seems like they do. But these aren't the people I was running for.

Over Eliza's shoulder, I see my mom and Monica coming

toward me and people are moving out of the way because Monica is pushing a wheelchair.

Marcus. He came. He saw me run. He saw me win. He was cheering me on.

I let go of Eliza and stumble toward my brother.

Monica is leaning against his wheelchair, smiling at him. No, his chair is leaning against her, *he's* leaning against her, and they smile at each other. I see that now. Their balance has changed and I think it's a good thing.

Monica is stronger than I thought she was. Stronger than Marcus thought she was. And I'm so grateful for it. He's going to need it, all that strength. His court appearance is in six weeks. We all know he's going to go to jail. But we got through this; we can get through whatever comes next.

I'm stronger than I thought I was too.

"You came!" I say, but my words tumble out all breathless.

Marcus grins at me, and it still isn't his full megawatt smile, the smile that could get anyone and everyone to follow him anywhere, but it's a smile and I'll take it.

"Of course I came, Wing! I said I would, didn't I? You were . . ." He pauses. "You were something else out there. Like nothing I've ever seen. I couldn't miss this."

A pause, and I know we're both thinking of all the things he missed while he was in the hospital. All the things he might have missed if he'd never woken up at all.

How lucky we both are that he didn't miss today.

I crouch down in front of him so we're at eye level, wincing because my legs are still shaking and my left thigh has started to spasm, and I hold his hands.

"I did it for you," I manage to say, and he closes his eyes and for a minute I think he's gonna cry, and then he says, "I hope you did it for you too."

I hug him as tight as I can and straighten up, aware that a crowd is gathering around us. The Riveo corporate team want me to start acting like the Riveo Running Girl right away.

Someone taps me on the shoulder. I turn, expecting it to be a journalist or Coach Kerry or a Riveo rep, and instead . . .

I'm staring at the most beautiful face in the world.

"You did it," says Aaron. "I knew you would."

"I didn't," I say, because I didn't know.

"Can I run with you now?" he says, and I know what he's asking. He's asking if, now that I've won, I can go back to running the way I used to, the way I love to. The way I want to.

There's only one way to answer him. I lean forward, putting my weight on him because my body is still trembling, and press my lips to his.

And it's like kissing and running belong in the same alternate dimension where time slows down and speeds up all at the same time, because our kiss lasts an instant and forever.

But everyone else is still in this world, and I can hear the clicks of the cameras and I can hear my brother going, "Christ, calm down, you two, everyone is watching," and I reluctantly pull back but keep my arms around Aaron.

"Sorry I'm so sweaty," I say.

"I like you like this," he says, and I hear a journalist wolf-whistle and write it down on his notepad.

"I like you all the time," I say, not caring who hears.

"You know what we need?" Marcus has wheeled up right next to us. "We need to go out and celebrate."

As we leave the stadium, after I take about a million pictures and answer about a million questions, I look up at the sky, hoping for one last glimpse of my dragon. I keep waiting to feel the familiar weight of my lioness's tail against my legs.

Nothing.

They're really gone now. And I don't think they're coming back.

"Come on, Wing!"

"Yeah! Hurry up, slowpoke!"

"We thought you were supposed to be fast!"

I take one last look at the track over my shoulder, just in case.

"Goodbye," I whisper.

And then I turn and head toward my family.

ACKNOWLEDGMENTS

BECOMING A PUBLISHED AUTHOR HAS BEEN SUCH AN AMAZING adventure, and I'm so lucky to have had so many wonderful people behind *The Heartbeats of Wing Jones*.

To my superstar agent, the incomparable and incredible Claire Wilson at Rogers, Coleridge and White, thank you for being my fairy godmother and making all my author dreams come true. Thank you for believing in Wing, and believing in me. There is no one else I would want in my corner.

Thank you to the rest of the team at RCW, especially Rosie Price, Lexie Hamblin, and Rebecca Jones. And to Emily Hayward Whitlock at the Artists Partnership.

I am tremendously lucky and so grateful to have not just one but two phenomenal editors who worked on *The Heartbeats of Wing Jones* and made it the very best book it could be. Thank you to Annalie Grainger at Walker Books in the UK and Kate Sullivan at Delacorte Press in the US. Thank you both for your brilliant, insightful, and thoughtful edits and for making the editorial process so wonderful. I've had so much fun working with you. I really do have the dream team!

Thank you to everyone at Walker Books, especially Gill Evans for her support and good cheer. And to the team at Delacorte, with special thanks to Beverly Horowitz.

A big thank-you to my cover designers on both sides of the pond, Maria Soler Cantón at Walker Books and Ray Shappell at Delacorte, for creating such stunning covers.

One of the best things about being a writer and a book lover is the amazing community. To the entire UKYA community, thank you for being so welcoming and so much fun. And a huge shout-out and thank-you to Claire's Coven for being so awesome. Special thanks and big hugs to Melinda Salisbury, Sara Barnard, Alexia Casale, Lauren James, and Katherine Rundell for making me feel so welcome and cheering for me and Wing from the very start. You ladies are fabulously talented, and I'm so glad I know you.

To all the fantastic people in the YA book community who have supported me in one way or another. Thank you to Maggie Hall for giving me invaluable publishing advice, to Nina Douglas for setting up my first-ever event (with the gracious and glamorous Leigh Bardugo, no less), to Louise Lamont for excellent early feedback, to Anna McKerrow for lunchtime writing sessions, to Jim Dean for shouting about Wing Jones from the rooftops, to Amy Harker for encouraging me in all my bookish endeavors, and to Anna James, for being just as excited about my book deal as I was.

Thank you to Kheryn Callender, Emma Dennis-Edwards, and Leyu Wondwossen for being brilliant early readers.

To Katherine Woodfine for all of her wisdom, wit, and wonderfulness. Don't know what I'd do without you, KWoo!

To my Team Maleficent ladies: Samantha Shannon, Claire Donnelly, Leiana Leatutufu, Lisa Lueddecke, and Krystal Sutherland—thank you for all the writing sprints, critiques, laughs, cheers, gifs, and brilliance. I'm ridiculously proud of all of us. Special thanks to Krystal for all the pep talks and for being there throughout this whole crazy and amazing publishing journey. I'm so glad we're in this together.

To Laini Taylor, who inspires me as a reader, writer, and human. Thank you for your kindness and encouragement.

A heartfelt thank-you to the NaNoWriMo organization for teaching me to be disciplined (*Wing Jones* started as a NaNo novel), to the British Library for the focus (most of *Wing Jones* was written in their magical reading rooms), and to Waterstones Piccadilly for being a book lover's paradise. I've spent countless hours on the fifth floor, in the basement, and, of course, on the children's floor.

To all my friends who believed in me and thought of me as a writer before I ever had a literary agent or a book deal. Thank you for wanting to hear about every tiny success, whether it was finishing a manuscript or getting interest from an agent. Thank you for sharing in my joy when I found out that *The Heartbeats of Wing Jones* was going to be published. To Fay and Janou Gordon, for the most imaginative childhood any writer could ask for and always believing that I'd be a published writer one day. To Courtney Dahl, for running by my side in high school cross-country and being there for me ever since. To Chloe Green and Jessica Herman for always cheering me on. To Caesar and Cynthia Maasry for wanting to know all the details and then wanting to celebrate every step of the way. And to Dyna Yates, Maarten Claessen, and Kris Barnes for all their support, encouragement, and excitement.

To my writing partner and dear friend Jennifer Ball. Thank

you for all the hours of writing in CozyTown and in the British Library. Thank you for reading and rereading my manuscripts, for brainstorming sessions and plot discussions. Thank you for being amazing.

A huge thank-you and big hug to all my wonderful family. To all my aunts, uncles, and cousins in the Webber, Hopper, and Tsang families, thank you for all your support and excitement. Extra-special thanks to my terrific in-laws, Paulus and Louisa Tsang; to my sister-in-law, Stephanie Tsang; and to my grandparents, Jack and Sharon Hopper and Bob Webber. And to my Grandma Kay Brockbank Webber, who was an incredible and inspirational woman.

To my brother, Jack, and my sister, Jane. Thank you for being the best brother and sister in the world and for being my best friends. Jack, thanks for playing football in high school—who knew it would inspire me so much? And Janie, thank you for knowing about all things YA—I can't believe my book is going to be on your shelves! Thank you to my wonderful parents, Rob and Virginia Webber, for always encouraging and supporting me. Dad, thank you for giving me your love of travel. Mom, thank you for giving me your love of reading and for being my biggest inspiration.

Finally, to my husband, Kevin: Thank you for staying up with me while I write, for reading every draft, for providing all my writing snacks. Thank you for all our adventures. Thank you for everything. I love you.

ABOUT THE AUTHOR

KATHERINE WEBBER WAS BORN IN SOUTHERN CALIFORNIA AND has lived in Hong Kong, Hawaii, and Atlanta. She currently lives in London with her husband.

She loves an adventure, whether it is found in a book or in real life. She has climbed the Great Wall of China, ridden camels in the Sahara Desert, camped in the Serengeti, visited sacred temples in Bhutan, trekked to Machu Picchu, and eaten her way through Italy. Travel, books, and eating out are her favorite indulgences.

Katherine studied comparative literature at the University of California, Davis, and Chinese literature and language at the Chinese University of Hong Kong. She has worked at an international translation company, a technology startup, and, most recently, a London-based reading charity. She spends far too much time on Twitter, so she invites you to come say hello at @kwebberwrites.

The Heartbeats of Wing Jones is her first novel.